MW00572421

FOLLOW

the

STARS HOME

Books by Diane C. McPhail

THE ABOLITIONIST'S DAUGHTER

THE SEAMSTRESS OF NEW ORLEANS

FOLLOW THE STARS HOME

Published by Kensington Publishing Corp.

DIANE C. McPHAIL

FOLLOW

STARS HOME

JOHN SCOGNAMIGLIO BOOKS
KENSINGTON PUBLISHING CORP.
www.kensingtonbooks.com

This book is a work of fiction. Names, characters, businesses, organizations, places, events, and incidents either are the product of the author's imagination or are used fictitiously. Any resemblance to actual persons, living or dead, events, or locales is entirely coincidental.

To the extent that the image or images on the cover of this book depict a person or persons, such person or persons are merely models, and are not intended to portray any character or characters featured in the book.

JOHN SCOGNAMIGLIO BOOKS are published by

Kensington Publishing Corp.
900 Third Ave.
New York, NY 10022

Copyright © 2024 by Diane C. McPhail

All rights reserved. No part of this book may be reproduced in any form or by any means without the prior written consent of the Publisher, excepting brief quotes used in reviews.

All Kensington titles, imprints and distributed lines are available at special quantity discounts for bulk purchases for sales promotion, premiums, fund-raising, educational or institutional use.

Special book excerpts or customized printings can also be created to fit specific needs. For details, write or phone the office of the Kensington Special Sales Manager: Kensington Publishing Corp., 900 Third Ave., New York, NY, 10022. Attn. Special Sales Department. Phone: 1-800-221-2647.

The JS and John Scognamiglio Books logo is a trademark of Kensington Publishing Corp.

ISBN-13: 978-1-4967-5088-4
First Kensington Hardcover Edition: September 2024

Library of Congress Control Number: 2024936511

ISBN-13: 978-1-4967-5090-7 (e-book)

10 9 8 7 6 5 4 3 2 1

Printed in the United States of America

To my husband, Ray, for his unfailing support through our own journey together.

ACKNOWLEDGMENTS

Although I grew up on the Mississippi River, until recently I had little knowledge of any segment of the river above Tennessee. I wish to thank my dear friend Meredith Creekmore for her insistence on a road trip together to New Madrid, Missouri, where we explored a portion of the river I'd never seen before. To that interesting exploration, I added a voyage on the American Queen paddleboat line from New Orleans to Memphis in order to experience the river from its center. I am grateful to all the staff and passengers who offered a warm welcome and made the voyage memorable and extremely pleasurable, and I am especially appreciative of the private tour of the engine room and its workings.

I am deeply grateful, as ever, to my outstanding agent, Mark Gottlieb, of Trident Media Group. I could not ask for a better working relationship or more supportive representation. It was through Mark that I came into an equally rewarding relationship with my most competent and proficient editor, John Scognamiglio, of Kensington Publishing Corporation. His unfailing precision, coupled with his expertise and support, make all my efforts that much more rewarding. His patience is a gift to my efforts. Many thanks belong to the skillful design, editing, and marketing staff of Kensington Publishing for their talented input. My immense gratitude goes to Vida Engstrand for her unfailing expertise in publicity and arrangements for touring and major book appearances, and to all the unnamed staff at Kensington Publishing who have worked to bring this book to the eyes of interested readers.

I am deeply indebted to friends and family for their support and unfailing interest in and enthusiasm for my writing projects. You all know who you are, and I thank you. As always, I am forever grateful to my husband, Ray, whose support has made my writing efforts possible, and to my children, Brad McPhail and Melissa Williamson, whose love enables me to create this rewarding life.

BOOK ONE

CHAPTER 1

Memory meanders however it will, in its own directions, serving functions entirely its own. Like this river I so strangely love, it may transport bits and pieces, both large and small for long distances, strange items long submerged bobbing now and then to the surface of awareness. These waters may muddy the clearest of things, may wash others free of collected debris, may deposit precious trifles in hidden coves to surprise some unknown finder down the years. Memory is like that: its flow self-defining through life, singular bits of lost perception surfacing now and then, evaporating sometimes entirely with the passage of time only to reemerge like one evaporated drop of rain, falling, joining others as streams and rivers, becoming the sea, like this river I am waiting to travel.

My memory, my small drop of history, which is about this river, begins with the sea. I was a child, five or so, when my mother died with her baby. That infant lies in the grave beside her, boy or a girl, no name, just Infant Latrobe and a date: its first and only, her last. My father is broken. In my memory, he sits alone by the window in a green velvet chair, silent. I want, need, to sit in his lap, but he waves me off. I know to go no closer. My nursemaid—I remember only that her name is Nanny and that a strand of orange hair is always escaping her cap—comes and takes me away. More than once. Much more. I stand at the door every day in the hope that he may change his mind.

Then one day he isn't there. I remember how vacant the room feels, how empty his chair. I climb up and sit, hoping to feel the residual warmth of his lap, but the red-haired nursemaid comes to fetch me. She carries a small bag of belongings for Henry and me. Perhaps you can imagine my distress, but only I can know it.

"Where's Papa?" I cry. I push her hand away.

"Hush, child." She tries to straighten my dress. "He's gone."

"Gone? Papa's gone where, Nanny? Where?" I am frantic. She makes it sound so final. Gone like my mother? I want her to leave me alone. I'm fighting her hands.

"Across the ocean, child. To the other side of the world," she says, snatching up a few toys. She repeats herself. Emphatically. "To the other side of the world."

That's all I remember until much later. Whatever there is of that lonely time is deeply submerged. It is years before I begin to comprehend his desperate struggle to escape his grief for my mother, for her and the unnamed infant beside her.

Nanny takes us to stay with some cousins; at least I think that's who they are. They are some sort of family, at any rate. I am too young to sort it all out, and later I don't care. There are children. Lots of them. I don't remember how many—six perhaps, some older, some younger. Henry and I tag along. Well, I tag along and drag him with me. I want so to belong. No one pays attention to us unless we misbehave, which we try not to do, in case we get sent away. That fear hangs heavy inside me. No one seems to think of us as another part of all of them, so we assume that we are not. Yet there are hard times when the difference is apparent. Times when I see one of those children cuddled in her mother's lap or lifted high on his father's shoulders. Such things don't happen for either of us, although both parents are kind in a nonchalant way, on those few occasons when they pay attention to us. No one comes when I cry in the night. We are afterthoughts to that family, Henry and I.

I remember the day someone takes Henry's hand and mine, leads us onto a massive ship. Named *Eliza*, I think. That feminine name seems strange for such a huge vessel, its towering masts, sails flying against the clouds. Truth is, that might be the name of the ship my father sailed on when he first left without me. He's told me his story a hundred times since we reunited, and I've long since mixed it all up with mine—or forgotten. So many things forgotten.

Awash in memories, floating somewhere in the past, when in truth I am right here. Here on this dock, waiting. Living my own story. Whatever the name of the ship, I remember that crossing as one long nightmare of dark and light, of nausea and vomiting, of someone cleaning up my mess and chiding me bitterly. Then hunger. So sick I could not have eaten had food been available. I wanted my mother. She would feed me, stroke my hair, and whisper in my ear. One day I sneak my way up to the deck, hunting for something I can't even name. I remember the sudden light and the blue of the sky as I climb out, the sound of sails flapping, air free of vile odors. I remember it well. Everything so wide, with no boundaries. The lapping sound of the water against the sides of the ship. And the wind, oh, the wind. I put my arms in the air and allow it to hold me.

I'm drifting again. Like the water, the sea, the river. Ah, the river. Begin with the river, this treacherous assemblage of untold drops of rain or dew or snow, collecting and seeking its way to the sea, the most major river of this new world, barely explored, waiting to be conquered.

Nicholas and I are prepared to do just that.

CHAPTER 2

There has been no calm water since the day we met, Nicholas and I. He is a close colleague of my father, nearly my father's age. So the problem was obvious from the start—he was too old for me by far, even in an era when men commonly were older than their wives. The larger problem, perhaps, was that I was too young, even in an era when it was common for brides to walk down the aisle to marry at only eighteen or younger. I was an emerging adolescent when he first knocked at the door of our house. He had come to propose some business to Father.

Since I happened to be passing through the front hall on my way to the library for an architectural reference I needed, I let him in. Yes, I opened that wide oak door as he stood with his hand raised, about to knock again. So handsome, he was and is: tall and angular, with narrow features and a thick head of wavy dark hair. Just the sort of man to capture a young girl's fancy.

"Miss Latrobe, I presume." There was a lilt to his voice as he tipped his hat and introduced himself. "I'm Nicholas Roosevelt. Here to see your father, please."

"Won't you come in, sir?" I watched him swipe his boots clean before entering.

He threw out some tidbit of humor for me to catch. I don't remember what. I tossed one back, which caught his attention. At least he laughed.

I gestured to Father's study and watched him walk with purpose down the hall. With each rhythmic step, his shoulders shifted as in an unfamiliar dance step. Something in me quickened. Something new and unexpected brought my body taut and urgent. I heard the enthusiasm of my father's greeting as he closed the door to his study. I stood there, looking at that door, holding those unfamiliar, imperative urgings within me until there was nothing to do but continue to the library and search for my architectural book. I had a drawing to complete, a drawing of a home we never had.

Yet in that moment, I knew in the core of my being that this man would be my life. And so he is. And has been. And will be until I die.

Ah, I'm adrift again. Time is almost irrelevant: the past and this present moment flowing together, as my own life flows here now into these turbulent Western Waters, this riverine network that forms the western boundaries of this new country. So, I'll begin, finally. You were wondering? Yes, I'll begin—here at the dock in Pittsburgh, waiting to embark on a journey that will alter history. At least we believe so, Nicholas and I, assuming that we are successful. There is every reason to believe that we should be. We have spent the last three years preparing for every challenge these waters may present to us. I am impatient to see my husband's face. The moment is approaching for our venture to begin. Along with the brave task it will involve.

Speaking of brave tasks, I am paying entirely too little attention to this unruly crowd amassing outside our doors, on the dock of the Monongahela River. "Falling banks," I'm told the name means. An alarming name for a river. Fortunately, our journey begins at the juncture where that river ends, where it flows into the Allegheny and becomes the Ohio. Our launch here, I presume, is well beyond the danger of falling banks.

Come now, Lydia. Pay attention. You must focus. It's almost time. I fix my gaze out through the dirty glass doors of the Mississippi Steamboat Navigation Company. A jostling crowd made up of every sort of person, from well-dressed Pittsburgh elite to rough-clad dockworkers, is forming. All waiting for me to join my husband—yes, my Nicholas—on his steamboat. More importantly, to see his remarkable vessel launched—the one the world deems an impossible folly. I am aware of many out there who actually wish to see us fail, if only to boast how righteous they are in their predictions of this venture's failure. More than a few even dare to make that plain to Nicholas's face.

Only yesterday a well-attired gentleman approached us on the dock. I thought he must be curious about our remarkable boat. Instead, he accosted my husband with loud, belittling insults.

"Foolhardy!" He tapped his cane at Nicholas's toes, almost striking him. "It cannot be done."

So rude!

He continued, looking about to see how much of an audience he'd garnered. He thwacked his cane, again barely missing Nicholas's foot. "And you are just the man to prove its folly." He laughed disparagingly. "Trying to prove you're a man, are you, Roosevelt?"

"Indeed, sir," Nicholas responded, his demeanor one of exceptional dignified calm. "And you are right, sir. I am the man to prove it! To prove it can be done." He paused. "To prove not only that it can be done, but also that it *will* be done. A simple matter of removing the *not*."

Nicholas took my arm, smiling down at me. We turned

away, as if the man's comments were nothing. Which is indeed what they were.

It seems only those who understand the powerful workings of steam comprehend how possible this venture is—enough to invest heavily in our endeavor, though the number of those who think toward the future is small. The steamboat *New Orleans*, built according to Nicholas's design, is funded by the two "Roberts"—Fulton and Chancellor Livingston. Its construction was based on information we garnered on our previous momentous, if disastrous, flatboat journey. Our honeymoon, that was—six months spent on a primitive flatboat, charting the river, with me at Nicholas's side. I believed in him then. That voyage is evidence. And I believe in him now. This steamboat journey with him, a feat never attempted before by anyone, will prove my husband's pluck and intellect and will confirm my confidence in him. Well, and if I must confess, I am seduced by the sheer adventure of it. I cannot resist this voyage any more than I could have passed up that ill-starred six-month honeymoon expedition.

Our honeymoon on the flatboat was an adventure like no other, in spite of my carefully designed living quarters, for which Nicholas gave me free hand. My simple training in architectural drawing with my father was brought to fruition, if only in a minor way. What pure delight it was to design my own parlor and fireplace on a boat that was otherwise equivalent to a cigar box turned upside down on top of a larger cigar box!

I could miss this embarkment, thinking back on that voyage! The night we woke in terror to a pair of Indians invading our sleeping quarters, demanding whiskey. Nicholas rose in trepidation and handed over a bottle to get them off the boat. In a matter of days, Nicholas, plus all three of the crew—Billy and Samuel, who are again on this voyage, along with my handmaid, Sarah—succumbed to the fever, leaving only me, pregnant and nauseated, to tend to the sick, the cooking, and the boat.

By the time we reached Natchez, all of them had recovered except Nicholas. The barely recuperated men dashed ashore for a boisterous night in that dingy settlement, notorious for its brothels and gambling halls along the shore. Natchez-Under-the-Hill, the locals have dubbed this district for the high bluffs that rise above and the obvious difference in lifestyle between the two levels. Sarah and I sat on deck, close enough to hear Nicholas in case he called. We amused ourselves in attention to the rowdy carousing in town and relished the cool night air which refreshed us. From nowhere came a deafening crack, and we were slammed from our seats with a violent drop in the river. Scrambling for footing, we sloshed through the water surging round our feet. Our hull had been punctured! We had landed on a snag. Water flooded in like the river itself. We clambered for buckets or pails. For hours we bailed, Sarah and I, bending, lurching, filling, sloshing, pouring, but to no avail. Exhausted, our backs and limbs aching and without further hope, we dragged my sick husband from his bed, clambered up the steep bank to dry land with Nicholas propped unsteadily between us. Unable to shut out the reverberations of the town's wild revelry behind us, we watched our boat sink. At dawn, I heard the men return, their low laughter halting as they caught sight of the three of us sprawled on the bank in the early light.

"Where's the boat?" Billy asked, almost as if it were an ordinary question.

I pointed at the vague outline of the rails under the waves of dark water. The awning I had installed on the roof of the cabin was ripped and flapped about in the varying current. Nicholas tried to raise his head, but he was still too weak.

An astonished silence ensued. Then chaotic noise: feet scraping down the bank, splashing into shallow water; slamming and banging as Billy righted the rowboat and landed it on the roof of the flatboat, where the now barely attached awning wrapped around him in the current.

"It's scuttled," he announced, defeat in his voice. "Ain't no way to get this thing off that snag." Wet boots sloshing, he heaved the rowboat to shore, and then the two men dragged it onto the bank. "At least we got a sturdy rowboat to handle this wicked river to New Orleans."

And we did. But that's another story altogether.

Wandering around in my head, caught in the past again. *Focus now, Lydia.*

I'm impatient, tired of waiting to board my husband's new vessel. I need this voyage. Need to be part of it. And Nicholas needs me to be. Like my husband, I ignore snide remarks as to our foolishness, especially mine, since I am a full eight months with child. With Rosetta, our toddler, in tow. This boat is assuredly safer than the flatboat that sank or the rowboat that brought us all finally from Natchez to New Orleans. I do not listen to the criticism. Nor does Nicholas. What would be the point?

Nicholas's keen mind has attended to every consideration in the design of this boat, including the side paddle wheels, which he suggested to Robert Livingston a good ten years ago, only to have his idea scoffed at and rejected, then subsequently appropriated and presented to Fulton as if the design were Livingston's own—Chancellor Livingston, who administered the oath of office to this country's first president. Now it is Fulton who gets all the credit associated with steamboats. But Fulton's boats handle only calm waters. The *New Orleans* is a different invention altogether, designed to conquer waters no one else would dare to defy. All the credit for this achievement will be my husband's.

This waiting! Time is stretching out. Discomfort gnaws at my legs. I shift from foot to foot, wiggle my toes in my boots to relieve the distress. At least they are dry. Standing is more and more difficult with my growing belly and a nagging pain in my low back. Only the windowed entrance to the offices separates me from the rambunctious crowd gathering on the dock. In a moment I must negotiate that crush. The glass doors, on which the company name is prominently painted, are smudged with handprints, despite being cleaned yesterday. No matter. I have a reasonable view. I am just awaiting the boarding whistle of the *New Orleans*. Though I am anticipating that jarring sound any moment, I fear I will jump at the whistle's explosive blast.

At the water's edge, heavy cinder-laden smoke from the boat's tall stack trails black across the murky sky, darker yet more alive with its embers than the gloomy industrial air of Pittsburgh, which we have been breathing for almost two years. I will welcome clearer air out on the river. Our boat is schooner rigged, with masts and sails, in case the engine should somehow fail—which it will not, as we will not. Here among keelboats and flatboats, our vessel's appearance is massive and unusual, its masts and smokestack like the offspring of a union between sailing ship and river barge.

My fingers are at work in the soft fur at the neck of Tiger, my great black Newfoundland dog, who will accompany us on our voyage. Another detail that elicits insults. I am trying to stave off anxiety. Close beside me, my friend Margarite—yes, I actually have a few friends from our long stay—seems to recognize the unease I am so attempting to conceal. She touches my arm, comforts me with a knowing smile. Rosetta clutches tightly at my knee. She's holding my leg and sucking her thumb, her little face hidden in the folds of my skirts. I lean down to reassure her, but she shakes her head and buries her face deeper into the white muslin of my dress. I'm hoping she won't leave it smudged before we walk to the boat.

I am considering the mud of Water Street and wondering how to hold my hem and Rosetta both when Bessie, our pretty young nursemaid, appears and scoops her up. Rosetta's little bonnet tumbles as she snugs her face into Bessie's neck. Quick as always, Sarah reaches to catch it. The friends who've come to bid me farewell smile at this simple domesticity. There is nothing either familiar or domestic in what is about to come. In a moment we will open these doors and make our way to the deck of the *New Orleans*—an untried vessel unlike any before it.

Beneath my fingertips, Tiger emits an unexpected low growl. Outside someone shouts in the crowd, and then another, then more. I stare through the dirty window as a chorus of bellowed insults rises dark as the smoke from the stack, insults turning into chants of mockery and worse. No wonder my sweet Rosetta is afraid. So am I. I want to cover her ears. My heart is racing. My fingers hidden in Tiger's fur are trembling. This jeering crowd is more frightening than any part of the river Nicholas and I traveled by flatboat—even with all the mishaps.

Here I am, surrounded not only by my few friends but also by an inelegant gathering of otherwise elegant women, almost all in fine white muslin dresses. Mine is a necessity for the show of our departure. Not theirs, which are nothing more than a show of ostentation, barely covered by short spencer jackets or fur-lined tippets hanging to their knees. A few wear less elegant redingotes, like mine, if they prefer warmth to fashion, which I do. More than a few are still intent on dissuading me from going, some from genuine concern, I'll admit, the rest out of their not-so-private sense of judgmental propriety.

Two of the women, with whom I have frequently dined, are whispering behind gloved hands with no shame whatever; they stop when they notice me watching. Another pair have the temerity to approach me point-blank, the feathers on their tall bonnets quivering. I straighten myself, pat Rosetta's back to hide my trembling hands. Ah, yes, I know them and wish I didn't. Mrs. Bellingham, if I remember her name correctly, seems to be the chosen spokeswoman.

"Out of great concern, I feel compelled to speak before it becomes too late to save you from yourself."

"What is it you wish to say?" I ask. I look her straight in the eye. I wonder if there is anyone to save her from herself.

She pauses, flips the corner of her lace handkerchief. "No lady, certainly no self-respecting lady, would consider such a voyage as you are about to embark upon, especially so heavy with child and with a defenseless toddler in tow. You should be at home. What sort of mother are you?"

My mind is blank for one second. Then flooded: *One who knows what it is to be a child without a mother.*

As for childbirth, I know too well its dangers; my own mother was buried back in England with her unnamed infant, dead in spite of the best care possible. If, like my mother, I could die at home despite excellent care, why should I not risk this daring adventure? All the contentions against my going mean nothing to me. Being with my husband is home and safety enough.

The other woman elbows her way forward. "And that dangerous Tecumseh stirring up violence among the Indians all along the west bank of the river. How can you dare put yourself and your family in that terrible danger?"

I do not bother to remind her that General Harrison marched out in late September with fourteen hundred troops to settle the Tecumseh problem.

Brashly, the woman at the rear of the group asks, "If you have no shame, what of your husband? Has your husband none himself that he would permit such behavior from his wife?"

I face them, holding Tiger tight—in truth, trying to hold on to myself. I take a moment, withhold my words, working to arrange them just so. I fix the first of the two women with my eyes before I speak.

"Ah, well, ladies!" *Do I honestly call them that?* "You must indeed count yourselves fortunate not to have adventurous husbands who desire to have you beside them."

I swivel a bit to address the woman in back.

"You pose an interesting question, Mrs., umm . . ." I hesitate, then continue. "Indeed, an excellent question. No shame?" I wait. I wait long enough to gauge her discomfort. "Ah, yes, madam, a very good question. Have you no shame?"

A small woman steps forward, inserting herself between us. It is Mrs. Melton, a lady of middle age, with whom we have recently spent a delightful evening discussing preparations for our voyage.

"We only wish you well, Lydia. This is quite an adventure you are undertaking. As you see, there is no little concern for your well-being." She speaks in a moderate tone. "For my own part, yes, genuine concern, along with the sincerest wishes for your well-being, but far more than that, an immense admiration for your spirit and courage to stand by your husband in this historic endeavor."

She touches my sleeve with light gloved fingers. I nod, take Rosetta's bonnet from Sarah's hand, and adjust it off-kilter on her little head. The baby shifts inside me as I tilt forward.

A bolt of noise, the jarring whistle blows a loud hissing that rises to a shrill hoot before falling and rounding out low. Blows again. I do not jump. I surprise myself, pleased to be composed. Perhaps the ordeal with these women has steeled me for the blast.

The door is open now. The chill air of Pittsburgh rushes in. My nostrils fill with the acrid smells of smoke and industry, mixed with the odor of the unwashed in the swarm of spectators outside. I long for a clean breath. It is time to make our way to the boat. I eye the dock ahead of me, seeking my best route through this deafening crowd.

Bessie looks me in the eye. "Would you like her to walk with you, Mrs. Roosevelt?" She sets Rosetta down beside me.

I nod. Rosetta does not raise her head as I take her hand. I step forward, chin raised. My daughter's hand in mine is cold. Tiger walks beside me, his leash taut. He steps in front of me. I pause to loosen the leash; he moves to the other side of Rosetta. She reaches with her other hand to grasp his ear and giggles up at me. My gentle giant of a dog, who snuggles and guards my little one, will be on board with us. Surely the smile inside me must show on the face I am working to hold deliberately still. In my peripheral vision I glimpse a gathering of smiles, nudges between spectators to call attention to this endearing moment.

I fix my eyes on the bold, colorful script painted on the side of the boat: the *New Orleans*—our vessel, our momentary home, our destination, our measure of success. I step forward. Relief flows through me as the difficulty of negotiating this tangled crowd begins to dissolve. The spectators cease their cat-calls, quiet themselves, and move back as we glide into their midst. I could be Moses parting the waters, except for the noise of my sturdy boots on the unmoving wood of the dock. Heels echoing, I accelerate my pace toward the boat where Nicholas waits. Ah, now I see him, his handsome narrow face, his white cravat, his dashing cutaway jacket in honor of the occasion and, best of all, his smile of reassurance. His eyes never leave my face as I approach. He steps down the gangplank, hand extended, to assist us across.

"Welcome aboard, Mrs. Roosevelt," he says, squeezing my hand.

I am smiling broadly now as Rosetta tugs at his jacket, calling excitedly, "Papa, Papa."

"Ah, and little Miss Roosevelt, too!"

Tiger steps back as Nicholas lifts her to his shoulders, where she squeals and comes alive, waves to the crowd as if they were cheering her. I survey the sea of faces, glimpse an older woman, cracked lips upturned in a smile on her rough, sun-weathered face. Her skin, her demeanor tell me she has lived a great deal, that she senses, understands what I am doing. Her eyes are kind. My face relaxes. After nodding to her, I take my husband's arm and turn with him away from the dock and toward the river. Rosetta, from her high perch on his shoulders, is waving and laughing now, the dancing giggle only a child can emit.

"We are about to embark," Nicholas says in a low voice, as if it were our personal secret, one I did not already know.

"Indeed, we are." I squeeze his hand.

"Are you certain, Lydia? There is still time. Is this truly where you wish to be?"

I hold his hand in both of mine. "There is nowhere else I would consider being, Nicholas. If I cannot be with you, then there is nowhere else on earth for me to be."

Someone in the crowd has overheard, laughs derisively, and whistles. Nothing is secret in front of an audience like this, the bulk of them hostile to one degree or another. We have been in this bustling port, this grimy hub of boat construction, for over a year, approaching two years, in truth. I tend to lose track of time, but we came here soon after Rosetta's birth in New York. From the time we arrived in Pittsburgh, Nicholas has been steadily occupied with supervising construction. His collaboration with Livingston and Fulton has resulted in a vessel they are all confident can defy the treacheries of the Western Waters and can navigate upriver against the erratic, overwhelming currents of the Mississippi.

The plan is for this boat to become a packet to establish regular upstream trade between New Orleans and Natchez. Now it is set, all 1480 feet of it, with a width of thirty-two feet and a molded depth of twelve feet. Even before the boat's keel was laid, the boatyard drew throngs of sightseers and naysayers. Its location is convenient to tourists, along with the adjacent glassworks, which is the pride of the city. I greeted a number of those visitors with Tiger at my side during my frequent forays to the construction dock. At last, we are waving goodbye.

"Here, Lydia." Nicholas swings Rosetta toward me. "Take her now."

"Come to Mama, little one."

I embrace her as she falls into my arms, cherishing her excitement and ignoring the impact on my extended abdomen. My own thrill is equal, if hidden. Though she has no way of knowing, my sweet girl has survived this treacherous river before, tucked safely in my womb, like this new babe I carry within me now. Her knowledge of that voyage will come only from the stories we tell her, the memories we share, just as I heard stories of my own early history from my father—my mother's death, my father's flight to America. Once I rejoined him, I clung to his presence like a shadow.

The two years of our separation had seemed eternal, somehow outside of time entirely. Time seemed not to exist. The exact date of our reunion certainly did not exist for me, as is the case for most children, certainly not after that terrible voyage. I'd have to go back to my birth and figure out the mathematics to get to a date, and even then, I wouldn't be quite sure. But I know that day, if not the date. It lives in my mind as if in the present: my father's exuberant, openhearted welcome, his wide-armed embrace of us both as we emerged from the boat onto the dock, the sun and the breeze, then steady planks under my feet. It would take me days not to feel as if I was still rocking on that ship and to trust that the surfaces beneath me would remain steady.

On the shore stood a beautiful woman, a warm smile on her face as she watched our excitement at reuniting with our father. "This is Mary Elizabeth. She is your new mother." That's how my father introduced her in his clear voice when we reached the end of the dock where she stood waiting. I was very shy around her at first, though I later came to love and enjoy her. Not so my brother, Henry. He threw his arms around her and wouldn't let go, overjoyed simply to have a mother. I wondered if he even remembered the mother we had lost back in England. For me, this woman was a stranger who shouldn't be, this new wife of my father's. I was simply overcome with the joy of seeing his kind face again, his round spectacles, the soft curve of his cheeks down to his full-lipped mouth. And having the security of his strong embrace. A new mother and a new home, however well designed, would take me a bit of time to accept.

My own designing skills came from my closeness to my father, who gladly shared his extensive architectural proficiencies with me. He loved how, even as a child, I understood his thoughts, his process from concept to drawing, from drawing to plans, right to his overseeing the construction of buildings as extraordinary as the new Capitol Building in Washington, DC. He designed the magnificent porticos of the White House under his friend, Thomas Jefferson, who bestowed upon him the official title: Benjamin Henry Latrobe, Surveyor of the Public Buildings of the United States.

He deserves exceptional recognition and will gain more, though his present accolades are fair enough. I believe he will be known as the father of American architecture. Of course, there is also brittle criticism of his work. The vast opportunities in this nascent country lead to more than a little nasty competition, and he is often a target, much like my Nicholas.

As a child, I had been lost without my father. Once we were reunited, I tagged along wherever I was allowed to watch him at work. He loved that I was more enthralled with poring over his designs, drawing my own plans for a family home—the one we never had—than with listening to his tales of visits with George Washington or Thomas Jefferson. Those were hardly more than grown-up talk to me, until I became a bit older and began to listen more intently than anyone knew, except Nicholas, of course. I grew quite proud, feeling that Father's associations somehow rendered me more important, more adult and notable myself, especially to Nicholas. Now I'm fascinated by the distinguished people my father knew to one degree or another: Washington, Jefferson, Madison. Dolley Madison, whose husband is almost as many years older than she as Nicholas is me, became my dear friend, even attended my wedding in her somewhat scandalous low-cut gown. There were those, of course, who had no faith in my father, who questioned his plan to provide running water for the city of Philadelphia. Well, he astounded them! Woke the whole city one morning with all the bells ringing and water pouring from newly installed hydrants into the streets!

Bells are ringing now. I hear them pealing in the distance over the noise of the crowd and the growing rumble of the engine, the slow splash of paddles gaining speed as the wheels turn. Nicholas and I stand at the bow, looking at the river, looking forward, his arm around my waist, as our keel slices the water beneath us.

"We are underway, my love," he says.

"Yes, *we*!" I say. "Here I am with you." I am my father's daughter, and I am my husband's wife. The bells are tolling onshore.

CHAPTER 3

Our first sunset is brilliant, the waters of the Ohio reflecting the peach and coral of the sky, lapping the deep blue sides of our boat with warm color. In spite of the glorious horizon ahead now that we have left the dingy air of Pittsburgh behind, our first evening on board is anything but peaceful. The steamboat is so different from the flatboat: the men shouting over the constant roar of steam, the pounding rhythms of the motors and paddles, the intermittent clang of shovels scraping and loading coal, smoke and sparks flying from the stack. There is no respite from the endless noise.

Nothing is familiar. Not even for the crew, who had the chance to take one brief, successful test run upriver from Pittsburg and back. These men are unsurpassed—Nicholas has made sure of that—proficient, well-trained boatmen who know in their bones the fickleness of these waters. Two have made this trip with us before: Billy and Samuel. All the experienced men of this crew know boats and navigation, especially Billy. But no one knows this particular boat. And on these particular rivers. None of us can. Nicholas and I know what we believe and expect. But how this boat will, in reality, handle the Western Waters—indeed, if it will, especially the Mississippi, that treacherous river ahead, capable of changing its mind in any given half hour—is only our best estimate, an act of faith buoyed by ambition.

Ambition is our key! If we succeed, history will be changed. We—Nicholas and I—will transform the face of trade in this new nation. We will break the formidable boundaries of its interior open to expansion. And finally, we will prove to my father that Nicholas, mature as he is and young as I am, is precisely the husband for me.

Our love was so difficult for my father to accept, even though he and Nicholas have been the best of friends and colleagues. He often depends on their collaboration and greatly respects Nicholas's skills. I know he has misgivings about Nicholas's business skills. But Nicholas's indebtedness is not a result of anything he did himself. The cancellation of his great contract to supply metal sheathing for numerous ships in case of war with France was due entirely to the election of President Jefferson, who happened to love France. No, it is the difference in our ages that created an immense impasse for my father, in spite of the reality that many wives are far younger than their husbands. Just look at our dear friend Dolley Madison. Perhaps it was not so much the age difference that was the actual problem as it was my own premature age. I was too young, he thought, to feel such love and to deal with such lifelong decisions.

I was so angry with him, even as he was with me, when he sent me off to boarding school. That day is etched in my head forever. I was separated not only from Nicholas but from my father and my family yet again. It was only two years later, when I reached the age of seventeen, that Papa realized the genuine strength of our love for one another, relented, and gave his blessing for our marriage. As I grow older, my anger toward him dissipates and my understanding of his misgivings grows. He was protecting me, I know, now that I am older. Angry as he was, it was only his love that sent me away.

A playful touch on my shoulder startles me. Nicholas chuckles. The noise around me is so deafening I failed to hear his steps across the deck. I lean back hungrily into the security of his encircling arm.

"I am so grateful you are here," he whispers in my ear, knocking my bonnet slightly askew, his warm hand caressing my shoulder. "Here with me in this new venture! With me for this coming birth." He strokes my great belly. "My intrepid Lydia!"

I turn my face to him, hold his cheeks in my palms. "Nicholas." I pause. "You once told me that you would never abandon me. And you have not. Nor will I abandon you. You, Mr. Roosevelt, flesh of my flesh, are affixed to me whatever adventures you dare!" I raise my lips and kiss his cheek.

The memory of Nicholas's promise when my irate father sent me away to boarding school in a vain attempt to separate us, is like a voice in my head: "Have no fear, Lydia. I will never abandon you." Even now I feel the profound sincerity of his promise. "We will be together. We will. You may be certain, Lydia. I will be here waiting when you return."

Oh, those memories! My father in the doorway of his study, shouting in rage at Nicholas when he came to know the attraction we had for one another! I cannot forget it! Nicholas had become uneasy and had decided he must speak to my father. I had followed a bit behind. Nicholas had spoken to him with the utmost sincerity, yet my father became enraged. So, at a mature fifteen, I was sent to Jaudon Female Academy, a good three hours away, where I was as alone as when my father fled England, and even more so, without my brother, Henry, by my side. But Nicholas had promised to be waiting.

Indeed, he was faithful through two years of separation,

sending constant letters of encouragement and love, which helped to fill the void of my separation from my family as well as from this dear man I loved. It was those letters that truly enraged my father—as if we had engaged in deception—enraged him to the point of canceling some business contracts with Nicholas. Yet Nicholas was there waiting for me when my father finally conceded the reality of our love and allowed us to marry.

It was that attentiveness, that sense of pure presence, conveyed even in his letters, that had first attracted me to Nicholas. It had somehow broken through the barriers of my perpetual loneliness one day in the library when he leaned down over my shoulder to see the architectural book I was studying. "Come," he said and led me to a desk, where he began to draw out his initial ideas of a boat based on the very principles I was examining. No one had ever been so present. And he has remained so. Nicholas did not abandon me for his work once we were wed, as is so customary for women in society. He scandalized Washington culture by giving me the unheard-of freedom to accompany him on that hazardous flatboat journey—our "honeymoon."

The genteel entertained themselves by condemning us as reckless. More than a few still do, as was proven shortly ago on the dock. But Nicholas knows me in a way no one else does; he comprehends both my venturesome nature and the lingering fear I knew as a child at being left by my father as he fled his grief. He shares also my grief for my mother, as his own died when he was only three. Indeed, I believe it may have been that very combination of unusual daring and leftover vulnerability that charmed him so when I was still an adolescent. I remember in our early conversations together the sparkle in his eyes when I would fairly explode with inventive ideas, ones usually related to architecture or design. Later he gave me charge of the design for all the living quarters on that flatboat, a home on the water, in spite of my reckless endeavor in agreeing to accompany him down the Mississippi on such a primitive vessel.

As darkness begins to meld with the sunset, the chaos of organizational chores diminishes among our six hands. The rhythmic slapping of the paddles is growing familiar.

I turn at an urgent tugging on my skirt and the sound of a whimpering voice.

"Mama, Mama. Where my teddy?" Rosetta is on tiptoe, balancing herself with a grip on my skirt. It is past her bedtime. Bessie is right behind her, trying to calm and contain her.

I hold out my hand to Bessie, reach down and pick Rosetta up. It is becoming increasingly difficult for me to do so as my belly protrudes more by the day.

Nicholas gives her a good-night kiss and heads up to the pilothouse.

"Where Teddy, Mama?"

"He's at home in his bed, remember? We left him there to be comfortable. It's winter, you know. That's when bears sleep all winter long."

Rosetta had been so excited as we prepared for the voyage, running on tiptoes with one toy after another.

"Mama, want Teddy!" She had begged more than once.

"Sweet one, Teddy is too big. He'll take up too much room in your little bed," I had said. Teddy is as big as Rosetta. "You know he has to sleep."

"But he can have my blankie, Mama. Sleep on the floor. He can, Mama." So insistent!

"But not on the boat, baby girl. It's not like home. The floor tilts back and forth." I rocked my body and let my feet slip around on the floor to show her. "He'll slide all over. Somebody might step on him and hurt Teddy." I think how injured one of us could be if we tripped on Teddy in the night.

So difficult to convince her that she could not bring every one of her toys, only a few favorites and nothing the size of her teddy. At last, she settled for her soft blue rabbit, a pull toy, a handful of stuffed dolls, and a wooden one, which hopefully will not break on the journey.

She seems a bit afraid as she cuddles up to me now, taking her thumb out of her mouth.

"Sweet Bunny can sleep with you tonight." I smooth her hair and hug her.

Now, in the excitement of being on board, it is difficult to get her to sleep. Some of the fault may be my own state of mind. On this larger boat, I feel somehow uneasy myself, unwelcome memories arising of that dark hole of a voyage across the sea to my father. Strange how memories will take you afloat from where you are. I must overcome that. I carry her to our cabin, snuggle Bunny into her arms, and stroke her hair as I walk her around the floor. I am tired. Finally, her head and her little hand droop. I grab at Bunny as he slips from her fingers. Gently I lay her in the bed Nicholas built for her, attached to the flooring so it will not be in danger of skidding about with the river's movement, unlike the big teddy bear she wanted so badly to bring.

After nodding to Bessie, I make my way back to the deck and absorb the final disappearing rays of gold and salmon. Thankfully, I changed those fine dress boots from the dock for my simple kid half boots. My toes are utterly grateful! I regret that Bessie is missing the end of this glorious sunset. Well, there will be others to marvel at—many more. Sarah is somewhere, doing something. I'm not concerned. She knows how to take care of herself.

With darkness, things begin to grow quiet. The three off-duty crewmen have gone to their quarters to sleep. I hope they will rest. Our pilot, Andrew Jack, and our engineer, Nicholas Baker, both experienced and of high repute, are at their stations, guiding us to the spot where we will tie up for the night. The coal shovel clangs now and then. Sparks fly higher. The rhythmic rumble of the engine and paddle wheels will be with us until we reach New Orleans. I will grow accustomed to the noise, I am sure. And we will reach New Orleans. Of that, I am certain. And not in a rowboat!

Ah, Nicholas is here. I am not startled this time. I turn for a moment as he comes to me at the stern, where I am savoring the reflection of the rising moon on dark water. Together we watch the flickering moonlight in the doubled, unifying wake behind us. It is somehow like a marriage. Two paddle wheels turning, moving us into the future, their separate wakes merging as one at the center, calming the motion, unifying our progress. Nicholas takes my hand, and I rest my head on his shoulder. His arm around me is snug and strong; his embrace is comfort to me. We stand here together, our unborn infant turning gently inside me, a little foot kicking out to the right, a habitual movement of this infant we await, this child to be born on the river.

The engine and paddles slow, and Andrew brings the boat around into a small hollow in the bank. Two of the crew, Samuel and Jessup, leap off to secure us for the night, then grapple their way back on board by the rope ladders they drop by the rails till morning. Night sounds reach me over the dying rumble of machinery: an owl, crickets, katydids and, best of all, the high trill of tree frogs so late in the season. Tiger comes and nudges his big head under my hand. I twirl the soft fur of his head.

"The world is before us," I say, turning my face up to my husband.

"Indeed, it is." He whispers against my cheek, his lips turning from words to soft kisses. "And you are with me. Your courage is a gift to me, Lydia. I'm grateful. I can't bear to think how lonely I would be here without you."

"You are making history, Nicholas. More than history . . . This country's future will shift. It will never be the same once we complete this voyage."

"You tend to exaggerate, my love. But yes. Certainly, river trade will be enhanced."

"And the ease of westward travel."

"We do not possess that land, Lydia. Except the Louisiana Purchase. The rest is Indian Territory. Our purpose is viable upriver trade, which will change the nation a great deal."

"Yes, I know. We will be in undefined territory for this journey. Our country to the east, and Indian Territory to our west. We will be in no-man's-land. Well, not exactly land." I laugh. "No man's water all the way."

Nicholas chuckles and gives me a kiss on the forehead.

"Look!" I say, pointing up.

Above us, high in the western sky, shines the brilliant comet with its long, wide trailing tail that first appeared in the heavens last March. The Great Comet of 1811, it has been dubbed. Among the superstitious, it is seen as a cursed omen of evil—against us, in particular. The cantankerous have said so, both to us and behind our backs, I hear. There were numerous trials in constructing this boat, each of which has been attributed to the comet. Nicholas faced so many complications: skilled worker shortages, supply shortages, an absence of adequate oak and even ordinary pine because of the widespread forest clearing, even the necessity of building new sawpits and workshops to deal with the size of the boat. Because of foundry limitations, he was forced to arrange for boiler plates from the East, hauled cross-country by oxen. Then came repeated floods that utterly destroyed a nearby dock, dislodging it and slamming the entire length of it onto Water Street, where it barely missed hitting the frame of our boat. During another flood soon after, the water rose so high, it came near to launching our partially constructed hull.

The comet gets the blame for even more sinister things. Rivermen all along the docks bear terrible tales of the water. Immense flooding has torn at roots and shallow graves alike, causing trees and bodies to float in the muddy water, they say. In its wake a deadly pestilence has spread among the scattered settlements. Squirrels by the thousands have leaped into the upper waters and swum south amidst an alarming din of chatter, and hundreds have died from their efforts, their rotting bodies floating down the Ohio. I pray we do not encounter them.

The men lower their voices when they speak of British conspiracies meant to provoke war to regain lost territory and of the Shawnee warrior chief Tecumseh and his brother, the Prophet, urging the tribes to join together in a league to guard the west bank of the river against American expansion. Wildest of all are the rumors of Tecumseh threatening to stomp his feet and shake the very earth itself. Now add to that the endless arguments among our business partners, who seem to need Nicholas to blame for every difficulty and its financial repercussions. All these dire things blamed at one time or another on that beautiful comet! Well, perhaps not the partners' arguments.

Yet here we are on October 20, 1811, having launched and cruised the river this first night of our journey. The light of the comet gleams on the water as we stand on the deck in the still night. Come Christmas, we will still be on this boat, with a newborn in our arms. Perhaps the comet is our guiding star.

CHAPTER 4

I wake feeling as heavy as the concentrated rumbling of the engine that fills our cabin. The engine and the paddles have priority here, and rightly so. Nicholas and I sat on the deck late into the night, satiating ourselves on the thrill of our early progress. My waking consciousness is soothed by the memory of gliding past dark forests, a canopy of bright stars above us, the brilliant comet guiding our way. And then the welcome quiet once we were moored and the engine and the paddles ceased for the night.

I stretch my neck, my cheek sliding over the smooth pillowcase, grateful I insisted on good linens. I roll over to Nicholas's kiss as he rises from our berth. I cherish his tenderness before I open my eyes to look into those of my handsome husband. Nicholas smiles at me as he tucks in his shirt. Then he is gone. I sigh, wondering how we both manage to fit in this narrow berth. Once again, I regret the redesign of our accommodations, not to suit ourselves, but for the benefit of the passengers we hope to entice. My freedom to devise the floor plan of our flatboat gave us a living space as homelike as possible, and our cabin was so cozy. This is a different vessel altogether, with a uniquely different purpose, of course—for trade upriver and to carry passengers in both directions. Our elegant accommodations and dining for as many as seventy-five was advertised in the *Gazette* as an enticement to passengers. However, we have none.

"That fine elegance will do them little good at the bottom of the river," said the wife of one gentleman, who seemed to be considering the trip with us at least as far as Louisville. He had even boarded and taken a brief tour. But her disparagement proved effective.

"Impressive accommodations, Mr. Roosevelt. Another time perhaps," he said. "When we have seen this vessel ply its way back to us. For now, I'll go by coach." He gave his arm to his doubtful wife and turned his back on my husband.

I'm glad not to have such a man aboard. Once Nicholas and I prove this vessel capable of enduring the vagaries of the river, there will be an abundance of trade and passenger travel. Indeed, a demand for it. That man will stand in line, wishing he could get a ticket. Livingston, and even Fulton, will express gratitude for the profits, and my father will ask my pardon for his distrust regarding our marriage. I know he trusted and relied on Nicholas's inventive design and engineering skills, but our union is playing out in quite an unusual way, which does nothing to assuage my father's concern for me. This journey is so untried, so dangerous. I understand his skepticism, alarm even. It is shared dramatically by a large portion of the population. At least my father has more faith in Nicholas's abilities than anyone other than Fulton and Chancellor Livingston. Or me.

On the other side of the green damask curtain, which provides us a modicum of privacy, I hear Rosetta waking. Sarah is singing a little nursery rhyme in a whispered voice to keep from rousing me. I listen.

Bobby Shafto's gone to sea,
Silver buckles at his knee;
He'll come back and marry me,
Bonny Bobby Shafto!
Bobby Shafto's bright and fair,
Combing down his yellow hair;
He's my love for evermore,
Bonny Bobby Shafto!

I cherish such moments as these. Sarah's plethora of little songs are a treasure to me. Such things were missing from my own childhood. My mother must have sung such songs. I can't imagine that she would not, but I have no memory of this. By the time my father met and married Mary Elizabeth Hazlehurst and brought me to America, I was too old for nursery rhymes and was already bent on copying my father's drawings. He might have designed a more comfortable berth if he had been included in the process instead of so bitterly at odds with us, joining Fulton and Livingston in blaming Nicholas for all the financial woes of this endeavor. Nicholas had been his re-spected—and, yes, trusted—colleague until he fell in love with me and I with him.

Though Father at last recognized the authenticity of our love and granted his permission for the marriage, he now waffles in his viewpoint of Nicholas: sometimes as favorable as before we fell in love and sometimes exactingly negative. The unexpected letter I received from my father before we departed, regaling me with his list of Nicholas's faults, angered me to an edge from which I had no response other than to ask with a bit of sarcasm why he had agreed finally to let me marry a man he found so terrible. I have had no reply from him.

What I haven't told you is that I fell in love with Nicholas primarily because he is so like my father. I love my father—his wit, his easy presence, his skill with a pen and willingness to share it with me. Yes, in spite of all this discord, I adore him. A tear or two slide from my eyes onto the pillow. With the back of my hand, I brush at them and push a bit of tousled hair from my cheek. I'm sure my father has little idea how alike he and Nicholas are.

The cabin is growing light. I hear Bessie rise and whisper good morning to Rosetta and Sarah. I clear my throat. Immediately Rosetta's little feet hit the pine floor, and she starts to run to me in spite of the women's protests.

"Let Mama rest," Bessie whispers loud. I hear the scurrying feet.

"All is well," I call to them.

I hear Sarah's soft laugh. "Go on now," she says and lets my little girl come to me.

Rosetta tries valiantly to climb into the bunk, her bare feet sliding against the drawers beneath. I scoop her up and snuggle her in beside me. Her cold toes push against my expanded belly. I allow this moment to fill me. Today will be the first day she will remember, if indeed she remembers plying these Western Waters, unknowingly a part in changing history. She has no idea what lies ahead. In truth, none of us do. Nicholas and I know full well the dangers of this trip, but he believes in this boat, and I believe in him. I do not want my children or myself to be separated from their father as I was. My mother dead—that is an emptiness too large to consider. I dare not think of it.

Rosetta is not nearly as eager to go out onto the deck as I am. She trundles back to Bessie and Sarah as I pull my simple cotton dress over my head, smooth the skirt, so tight now, down over the flesh that protects my baby. I have brought three of these ordinary strong-fabric ones, as easily washed and hung to dry as my chemises and petticoats. I am reserving my white muslin dress and my one striped spencer, decorated with red and gold cords and matching buttons, for the stops where we need to make a favorable impression on potential passengers and investors. And for our triumphant arrival at New Orleans, to be sure.

I pull at my hair, secure the plait into a knot above my neck, and brush back the tousled escapees from my sleep. They curl naturally enough to fringe my face. For the moment, I'm simply eager to see these riverbanks in daylight—not the Monongahela, with its falling banks—so full of every sort of wildlife, if our noisy engine doesn't frighten them all away. Such a vast difference from the peace of the flatboat, with its quiet oars and long rear steering rudder.

On the deck, I regret not taking time to wrap myself in something warmer. The air is chill, thanks to a southwest wind blowing in. Much of that "wind" may be due to our own rapid motion, though I also see the glorious autumn leaves whirling high out beyond us on the shore. I turn so as to have the wind full in my face. I relish the feel of the wind against me; I have since early childhood. I want to simply raise my arms in the air but fear the crew will see me as unladylike. Nicholas is talking to Baker. I shall have to call him that from now on, to keep the two Nicholases—should I say Nicholi?—straight. My Nicholas sees me and lifts his finger to Baker to wait for him. I am shivering when he puts his warm arms around my shoulders.

"Couldn't wait to see, then, could you, love?" he says.

I shake my head. "I needed to see all this in the light." I snuggle against him.

The colors overwhelm me, golden yellow, orange, deep red-wine crimson, though a few trees are yet green and some evergreen. The sky is a perfect blue, and the air clear as fresh-cleaned glass, so unlike the smoke- and soot-filled atmosphere of Pittsburgh, now behind us, there where even the snow turns black. Our own smokestack is throwing a trail of dark stain behind us, spark-filled smoke shooting upward yet incapable of affecting the swaths of white cloud far above. I'm shivering more now as the wind picks up. Nicholas laughs at me, pinches my cheek, and shoos me back to fetch Rosetta and my warm green redingote, which will hardly close around me now.

"Morning, Miss Lydia." Sarah has the bread and tea set out for us, Rosetta's bread soaking in warm milk.

"Good morning to you all." I step toward the little group. "Bessie, you have her dressed already." I reach down and pick Rosetta up. "Good morning, pretty miss." Her high-top boots are laced and secure. She's waving her little spoon in my face.

Nicholas's boots echo loudly as he lopes toward the door, hops over the threshold, his fresh high energy filling the cabin. Rosetta drops her spoon, and it clinks as it hits the floor.

"Papa, Papa," she cries as she reaches for him, arms outstretched. She loves for him to twirl her round, her legs flying out as he spins.

By the time he sets her down, Sarah has a clean spoon in her dish, tea and bread for him, and all of us are laughing. I am gratified for a moment with a warm feeling of home. My tea is warm and sweet with honey. I lack only the fireplace of my flatboat.

Once we are finished and the table is cleared, Bessie fetches Rosetta's warm coat. Nicholas has already returned to the deck. We women bundle ourselves up and go out. I am in the lead, holding Rosetta's mittened fingers steady as she climbs over the threshold to the deck, and Bessie is behind, just in case. We have treated this morning's adventure as a great surprise for Rosetta. I pray it succeeds. The smoking stack and the slapping paddles may frighten her, but we are counting on the river, the forest, the colors, the sky to delight her. And they do. Her father is there waiting for her. He lifts her to sit on his shoulders, then points to the clouds, the blue sky. A great blue heron swoops in, its perfect timing setting the tone for adventure, its grand wingspan hovering over us, and then it soars out ahead along the river.

Rosetta squeals. "Birdie, Mama. Birdie." She points to the heron, claps her hands, kisses the top of Nicholas's head.

One of the crewmen leans on his shovel and grins. "She's got the feel," Ezra says, smiles again, then lifts another shovel load of coal into the furnace.

We are all of us mesmerized by the day, the sky, the boat, each other. Machinery, crew, weather all working together. We have the day to reach Wheeling. We are hardly alone. The river is dense with traffic on this perfect autumn day: keelboats and flatboats of all sizes, family boats of every conceivable design, great barges and arks filled with produce and livestock for trade. We are not the only noisy ones. There is a general cacophony of chickens and cattle.

Families and rivermen, hallooing and waving their hats, gather at the sides of their vessels to see this fiery monster go by. Almost alarming! I pray they don't tilt their boats! They appear as excited as we are on board as we pass them at a speed I find hard to comprehend. Though I understood Nicholas's design calculations for this boat, thanks to my education with my father, I could never have imagined this experience itself. The speed is almost unimaginable—perhaps near to ten miles an hour. A surge of surprise rises in me, and I tingle with antic-ipation. The feeling envelops me in much the same way the light and the air held me on deck when I was a little child. I want to squeal and throw my arms in the air with Rosetta. What I do instead is run from one side of the boat to the other, waving to the gawkers until my arm grows tired. I lift my skirt and run to the stern, afraid suddenly at how our wake will af-fect those we pass. They have spread their vessels far enough from our path to be out of our wake, though I see the sec-ondary waves rocking them with no little vigor.

Near the bank a few keelboats are working their laborious way back upstream, setting and lifting their poles and making little progress, especially as our wake adds to the current of the river. They wave, call out, but with less enthusiasm. Hardly any work is so difficult as theirs. These are seasoned men. They surely know that if we succeed, it will stifle the need for their poling services. We have heard rumors of their antagonistic talk. Here and there along the banks, I glimpse small bands of settlers gathering among the trees, some silent, some calling out, some holding back or hiding behind the trees in fear. Settlements along this stretch of the Ohio are few, and there will be fewer still once we advance onto the Mississippi.

"Wheeling, at Virginia's northwestern point, will be our first stop," Nicholas says to me, as if he has not told me this ad infinitum already. "We will spend the night at the dock and will stay awhile tomorrow. I want enough time for folks to come on board. We'll charge a small fee, of course."

"Twenty-five cents?" I say.

"Yes—for a tour of the boat. To raise excitement and entice a passenger or two, perhaps. You never know." He laughs. "We might just fill the boat."

Nicholas is ever the entrepreneur, alert for any opportunity to spread our fame abroad among the populace, plus add to the purse to assuage the partners. And Father.

"Once we resume," he says, "we will have a brief stop to on-load more fuel at Point Pleasant, then nothing else till Cincinnati." He squeezes my shoulders.

We must have a talk about that plan. Advantageous as he feels Cincinnati will be for recognition, I am anxious to get on to Louisville before my confinement. I suppose if we must stop, we will. It depends largely on how I am feeling by then.

The Wheeling crowd is astonishingly large for a small town. Every citizen here must be waiting to see us. People are already lined up, excitedly patient, fingering their coins for entry once the crew has secured the gangplank. It has hardly clanked onto the dock before a man or two are on it. One elderly lady seems to lose her balance as she tries to cross, but a rough-clad fellow behind her catches her elbow, quite gently it appears. She smiles a rather crooked smile at him over her empty gums. He guides her all the way to the deck; then I see him shake his head at Nicholas as she extends her coins. He digs in his pocket and drops more into Nicholas's outstretched hand. Nicholas regards the coins, takes one, and hands the rest back to the man. Their mutual smiles are contagious, and I find myself joining them, until I feel a tap on my shoulder.

A fetching young woman in a blue checked dress, wrapped in a raw wool shawl, says, "We were told to ask about the quarters."

My mind still on the scene before me, I momentarily mistake her remark as referring to the coins, then realize my mistake. "Of course. We are happy for you to see the cabins. I'll take you through myself."

A line of folks, both men and women, follow me over the precarious threshold to the quarters.

"Watch your step, please," I say. I'm nervous someone will fall, including me, but all goes well. I spend my day conducting tours of our accommodations, designed not by me, but by Nicholas and Fulton.

"From here to the aft are the women's quarters," I say. "Smaller, but nonetheless comfortable and gracious, thanks to the quiet carpet, the damask drapes for privacy, and the fine bed linens. You see the comfortable accommodations for sitting and small meals. And the cribs for any little ones. Secured so as not to slide, as you see."

The partners complained of the expense of outfitting the guest living quarters, but how else do they expect to entice paying passengers? Townspeople of both genders exclaim in admiration at Nicholas's detailed elegance in the gentlemen's quarters. He is so proud of the fine-carved oak trim and the gleaming dark-stained paneling, the berths lining the quarter's interior, the comfortable leather chairs and card tables. I had nothing to do with any of that. Of course, my suggestion to lay down carpet in the gentlemen's quarters to reduce the din was met with refusal from not only Fulton but my husband, as well. A man among the visitors notices the floor. And the spittoons arranged in strategic spots.

"Well done," he says. Several men laugh. "Imagine just what pattern a carpet might take on after a few juicy spits of tobacco!"

So, it's plain pine flooring, noisy as can be, even though not one passenger is in there yet. The crew have other living quarters. Andrew Jack and Baker have their own private cabins. So the gentlemen passengers are the ones who will deal with the noise. We women savor the subdued sound of my woven woolen carpet. Warmer on the feet, as well, I must say.

The day has tired me out. Rosetta, as well, and with no nap, she is fussy as can be. So many people coming through, so many questions. All in all, a satisfying day, however. The enthusiasm has been utterly contagious. Our boatmen are whistling merrily, joking with one another and exchanging cheery insults. Those off duty are sitting round the deck, smoking cigars and playing cards. Nicholas approaches them, taking his long Dutch pipe from his mouth.

"Hey, Cap," I hear Oren call to Nicholas. "We could've been the Pépin and Breschard Circus today!"

The laughter follows me as I duck into our quarters to rest. Yes, we seem to be making quite an impression. The enthusiastic kind we are seeking. Now to garner some passengers.

CHAPTER 5

Another morning comes. I must say I hardly remember being so tired from carrying Rosetta as I am with this one on the way. Yet I was working harder before her birth. Oh, by far. The flatboat required everything I had to give. In comparison, I have little to do on this vessel other than the tours and a bit of sewing for the baby. I sit perusing Parson Weems's *The Life of Washington*. I keep turning the pages, though it doesn't hold my interest. I'd much prefer my father's adventurous tales of traveling the indistinct roads of this new country and getting himself lost. I miss his tales. And him. But I am living my own tales to regale him with someday soon.

After a bit, I shuffle my deck of cards. I like the slight click of them as I lay them on the table to play a solitary game of Patience while Bessie takes Rosetta outside. Patience—could I find a more appropriate name for a game to play here alone? I'm trying. I am. I'm trying to be patient, but I must confess to my apprehension that labor might commence at any time during these late weeks. The awareness that women die, like my mother, is keen. That won't happen. But the thought hovers and intrudes. I may say it can't happen, but realistically it can.

I'm ready to have this over and done with, to have my infant at my breast. I must discuss with Nicholas my sense of urgency about getting to Louisville. My friend Lucy Audubon is there with the midwife she recommends so highly. Getting to Louisville is quite doable if we skip Cincinnati. I'm almost terrified of going into labor early with no midwife, in the midst of some unforeseen navigational crisis, with everyone scrambling and occupied. My head is spinning.

I should not be afraid. Andrew Jack is an exceptional pilot. I've watched him spot dark water, veer the boat to avoid submerged dangers no one else noticed. However, I also know how full of such unseen dangers this river is. Memories of our mishaps on the flatboat flicker in and out of my head.

I pull a card—the jack of spades, the very one I need. It snaps as I lay it into place. The sound somehow reminds me that downriver we will need to make any number of stops of several hours each for the crew to cut and gather firewood for the day. My anxiety rises. So much for Patience. I gather up the cards, tap them even, and drop them into their box.

I have wasted away the morning in our quarters. We have a stop ahead at Marietta, thanks to a shift in plans. Today is Wednesday, the twenty-third of October, and we are traveling fast, eight or nine miles an hour. If this baby stays on schedule, all will be well. The weight of my pregnancy slows me down as I make my way to the deck, holding the bulkhead for safety. Bessie and Sarah have been out with Rosetta for nearly an hour. She darts to me, chattering and pointing.

"Mama. Look, Mama. It's friends!"

I scoop her up and balance her against my side, then set her down quickly. Onshore I see a virtual parade of children laughing and waving and running along the shore. Ah, yes. I remember this place from the flatboat. Children everywhere. And only a handful of parents. Some of these men have as many as fifteen or more children, generally by more than one wife. The wives die from bearing so many children so quickly. They die in childbirth, like my mother. Like any woman could. Exactly as I could. I shudder. Then look back at this unusual gathering.

The men go on to have more children, like the father of Nicholas, who is the youngest of eleven. Like my father, who had six more children with Mary Elizabeth, eight of us in all. That is an ample number of children. I love each of them, but Henry most of all. We shared the years of our separation from Papa in a way the others cannot imagine. I digress. The proliferation of children and the range of ages here is like nothing I had heard of before, let alone encountered, until our flatboat voyage. It's unlike any other place I have encountered. Rosetta grasps my hand and pulls me to the rail with a surprisingly hard grip. She is calling out to the children, waving and laughing, tugging my hand and pointing to them, as if I actually might not see them. She can hardly wait for us to dock so that she can run out among them. She pulls me down and whispers in my ear, as if not to frighten them away.

"Mama, are they real?"

I laugh and lift her up again. My goodness, this is hard. I rest her feet and weight on the rail, one arm around her, and with the other, I wave as I call out to the running, skipping children as a way to answer her question. A change in the engine tells me we are docking.

"Mama, I go play?" She's tugging hard. I set her back down on the deck, afraid she'll fall. "Can I?"

"May I?" I correct her. "Yes, dumpling, you may go and play all you wish. But we have to get the boat docked first."

I give her a squeeze before she runs off, straight to Bessie, the dark ringlets of her curly hair bouncing in excitement.

As we round the bend and pull toward the mouth of the Muskingum, I am suddenly as surprised and excited as Rosetta. There, stopped in the river to regard us, is a ferry operated by ropes attached to windlasses on either bank. Run by pulleys for crossing the river, this ferry is a new invention since we were last here. Ingenious. But not as ingenious as our own steam-powered paddleboat. I am profoundly impressed, nonetheless, at the sheer ingenuity of human enterprise.

Much to Rosetta's disappointment, our stop in Marietta is not an extended one, and so her playtime is cut shorter than she would like. Of course, any end to playtime is too soon! The settlement is quite small, considering all the children, so the tours go quickly. The collection of quarters seems hardly worth it.

The crew have been off purchasing firewood where they can find it. Our furnace is voracious. Purchasing fuel is more expensive than making afternoon stops to cut wood from the forest, but it is also considerably speedier. It's hard to tell whether speed or expense is of greater value to Fulton and Livingston—they are so unyielding on both counts—so we take advantage as the opportunity presents itself. I suspect whichever way Nicholas chooses will bring criticism that he should have done it another way.

For the moment, I simply want to enjoy this glorious autumn weather, to sit here on the deck with Rosetta, watching her play, hearing her gleeful chatter as she runs about with Tiger, trying in her childish way to tell me story after story about her afternoon adventures with the scores of children.

"Mama, me runnin' with friends! Runnin' so fast! Tiger too."

"What did you have the most fun doing, Rosetta?'

"Play ball! They have wood ball, Mama. Me have one, too?"

"May I have?" I do not like correcting her. "I'm afraid a ball would roll right off the boat, Rosetta, and you would be so sad. So would I!"

"Us play tag!" She reaches out and pokes me. I poke her back. "You it!" Her squealing laughter attracts attention on the deck.

Bessie is watching from across the way, engaged in conversation with Baker. Not the first time I've noticed them chatting when duties have lightened enough to allow this. Their apparent interest in each other delights me. Sarah unexpectedly sets a footstool in front of me, reaches down, and lifts my feet.

"There," she says. "Your ankles are getting swollen. You need to keep off your feet, Miss Lydia."

I know it is only out of customary respect, but I cringe when she calls me that—this woman who has been through so much with me, who battled the trials of these waters with me before, who dragged herself to her feet with the fever to help me nurse the rest of the crew and Nicholas. I am younger than she and far less experienced, though that flatboat taught us both more than perhaps the rest of our lives well may.

I'm ruminating here.

On the skirts of the water, the sun is shining through the not yet bare branches. The light glows through the vivid reds and golds of the remaining leaves as if through magnificent stained glass. A sense of awe awakens in me. No church I have ever seen quite compares to this moment.

The noise of boots snapping against the deck makes me lift my head. Nicholas rounds the smokestack with a chair of his own, bangs it down with a whack.

"Nicholas!" I am instantly provoked by the habitual noise of his impulsive nature. Before I can say another word, he slides the chair closer, drops himself into it, and takes my hand. He raises it to his lips and kisses my palm. Then stands again, walks to the rail and back. He seems incapable of ever sitting still.

"Lydia," he says, "we will succeed. There must have been nigh on a hundred folks here peering at us today. Do you know they even recessed court for the judge and lawyers to come see our boat?"

"Wait, how can that be? This village is so small."

"Large enough, Lydia. Large enough to demonstrate the enthusiasm and interest this voyage deserves to generate. Just imagine when we dock in the larger cities!"

He strikes a match on the sole of his boot to light his pipe. For a moment, the tobacco flares in sparks and smoke trails up, the pipe an echo of the tall stack behind him. He appears at one with his boat. He exhales and speaks again. "Yes, Lydia. We will succeed. Together! Imagine Cincinnati!"

Tired, Rosetta is whining now and tugging on my hand for attention. Nicholas stands. I rise, feeling the weight of this child so near to being born, tilt my head up to my husband for his kiss. Bessie comes quickly, glancing back over her shoulder at Baker. I regard his look at her with an inner smile. Rosetta is pulling at my skirt. Her tugging bothers me, but I restrain myself. I take her hand, and we negotiate the darkening passageway to our cabin to prepare for bed. Bessie takes charge of Rosetta. I am more tired than I should be. The excitement has worn me out. That and the weight of my belly, which now makes eating much supper uncomfortable. Even the yeasty scent of fresh bread out of the oven has little appeal. The baby is growing so big that more than the smallest amount of food gives me heartburn. I have resorted to sleeping upright, propped up with a pillow behind my back to stave off the discomfort.

I need to talk to Nicholas about Cincinnati, but all I want now is to rest.

The Great Comet above will lead us tonight without me.

CHAPTER 6

The day has passed well, with little to note. I'm almost on deck, anticipating the late afternoon sunlight, when from behind me, I feel Nicholas's restraining hand on my elbow. He squeezes past from the passageway and plants himself in front of me.

"Lydia, think carefully now."

"I am not thinking carefully, Nicholas?" I am aware I sound petulant.

I don't like being told how to think, or even to think. I think on my own. No one needs to tell me to think. Not even my husband.

"Cincinnati is a thriving city, Lydia. The population is well over two thousand these days, I think."

Oh, he thinks? Thinks Cincinnati is a thriving city, does he? Well, I agree. There could be any number of investors there. I don't need to be told Cincinnati is important. But this babe I am carrying is more so. I need the security of a midwife I can trust. That midwife is in Louisville, not in Cincinnati. If this boat proves itself, we will be turning away investors. But there is only one opportunity for a baby's birth.

"We have made such valuable friends there already, Lydia, when we arrived on the flatboat. What will those friends think when we just pass them by? Dr. Drake and Jacob Burnet, who entertained us well on our previous voyage, are two who for certain will be puzzled, likely even offended, if we do not stop. A whole list of others. We could lay in a good supply of beer and porter from General Harrison's plantation for our guests in Louisville—even in his absence to subdue the Indians."

I wait. I tick off these names of Cincinnati leaders: Dr. Drake, eminent physician and a founder of Christ Church; Jacob Burnet, renowned lawyer; and William Henry Harrison, previously the governor of Indiana Territory and now a general. General Harrison was leading his troops toward Prophetstown to take advantage of Tecumseh's absence in his campaign to unite the disparate tribes against US westward expansion. These men are important. I know that. And they were quite gracious to us on our initial voyage. I try to gather my wits. And to tame my bad humor.

"You are right, Nicholas. We made extremely important friends on our first voyage. And the population is impressive, I grant you. But the population of this family," I say, staring him straight in the face, "is quite soon increasing by one. This baby is more important than the most prominent friends. Certainly, more important than future guests or beer or porter, even that brewed by General Harrison, off on his Indian campaign. Think carefully now, Mr. Roosevelt."

There is a long pause before Nicholas responds.

"I am trying, Lydia," he says at last. "You know in a town the size of Cincinnati, there will be midwives. It may be days yet before this baby decides to make its appearance. How can we just pass by? As if Cincinnati matters not at all."

"I'm sure there are any number of midwives. You may be certain of that. But none whose name or reputation I know to trust as I do with Mrs. Morgan in Louisville, thanks to Lucy

Audubon." I pause, take a deep breath. "As for Cincinnati, we can just come back to it."

"Come back?"

"Isn't that the point of this boat design? To return upstream as easily as you go down?" I'm making my argument up as I go. "Isn't that the difference this boat is intended to make? Upstream journeys against the current, for trade and passenger travel? What better time to prove it?" Yes, I am making perfect sense. "Cincinnati will be well aware we passed them by. You can be sure of that. I expect it will be in the headlines even." I hesitate. That one may have been a step too far. Nicholas will be wary of negative publicity. "Louisville will be extremely impressed that we came straight there without making a stop. That should make the headlines, for certain. Imagine the surprise then"—I raise my hands in mustered enthusiasm—"when after the birth of this baby, Louisville watches us go back upstream and Cincinnati sees us returning."

I'm too tired for all this at the moment. My feet and ankles are swollen twice their size. My spirits are sour. The waiting seems endless these days, and I want this birth to be safely over. Yet I'm anxious beyond words that my labor may start before I get to Louisville and Mrs. Morgan. I'm ill-tempered and hard to deal with, I know. It takes such effort to keep my temperament easy. My logic makes sense, is surprisingly better than his at this point, I must say. No one believes this boat can go as well upstream as down. If he wants to prove his critics wrong, then we should do it now along the way, so folks can be impressed with more than just the looks and downstream speed of this vessel.

I have to sit down. And I do.

Nicholas twirls a chair around and straddles it. He is about to make one last appeal to me, and I haven't energy left for it. I'm afraid I will be not just difficult but actually quite ill-tempered, too. Luckily, there is a pause.

"Lydia," he says, "I believe you may be right. I have been so intent on the New Orleans–Natchez round trip to prove our success at maneuvering upstream against the current that I haven't thought about how we could prove it along the way. You are right, Lydia. Cincinnati will be astounded to see us pass by and then return in no time at all. It will be proof of our capabilities as a packet not even halfway into this journey. I can see the headlines! Word will pass downriver and across the country. We will reach New Orleans as victors, our ambitions not unproven and still in serious doubt."

I sigh, breathing in the earthy scent of the river. A billowy waft of fresh air blows at my hair. My relief is immense. It must show on my face, for he smiles at me with the kindness that won me to him in the beginning.

"This is the very thing for which I first loved you, Lydia. Your brilliant ingenuity. Presented with such charm!" His face breaks into that smile I can't resist. "Even so young, you had a maturity, a wisdom beyond your age. A way of thinking so clearly, so precisely. How could I not have loved you? Then and now. And forever."

He rises from his chair and stoops as close as our awkward positions and my bulging abdomen allow. He has an embrace that makes me feel complete.

I lay my hand across his arm as he reseats himself.

"You need some rest, Mrs. Roosevelt. You'll soon be adding a Louisville baby to this household. Or this vessel hold, as the case may be." He chuckles at himself, leans in to give me a brief kiss. "And we have plans to make for an upstream celebration in Cincinnati."

"And you need to keep this ship moving, Nicholas. We can't be wasting time." I need to lighten my mood. "We will need to load wood in the morning, and I truly want to be in Louisville by nightfall tomorrow."

We will make quite a ruckus, I think, passing Cincinnati at

dusk, our fires stoked and the cinders flying into the sky. "We can garner quite a bit of attention as we go by in the twilight," I add. "Maybe they'll think we're the comet itself blazing to the earth."

He laughs, as I intended. I don't want this crucial phase of our lives and this journey stained by my temper or my fatigue.

"That may be more truth than joke, my love, out here on the frontier. You never know. Now, let's get you some rest."

I treasure this man, his kindness, his energy, his intellect, his willingness to hear my voice. I will rest well this night.

CHAPTER 7

The morning is done. We loaded sufficient wood and will make it into the Louisville port the following day, by midnight. That should give us a day at least to set up for the birthing. Our needs will be amply met. The port is as fine as one could wish for, with a twelve-foot depth even in dry periods—so no running aground or drastic fluctuations like we had with the flatboat. The harbor extends well out into the river, past town, and offers good protection from extremes of weather. Fortunately, we launched from Pittsburgh in advance of the winter ice. Nicholas still worries about any delays for fear the winter ice could catch us. It can be so deadly. High winds, of course, are a threat during any season, but this port is well protected. Fortunately, we are still benefitting from the extended and unusual warmth this fall.

I am grateful.

Grateful, also, for Bessie. Rosetta is resisting bedtime and has been more irritable even than I have been today. And she continues to be tonight. Bessie is doing her best. We all are. But we are too tired and too excited simultaneously to handle ourselves as well as we might wish. We have been on the river for eight days; we have entertained and given tours to multiple excited crowds. We have marveled at the power and speed of this vessel, which is even faster than I thought: a consistent ten to twelve miles an hour, according to our competent engineer, Baker, who seems quite entranced with Bessie. I'm not surprised. She is energetic and lovely. I try to give her free moments that might correlate with his less busy times. The attraction between them seems mutual and appears to be growing.

I must go outside. I have to get away for a moment. Rosetta's refusal to sleep is wearing me down. I'm already worn down. And pacing. If I'm going to be pacing, it might as well be on the deck, with stars and a brilliant comet overhead. Sarah watches me struggle to find my redingote. My hands are more than a bit frantic. She reaches behind the privacy drape, lifts the garment from the hook, and hands it to me, clasping my hands in hers as I take it from her. She wraps her arms behind me and holds the coat for me to slip my arms into the sleeves. The two edges will hardly meet around my body, and only one ivory button will slip through its buttonhole. I am distracted. Sarah slips my linen bonnet onto my head, then my wool high-top hat over that, smiles as she ties the wide bow under my chin. As I turn, she takes hold of my elbow. What now? She flips my gloves into my hand. I purse my lips and nod. I'm off to the deck. Escape.

Yes, I am fatigued and too anxious to be myself at the moment. No, that isn't true. I am being utterly myself, my actual self—fatigued, anxious, and ready for this birth.

"Lydia!" Nicholas dashes toward me. "Shouldn't you be in the cabin, resting? There is nothing you need to do out here." He takes my arm. "And it's getting chilly."

"I'm fine, Nicholas." My smile must look as strained as I feel. "Snug and warm."

"The sun is setting, and the wind is picking up. You need

something warmer, Lydia." He wraps his arm around my shoulders, tugs at the edges of my redingote. But even his strong hands cannot make it quite close around me. "Aren't you tired, Lydia?"

"I'm exhausted, Nicholas. But I can't stay still. Can't find a comfortable position. And Rosetta is cantankerous, too tired herself to go to sleep." I lay my head against the soft wool of his greatcoat, reach up and hold his collar. "I'd rather be out here. At least for a bit. Where are we? Shouldn't we be passing Cincinnati soon?"

"Your calculation is right on target, Mrs. Roosevelt." He looks down with a slight chuckle. "Have you been on this river before?"

I laugh. A moment of jest between us relieves my lassitude momentarily.

"You should see the lights of that city just round the bend ahead, my dear." He is leaning against me and pointing far out to the right. "I'm expecting all two thousand and some-odd citizens to be out on the shore to greet my brave wife as we go past." He hugs me to him.

An immense gratitude fills me at his humor. He had counted on Cincinnati. Hoped for paying visitors, investors, publicity, and possible passengers. We are, indeed, passing up potential, prospects and I am to blame. But it is not in his nature to blame. Nonetheless, I cannot release myself from my deep sense of guilt.

What if I'm wrong? Maybe I have more time than I think. More time than my body is feeling. What if we make it to Louisville and days pass before I deliver? Would he blame me then for this missed opportunity? I have to stop thinking this way. I know I am right. I will concentrate on what a great and unprecedented victory is in store for us when we come back upstream, against the current of this river, from a Louisville birth!

"Look, Lydia. There are the lights! There's Cincinnati."

Andrew Jack has negotiated the bend so smoothly that I have hardly been aware of it. The lights onshore are glowing from various structures and flickering from torches and lanterns onto the darkening water as the lingering light of the day continues to diminish. The noise! I realize how accustomed I've become to the din of the engine and paddles. Crowds are gathering along the docks, pointing and yelling, pushing to get a clear view of us.

"What a crowd! Baker, Andrew, look at this!" Nicholas calls to our men.

Nicholas is hardly conscious of me now. Leaning far out over the rail, hallooing at the limits of his voice, he waves wildly. Pain shoots through me like lightning as his moving hand strikes my breast. He doesn't even realize he's hit me. Two or three of the crew run up and press themselves against the rail, yelling and waving. Someone steps on my foot. An elbow jabs my side. I am invisible. I do not exist in the midst of this furor. The agitation has captured these men. Onshore, people are running along the dock, along the bank to keep up with us. A group of men mount up and race along the shore, as if competing with our smoke-fuming monster of a boat. One straggler perseveres, slapping the sides of his horse with the reins, until finally we outdistance him downright. He pulls his panting horse to a halt and waves his hat in the air.

The lights and shouts of Cincinnati are fading into the descending darkness. A fog of anticlimax seems to fall over the men as they back away from the rail. Baker almost runs straight into me.

"So sorry, Mrs. Roosevelt." He stops. "What a crowd! Too bad we couldn't stop—" He halts himself. "Forgive me, ma'am. I wasn't thinking."

"No need to apologize, Baker. It is, indeed, too bad not to stop. But we shall return. Mr. Roosevelt has a plan. One to prove this vessel's capabilities once and for all. Just be patient."

After touching his sleeve in assurance, I head for the ladies' quarters to check on Rosetta. My boots sound outrageously loud after all the commotion. I will have to send Bessie out to hear all about it from Baker himself. Surely Rosetta has settled by now. But the excitement has been contagious. She is still awake, though in her bed with her blue bunny.

"Bessie, it's a lovely night. Perhaps you would enjoy a turn around the deck now that some of the excitement has died down."

She is grateful, as I suspected she would be, and gathers her warm wrap to go out. Sarah and I sit with Rosetta, whispering about Cincinnati, as she finally falls asleep.

I have only one more day to go before Louisville and our calculated midnight arrival.

CHAPTER 8

Women say the second birthing is easier. I hope that is true. But "even easier" is relative. That doesn't mean easy. Ever. I don't want to be screaming for these men to hear. Or for Nicholas to hear. He sometimes mentions my crying out with Rosetta. I hardly remember that, except as her head was crowning, that moment ripping me as if my total existence were pain. Then, almost instantly, there she was, warm and wet in my arms. Everything about her beautiful, in spite of her wrinkled little red face and the waxy white birthing custard covering her. How I loved her! Love so beyond me that I had never imagined it possible. Love, like the pain, as if nothing else existed, floating me forward.

My mother must have felt such love at my birth. And again, at Henry's. I must believe she felt that sensation one last time while she and the unnamed baby were dying together when the birth was complete. Perhaps she floats on that love somewhere even now. If not for complications, I would not have lost her. What if I have such complications? What if I die? On this boat, with Nicholas and Rosetta? Nicholas having to witness such a thing, then raise two children alone—or only one? It happens. What would it be like to die? Would I see my mother? And what would Nicholas do with my body? Bury me there in Louisville, alone, with no way to carry me home. Where is home? My only home is wherever my Nicholas is.

Stop, Lydia. What useless thoughts. Focus on the night and Louisville.

Yes, look at the sky. At this brilliant moon. At the Great Comet there, giving that moon competition, not in size, but in brilliance, as it trails its light like a bridal veil. The whole sky is glimmering. We should soon be approaching Louisville. Over the noise of the engine and the rhythmic slap of the paddles, I hear the men's voices calling out to one another.

"Nicholas?" I call, recognizing his silhouette near the helm.

He hurries to me. Perhaps it is the first thing I loved about him, his quick attention to me, even among a multitude of diversions.

"Is it time? We are almost there, Lydia. I'll have you there in time, I promise. We'll fetch the midwife immediately."

The sudden concern on his face makes me smile. He holds my gloved hands in a mild sort of desperation.

"Is the baby coming?"

"No, Nicholas. It's not that. We have time yet, maybe even a day to prepare, though I have a bit of an ache in my back, so it will surely come soon. I only needed to be outside in the air, to see the moon. And the comet. And you, of course. To quiet my nerves. Everyone seems a bit anxious."

"We are coming up on Jeffersonville. Over to starboard." He guides me toward the rail. "It looks a bit more expanded than when we were here before. But still hardly out of the wilderness. You remember that settlement across the river from Louisville, barely hewn from the forest there?"

He is pointing. I can barely see vague outlines in the dark— houses, chimneys, buildings tucked into the moonlit forested bank, like a child's make-believe village among the spreading roots of a tree.

I nod, slipping my arm round him. Yes, I remember. How could I not remember? I was tired then, too. Exhausted for no seeming reason. But newly pregnant. Or so I hoped. I wondered at the first monthly I missed, and suspected, hoping; then was ecstatic at the second one missed, even welcoming the nausea, unlike my remembered childhood seasickness. This nausea woke me of a morning, and I would lie in my warm bed beside Nicholas, trying not to gag. He was so quick to jump up and fetch me a crust or two of bread to stave off the nausea. It always worked. The quesy feeling would pass, unlike my unrelenting childhood seasickness. I was ravenously hungry all the time there on board, with our carefully stored provisions for different legs of the journey. I found myself sneaking into the galley, standing near the fireplace I'd insisted on, repeatedly tasting whatever was cooking on the pretext of making sure the dish would meet Nicholas's approval. I imagine he suspected my true motivation. Actually, I imagine everyone on board might have had a good chuckle behind my back.

I look up into his handsome face, his narrow dark eyes. I adore this man. I have since he first became a fixture in our household, collaborating with my father, who loved him—no, loves him still, I have to believe. Nicholas is, after all, the same man he always was. Father was so utterly opposed to our marriage. Thank goodness for Mary Elizabeth's intervention. She was always as kind to me as if I were her own. It is thanks to her I am here now. I understand Father's abysmal concern about our age difference, but there are times when age is immaterial. *Love hopes all things.* Do I remember that scripture right? Well, right enough for us.

The night is so clear, so bright under this moon. Our shadows lie behind us across the flat pine deck. The constant noise of the engine and paddles has become so familiar I hardly hear it unless the men are stoking the engine, which they are beginning to do now. I look back toward the open door of the firebox, where the blaze is mounting in intensity. The shovel clangs repeatedly above the roar of increasing steam. A shower of sparks flies from the stack into the night, mixing with the stars and the bright tail of the comet.

I can see Andrew pulling hard at the wheel. We have reached the mouth of Beargrass Creek and are beginning the turn into the port at Louisville. Louisville, at last! Before us is Corn Island and the town, lit by the moon in the darkness of midnight. Vague shapes of keelboats, flatboats, and barges emerge packed close together in the port. Here and there I see the movement of a bit of light. Fiddle music and drunken voices drift across the water, keeping time, it seems, to the slapping waves. A pair of men stagger away from one of the numerous taverns—or perhaps it's a brothel—lining the docks. The town proper is high above us on the bluffs, at least a good seventy feet. I am struck with awe, as on our first arrival here two years ago, at the realization that the White House, on which Father has worked with President Jefferson, is approximately the same height. It is monumental! And monumental that Father is so highly respected as an architect for the Capitol, the White House. I don't have time to think of his accomplishments now. We are arriving!

Our competent helmsman is easing us into the crowded waters as Baker and his crew work to lower the fire. The steam is shrieking above us as we pull into port. Even with my wool hat, I instinctively put my hands over my ears, laughing. Nicholas turns and points. Bessie is running toward us in pursuit of Rosetta, Sarah close behind. Rosetta squeals in excitement, her arms thrown up in the air, head tilted to the sky. Nicholas catches her. She seems hardly to know she is aloft in his hands, but then she claps his cheeks in pure delight.

"Sarah finally got her to sleep. Then all this noise woke her back up. Nothing to do but let her come see," said Bessie. She glances back toward the furnace, where Baker is focused on his work. Her gaze is locked on him. She turns back at the sound of Nicholas's voice.

"It's all right, Bessie," he says. "She's not likely to remember much from this age, but hopefully, she'll remember this night."

Rosetta sees me now, reaches for me with her whole body. Nicholas hands her over and hurries to the side of the boat, looks back and forth into the black water and the tight quarters of the dock.

As I take her, I'm suddenly aware of a cacophony of voices, of seemingly frightened folks dashing about, some cursing, screaming as they call out that we are the Devil's ship. A virtual bonfire of torches lights up a crowd of faces marked with fear. From various boats, rivermen are yelling now, and our crew yells back, recognizing familiar faces from their working history. Such recognition should settle some of the fright at the unexpected midnight arrival of our noisy, fire-belching steamboat. Muted light from fresh-lit lanterns glows in one window, then another, in houses high up above. A virtual parade of torches and lanterns descending the hill is mirrored on the water as residents of the high bluffs run down to see what is amiss.

Rosetta claps her cold little hands on my cheeks. I strain to pull my coat around her legs and feet. Its slight scratchiness is worth the warmth for both of us. She is high in my arms, balanced atop the protrusion of her coming sibling. I am suddenly, unexpectedly afraid. What if I have chosen wrong? What if this was not the thing to do? What if I have put us in danger of failure? What if I have simply put us in danger?

Sarah reaches for Rosetta, who readily throws herself out of my arms into hers. She kicks my abdomen with her little stockinged feet. The baby kicks back. Sarah looks steadily at me, even as she holds my swaying child. I cannot let her see my fear, though I know she does. She has been with me through so much. She will not fail me now, I know. I trust her strength and look straight into her face. My vision is blurred by unwelcome tears. She takes my hand in hers.

"You go find Mr. Roosevelt," Sarah says. "This is a right fine moment for him and his boat. He'll be wanting to share it with you." She squeezes my shoulder.

"Thank you, Sarah. Keep Rosetta warm for me. Someone needs to get her slippers on and a blanket around her. I know she ran right out in her excitement, but it's no time for her to get the sniffles."

I am choking on my tears. I will not cry. Nicholas has brought me to Louisville.

"Where is he?" I ask.

She points across the deck, toward the bow. Nicholas stands with his arms aloft, hallooing to the swelling crowd. This crowd has waked from sleep in utter fear and puzzlement as to who— and what—we are. Screams of panic pierce my ears.

"Brits," someone yells. "It's Brits with their damned Indian allies!"

"Get the guns!"

"It's an invasion. An outright attack!"

Nicholas's reassurances, as loud as he can manage, do not assuage them. The crack of a gunshot tears the night. Someone is firing a musket. I smell its odor like rotten eggs. The explosion of another shot splits the air. The rotten-egg stink increases.

Baker reverses the engine, and the paddles struggle to change their push against the dark waters. We dare not dock. They believe us an attack of the enemy.

I cannot focus. My mind is blank. Where is Rosetta?

Suddenly I remember the flag attached to the stern, and I run, stumbling on my dress, holding my heavy abdomen with both hands. I find the pole, but it's empty. The flag is not there. Taken down, of course, at nightfall. I cannot get my breath. I run to the wheelhouse, where Andrew Jack looks at me in consternation. I'm scrambling among the shelves of maps and charts, flinging things out of my way.

"What are you doing?" he snaps. He is desperately trying to back us away.

"The flag. I need the flag," I cry. I am beside myself.

"The flag?" His voice is sharp with annoyance.

"Now," I wail. "I have to have it now!"

Andrew Jack releases the helm just long enough to reach above his head and slide the carved chestnut box holding the flag from a high shelf. He thrusts it at me and grabs the helm again.

I am running, sliding on the deck, jerking the latch on the box, dropping it with a crash on the floor, pulling at the flag without regard for its unfolding. My foot catches a corner. Nicholas turns and seizes me at the rail. The flag is half-open, its thick weave in my hand. I am clutching hard so as not to lose it. I wave it in the air, flapping it wildly in front of me, the snap of it crackling in my ears. Nicholas looks at me as if I'm insane. I feel insane. And then he understands. He grabs one corner, tries to hold it upright, the blue square filled with stars in his hand. With the other he clasps mine tight and lifts. The flag, fully visible to the crowd, all fifteen stars and fifteen stripes, drops over the side and quiets save for a small flutter in the breeze of the night air. Stillness flows through the gathering. Then the crowd begins jostling for a better view.

A shout! "Who be you, then?" The man lowers his musket, looks at his neighbor, then back at us. "Is your boat on fire?"

One of our crewmen laughs. A riverman who has recognized one of our crew from previous trips yells halloo over the side of a nearby flatboat.

"It's Mr. Roosevelt's steamboat!" another calls out.

"He said he'd be back! Two years and here he is! Just like he declared."

The crowd's mood shifts from alarm to amazement.

"Never believed he'd do it," cries a gentleman in a robe wrapped over his nightshirt.

"Don't believe it now." A gruff man spits tobacco as well as words.

"Impossible!" I hear an older gentleman in a heavy overcoat and red nightcap cry out. "It's impossible, I say!"

"Thought that damned comet'd fallen in the river," one gruff riverman proclaims, to a raucous round of laughter and jeering. The fulfillment of my humorous prediction!

As the chaos and noise diminish, I feel the paddle wheels shift. The boat begins a slow advance. Nicholas hands the flag to a pair of crewmen, who fold it properly, while a third retrieves the box I sent skidding across the deck. My husband's arm is firm round my shaking shoulders, holding me steady as the boat slips toward the dock under Andrew Jack's skilled hands. Some in the crowd begin to cheer.

"Well, sir, glad you ain't the Brits! Best you be glad of it yourselves!" The cry is followed with echoes and laughter from others.

The jostling of the crowd increases as we near the dock. I notice some feet with slippers, others bare, an indication of the residents' rush out into the cold. Citizens in nightclothes become differentiated from rivermen in their rough working trousers and coats. Here and there are a few women, some less than well clad. Unsurprising along the dock.

"Thought sure that damn racket was the Brits's canons, come in the night to take us by surprise." The comments continue.

As we pull in, the yelling dissipates, but not the crowd or their curiosity.

Slowly the mingling crowd thins, but still the dock is alive with people, mostly working men.

"We must send for the midwife," Nicholas says in a quiet voice, leaning closer.

"There is time," I say. I am depleted, overwhelmed by the aftermath of my burst of energy while I was in search of the flag. But, thank goodness, no labor just yet. "Morning is soon enough."

"You are sure?" He turns me toward him, his hands on my shoulders. His eyes reflect the flickering light of the torches.

"Yes," I say. "I will know. And so will you. Rest assured."

But rest is not assured. The noise and excitement on the dock continue. My sleep is shallow and fitful. The chaos and danger of our arrival stay with me through the night. I am wakeful, anxious for the morning to summon the midwife.

Rosetta crawls into my bed. I hold her close, thinking of my mother, remembering her arms around me, around Henry and me both, laughing with us, saying, "Just wait. There will be three of you, and you will have to share me." I knew already about sharing her with Henry. That was hardly difficult, as he was so sweet, and she had an arm for each of us, a knee for each of us. But what would happen with three? How would she share her lap with us? I wondered. I tried imagining her with three arms and three knees, but then I thought of families with ten children and their mothers with only two arms, the children taking turns for hugs if their mother was the type. I knew other mothers who were so tightly prim they never hugged their little ones. I was glad not to have a mother like that.

Then I had no mother at all, no third baby to share anything with, and a father who fled his grief and left us behind, with no parent at all. Just us two children to share our own grief. And kind relatives, of course, but only us two who felt our loss. Henry felt it as deeply as I, if not more so. I doubted that was possible. But then he would come to me with a sad blankness on his face. Once he was sure I had noticed, he would fall into my arms and hide his face against my shoulder. Still, he rarely cried. But I did. For both of us perhaps.

Holding Rosetta like this, rocking her back and forth in my arms, I am overwhelmed at the thought that I could be taken from her, that I could die, that this baby kicking away at me beneath her could be one whom she would never see. An unnamed grief floods through me, like the waters of this river when our flatboat hit the snag. What is this ragged grief? I have lost nothing but the loosely remembered mother of long ago. How can I be grieving for her all these years later? The tears are stinging my eyes.

This is not the time to cry. This is the time to rest.

CHAPTER 9

At long last, I must have slept awhile. I wake to the thud of heavy footsteps on the deck. I half roll and stretch my arm. Nicholas is not there. Perhaps I've slept more than I thought. I've no idea what time it is. Sarah must have taken Rosetta at some point. There is no noise from the other side of the privacy drape. Rosetta and her nursemaids are still sleeping. What a night this was! I slide my hands over my abdomen. Soon I will hold this new one.

I stretch and think back on my sudden panicked dash for the flag, a gift to my father from President Jefferson upon the completion of the first phase of their collaboration on the porticos of the White House. The flag I begged to hang at the stern of this boat for our history-making voyage, which my father, relenting, hesitantly gave to me. The flag that saved us from who knows what if anyone on that dock had decided we indeed were the British attacking by night, had aimed those muskets for more than a warning. The flag, with its fifteen stars and fifteen stripes, now that Vermont and Kentucky have been added as states. How will they manage to adjust the design, I wonder, if, or as, more territories become states with the push toward the West? This push the British are determined to block. Can we avoid another war? But *what if*, I stop to consider. What if indeed this boat, meant for passengers and trade, opens up access to the West?

Ah, well, does any day pass without a *what-if*?

There is bustling noise coming from the gentlemen's quarters at the other end of the boat. I roll my feet onto the floor. What can be happening? Well, after last night, I find anxiety is easily triggered. The noise is louder now, and I can make out men's voices.

"Well done, Mr. Roosevelt! Very handsome it is, with this outstanding hand-carved woodwork. The berths with privacy drapes, the chairs, even the spittoons! Seems you've thought of everything."

"We fully intend to be a luxurious passenger boat as well as a trade packet, Mr. Walton."

I recognize Nicholas's steady voice. I picture him leaning toward whoever this is as he speaks, almost in his face, but with enough restraint to make the man feel as if he is the recipient of important confidential information. I smile to myself. The potential investors are here quite early, and Nicholas has them aboard, already at it, taking advantage of every moment. Our dramatic arrival is now an advantage, I gather.

"Indeed?" a deep voice breaks in. "This fine boat you are so proud of will never make it upstream. No boat can defy these treacherous currents. This river has a mind of its own, and it's not in conjunction with yours. You'll be sitting in New Orleans, with your paddles going like one of those paddle-driven sawmills, to entertain folks idiot enough to spend their money coming out to see the fancy boat. This investment nonsense is exactly that—nonsense."

Then again, perhaps not. It will take more than drama; it will take a successful upstream jaunt.

"Ah, Mr. Blackwell." From Nicholas's tone of voice, he might just as well have received a compliment. "What a delightful concept! Such an idea never entered my imagination. That could raise a fair amount of money while we are in harbor, more than simple tours on board. I'll keep that one in mind. Perhaps I'll see you in Natchez when we steam back upriver, and I'll give you a report on how that project went."

I move away from the wide doors between quarters. I've heard enough, and I desperately need my little privy closet. I know my husband. This is one of the myriad reasons I love him. He might as easily have been a diplomat as an inventor.

By the time we are fed and dressed, Rosetta is dancing on her toes to get to the deck. Bessie takes her ahead, while Sarah comes behind me as I plod along the narrow passageway. I reach the deck to find it nearly as crowded as the dock was last night. Nicholas is clearly ecstatic at the excitement our arrival has generated. The wild commotion of the unexpected midnight arrival in Louisville has made it worthwhile to bypass Cincinnati, then. We'll have another chance at Cincinnati, I trust. A chance to prove wrong the gruff-voiced prophet of failure this morning. I chuckle to myself as I think of their next exchange.

I see a steady gathering of men of all classes crowding in groups at various points of interest. Questions are flying about like mosquitoes. The roughened rivermen lob theirs at our crew, clearly with respect and a bit of envy, and pay close attention to the unfamiliar explanations of engine duties. Other gentlemen, tradesmen perhaps, smithies, and men who understand the relationship of fire and production, gather around Andrew Jack and Baker and peer into the combustion chamber, run their palms along the seams of the smokestack, poke their heads without caution right out between the spokes of the paddles.

Yet another group, clearly from the three-story-high brick

homes built on the bluffs and singularly well dressed—are they trying to impress us?—are conversing with my husband. He is holding court! In his element now, although he seems always in his element, Nicholas is extolling the power of steam for the future and, like any good pastor, preaching for conversion among his listeners. We are in need of converts; that much is certain. Fulton and Livingston are looking to Nicholas to find investors to help fund this ambitious project and future ones. And my father is watching for the outcome. Of that I am acutely aware.

Soon Nicholas comes to me, his arms outstretched. "We have a tiny lull here, Lydia. I am sending one of the men to fetch the midwife. Would you like for Sarah to go, as well?"

"Ah, Nicholas, this is your moment. I can arrange to send for her myself."

"No, Lydia, I want to be thoroughly prepared for this baby. And for you in your delivery. We bypassed Cincinnati to be here with the recommended midwife." I detect an irritable undertone in his voice. "There is no reason to delay sending for her. If she has to remain on board for a day, so be it. Now, do you want Sarah to go with Billy or not?"

I am taken aback but recover immediately. "Yes, Nicholas. That is a far better idea. I'll fetch Sarah. She will be able to explain to Mrs. Morgan who we are, who I am, a friend of Lucy Audubon, and just what our unusual situation is. I'm sure she has never delivered a child in quite such circumstances before. We can have everything fully set up and arranged for the lying-in, even if we have to wait a bit for this baby to decide to greet us. I'll go for Sarah right now."

Indeed, it is entirely at my insistence on reaching this midwife that we arrived last night and are here today. Why am I put out at his concern? My unspoken fears? Perhaps due to my own uncertainties as to whether the boat can make it back upriver after the birth, making me to blame for missing Cincinnati. Or what if the river rises quickly on us and we will need immediately to push forward through the Falls of the Ohio, with no chance of turning back? Perhaps I'm not as at ease about this process of labor as I would like to believe I am. Whatever the case, Nicholas is correct: the wisest course is to fetch Mrs. Morgan and make all necessary preparations ahead of time. I thread my way through the tangle of visitors to find Sarah.

As the morning progresses, more women of the town, finished with household chores or ignoring them, begin to appear. Nicholas has stationed himself near the gangplank so as to miss no opportunity and, always the consummate gentleman, holds out his hand again and again to one lady after another, nodding to each yet hardly breaking off his conversation with the gentlemen around him. Just a simple hand gesture in my direction sends them toward me. I'm wishing for Sarah, as I do not feel up to conducting tours of the ladies' quarters as I have at previous stops. However, I'm greatly surprised that few of these guests seem at all concerned about the boat and its luxuries. I have met a number of these ladies on our previous voyage; they seem concerned about me in a rather personal way. Perhaps too personal.

"Have you a room in town for the birthing, my dear?" Mrs. Dalton asks.

"No," I say. "I intend—"

"There is a nice inn just up the way a bit." She seems unaware of her interruption.

The thought of an inn makes me want to flee. Oh, those inns below Natchez after our boat sank! How raucous and filthy! Nothing but bawdy shouting all of one night and a bed so dirty we spread our cloaks out on it to sleep—which we never did. After that, I preferred to sleep on the shore, wrapped in buffalo hide. An inn is most certainly not a place to birth my baby!

"You look quite ready to bring this one into the world, my

dear. How soon? Have you a midwife? I can recommend Mrs. Daily. She is so good that the town provides her a house and fees."

"Thank you very much. I've summoned Mrs. Morgan, who is recommended to me by my friend Lucy Audubon."

"Oh, yes, Mrs. Audubon! So sad her husband failed to focus attention on his business in town. Lost his store, he has. His bird sketches may be admirable, but they don't feed a family. I believe they are quite dependent on her money now. Such a shame. As you are her friend, I presume you know all of that and share our concern for her."

"Of course," I say. I want my privacy. I want these women off my boat. I want my rest before I labor. "Lucy is wonderful at correspondence, far more so than I. I owe her a letter. Actually several, I believe."

"May we see the living quarters on the boat? We understand you are setting up there for the lying-in. Of course, that means you are quite busy, so we won't be bothersome," says a narrow-faced lady who looks familiar but whom I cannot place. "That was quite an entry you made into port last night. Woke me from a sound sleep, but oh, so worth it to come down the hill and see the show."

Not bothersome? These ladies are nothing but bothersome.

"Indeed," says a short lady, looking a bit chilly in just her red spencer over her white muslin. Dressed up fancy to visit our boat. "This vessel fairly outdid the Great Comet itself, with all its sparks and flare. Quite exciting, my dear, especially your exhibition of the flag. That one surprised us. To think you had one on board!"

"A gift to my father from President Jefferson." I turn toward our cabin, my hand tight on the rail, ignoring their surprised exclamations.

The women cluster in twos and threes, exclaiming over the luxury of the quarters.

"Oh, look at the damask drapes!"

"How beautifully the woodwork is designed!"

"My, my, who would have expected such comfort in these berths?"

"Yes, designed for the comfort of our lady passengers," I say.

Bessie has been in the process of removing Rosetta and herself to the gentlemen's quarters, where they will stay for my lying-in, since we have no passengers. The women seem surprised to see this toddler running round the heart pine floors with her wooden horse pull toy, until they realize her nursemaid has her well supervised. I'm beginning to feel a bit claustrophobic as they crowd about me.

"Do you not think you should send her into town for a few days for fear she will hear your screams, my dear?" It is the short woman in the red spencer again. "We can certainly make her at home among our children."

"You are most kind to offer such hospitality, but I have the greatest confidence in Bessie's care of her. We have separate private quarters for both our pilot and our engineer, quite distant from mine, should we need to utilize one of those. We also have a rather noisy engine, as you discovered last night, with which we can cover virtually all other sounds if need be."

Why am I insulted? And in danger of being insulting?

"But, my dear, then the boat would be moving—either upriver, against the current, or down toward a deadly encounter with the falls. The water is far too low."

"Or right here in dock," I say. "With the paddles disengaged. Of course, then, the noise might alert the entire town that we are about to welcome this new soul into the world. Fitting fanfare, don't you think?" I lean forward, as if I'm conveying a confidence. "I'm quite sure this is a boy. He's lying very low."

"Several of us are available to help," says the one whose name I can't recall. "We've discussed arrangements, even for various shifts, to be of assistance, you know."

"Oh? Well, how grateful I am to all of you," I say, looking

around at the women crowded into the space. "However, these quarters are somewhat confined, as you can tell already, and with two cribs, it is really only large enough for Mrs. Morgan and my Sarah to operate efficiently. They are quite competent, so rest assured I shall be fine. Though I expect my child to be a boy, a little prince, if you will, I am not Marie Antoinette. My lying-in will not be an event for public spectacle."

Have I truly been so audacious? I hardly know myself these days. I vacillate between that wildly intrepid girl I was on the flatboat—only two years ago?—and the frightened child I was after my mother's death. And this woman I am, about to birth my second child. I am suddenly wanting my dear stepmother, Mary Elizabeth, with me, close by, holding my hand, encouraging me, telling me I can do anything, as she has ever since marrying my father. Was I wrong to leave them? To be on this journey with Nicholas? No, I hear her now, her quiet motherly voice in my ear.

"Lydia, if you love him, I will stand by you. I will help convince your father. Nicholas is a good man. And a talented one, with great skills. What has age to do with love? If you truly love him, age is irrelevant." And then she added, "As long as you are of an age to be a bride."

I gave birth without her in New York, at the Markses' home, and succumbed to Nicholas's notion that I name our daughter for Rosetta Marks and not for Mary Elizabeth, displeasing my father utterly. He persists in calling her Mary, regardless, for which I am grateful. She answers gladly to that name for him. If this is, indeed, a boy, Nicholas will expect me to name it for him and not for my father.

Well, we shall see.

CHAPTER 10

I bid these ladies a welcome farewell, with effusive thanks for their offers of help. Bessie senses that I am flagging and hands Rosetta off to me as she scurries to usher the last of our visitors away. Rosetta is snuggled against my chin when Bessie returns to take her. She throws her arm out toward Tiger, who is lying on the floor, yawns and rubs her eyes as Bessie lays her on a soft cotton pad beside this giant dog. He lifts his head and snuggles it around the top of hers, their dark curls barely distinguishable. I pick up my basket of yarn and the unfinished blanket I am trying to finish knitting. I pull out a few stitches to correct the pattern, though I'm sure this new infant will have no objections to a missed stitch, as long as he is snuggled soft and warm. The click of the needles lulls me almost as much as the softness of this blue yarn. Yes, I'm that convinced of a boy, who is lying so low that I have appeared near delivery for two months already. Now I await his willingness to leave my warm body and for Mrs. Morgan's arrival.Hopefully, I'll have this little blanket complete for him. I do knit very quickly, even with a few mistakes.

Since we cannot reposition a built-in berth, designed as it is to accommodate passenger travel, a comfortable padded armchair has been brought in from the men's compartment to serve as a birthing chair and has been ensconced in canvas to protect the fine upholstery. I'm counting on the softness of a fine bedsheet to make the rough canvas more comfortable. A pillow from the berth will cushion me, as well. We have footstools for the leather chairs in the gentlemen's quarters. Bessie and Sarah have arranged two of them to accommodate my feet. Higher ones would give me more support, but this is what we have. I will be glad of them. The boat is not designed, I must admit, for lying in. This is all by my own choice.

My needles click in a familiar rhythm.

Ah, I hear another click—the distinct sound of women's boots—and Sarah's voice as she leads the midwife down the hall. She is short, wiry, middle-aged, and quick about everything. Assured that no labor has begun, Mrs. Morgan casts her eyes about our makeshift birthing arrangements. Instantly, she waves her hand toward the door, where a folding birthing chair now appears in Billy's hands amidst a good bit of clanking. For a few minutes chaos reigns as Billy and Sarah drag the armchair and stools back to the gentlemen's quarters. Billy hurries back out, embarrassed perhaps, at the scene with the unfolding chair. The finely proportioned birthing chair is outspread and stabilized, with footrests at an adjustable height, I am relieved to note.

Mrs. Morgan has brought her own fine caudle concoction of red wine and oatmeal for pain relief. There is only to heat it. She offers me a sip, and I taste a hint of cinnamon. Ah, the flavor has overtures of Christmas. Yes, I think, the comet, our star leading us on. We will have our baby for Christmas. My metaphor is a bit skewed, I tell myself, but I love the thought regardless.

Almost on cue, as if I've just been waiting for preparations to be complete, a familiar heavy pain in my back curves round to my abdomen. My breath comes too deep, like a gasp. Mrs. Morgan is beside me instantly, her hand on my contracted abdomen. Bessie brings Rosetta to me for a kiss before they retire to the gentlemen's quarters, set up now just for them. As they leave, Sarah and Mrs. Morgan are busy loosening my clothing, pulling it over my head as another contraction hits, and warm dampness soaks my lower body. Sarah brings towels, then a loose, dry gown and a quilt to keep me warm. I am alarmed at how quickly these contractions come. Mrs. Morgan soothes me.

"Sometimes it happens that way with a second child. Often early contractions may not even be felt, and it's only when we get down to business that they come on fast and hard. I imagine you will have this baby quickly."

I am breathing with Mrs. Morgan's guidance. I am not screaming. The breathing keeps my mouth occupied. And between contractions, Mrs. Morgan offers me her caudle. I take only sips. I do not want to be drunk when I put this baby in my husband's arms. There is no turning back from this, no pause to gather myself. There is only to bear it courageously, if I am able, until I hold this infant to my breast.

"Here is your firstborn son." Sarah almost whispers, speaking just to me, as she puts him in my outstretched arms, still red-faced and waxy, while Mrs. Morgan cuts and secures the umbilical cord and seals it with a bit of lard. Lard, of all things. Whoever heard of that? That makes me laugh. This baby makes me laugh: so energetic, so eager for my breast.

"I need this little boy back now," Sarah says. "Just for a minute or two."

Sarah urges me to release him briefly so that she can clean him, while Mrs. Morgan delivers the afterbirth and makes certain it is all there. She looks up from her less than lovely chore and smiles.

"A good birth," she says.

Gratitude floods me, just as an intensity of love flooded me when I first felt the wet warmth of this child at my bosom. Sarah leans over and puts him back in my eager arms, all clean and soft and warmly wrapped. Now he is truly ready to suck. The milk is let down, and I am in some heaven I have been lacking since Rosetta weaned herself. I have missed nursing a baby. His cheek is soft against my fingers, moving in a soft rhythm as he sucks. I think how he will never remember his first taste of my milk and how I will never forget.

There is a bit of shushed noise. I look up to see Bessie darting to catch hold of Rosetta, Tiger tripping along behind them. I wave Bessie away and pull Rosetta close to the baby with my free arm. I give her a kiss on top of her head. Rosetta's little face is puckered in a sort of wonderment. Timid at first, she begins to run her gentle fingers along his tiny arms, then tucks a finger into his curling hands.

"My baby," she whispers. My heart melts to hear her call him "my baby." She turns to Sarah and, in a very loud voice, repeats, "My baby!" Laughter fills the room.

Nicholas is nearly at the door. The snap of his boots is as loud and as fast as can be. Eagerness rises in me as Rosetta runs to greet him, take his hand, and bring him to us, chattering all the while.

"Papa, Papa, my baby so soft." She's tugging hard at him. "Look, Papa, so tiny. See, Papa? My baby so sweet." She does not let go of Nicholas as he bends toward us and buries his face against my neck.

"I love you so," he says before he pulls back enough to see his new son.

I lift the linen towel over my breast and break the baby's hold. He makes a tiny, scrunch-faced cry as I hand him into his father's arms. Nicholas rocks him side to side, cooing nothings to him and kissing his forehead. He bends level with Rosetta and holds the blanket back for her to see. She kisses the top of the baby's head, continuing to murmur, "My baby, my baby." I am enamored, as always, with my husband, but especially while watching him in his introduction to his first son and his gentle, affectionate inclusion of Rosetta.

"He is a beautiful boy, Lydia. Imagine the tales he will tell his grandchildren about his birth! Have you considered a name for him?"

He hands the baby back.

A sigh escapes me. Oh, how I have dreaded this question.

"Yes," I say. "Actually, I have given a great deal of thought to this, Nicholas. And I must admit, I am torn." And I am. I'm fiddling anxiously with the edge of the blanket. "I'm aware a first son ought to be named for his father. And I know, beyond doubt, that is what you would want."

The expression on his face is one of puzzlement. He is think-ing of another Nicholas, I know, but hears in the tone of my voice something else.

I look up into his eyes to be sure I see his reaction. "I wish to name him for my father, Nicholas." I hesitate a moment to let him take this in. "We failed to name Rosetta for my dear step-mother, Mary Elizabeth, as would be customary. I know that added to the rift our marriage created." I pause yet again, work-ing to get this right. "As to you and my father, you loved—no, still love—each other, in spite of the disruption our marriage has caused. I wish to heal that where I can. I wish to name him Henry Latrobe Roosevelt. But more than anything, Nicholas, I don't want to hurt you."

A long silence ensues. Nicholas turns away from me for long minutes while I wait in silence. I am filled with dread that I have truly injured my beloved husband. I kiss the unnamed baby's head. Nicholas returns to stand beside me.

"You know, Lydia . . ." His hand is quiet on my shoulder. "When Rosetta was born, I was so full of gratitude that the

Markses were hospitable enough to take us in that I lost my focus. I should never have disregarded your wishes. I overstepped. I hope you forgive me."

My free hand comes across my swollen breasts to enclose his. I look up and am unable to read his expression.

He takes our son in his arms again, lifts him high, says, "Welcome to the world, Henry Latrobe Roosevelt."

CHAPTER 11

The river remains low. We hear of boats that have waited a year for it to rise enough to negotiate the two miles of deadly protruding rock formations that make up the Falls of the Ohio. We also hear tales of disastrous shipwrecks befalling those who dared the rapids without enough depth to spare. The waiting seems interminable. The boat sways quietly in its dock. The sun shines over Louisville with a benign warmth that breaks the chill of early November—at least Bessie tells me so on return from her outings with Rosetta these three days since the baby's birth. She also tells me the exciting news that the Audubons are expected for a brief visit in town on their journey from Henderson back to Lucy's Pennsylvania home. I am tingling with joy at the thought of introducing her to my baby, brought into this world by Lucy's trusted midwife. Henry sleeps around the clock except when it is time to nurse. Rosetta slips her hand into the cradle Nicholas built, attached to the flooring like hers so as not to slide, and pats the baby's head.

"When my baby talk to me, Mama?"

"Not just yet, honey."

"But when?"

"Oh, I expect we will have another birthday cake for you before that happens, love."

"What will he say, Mama? He sing me a birthday song?"

"Well, first, I imagine he will say, 'Mama' and 'Papa,' just like you did."

"I did?" She giggles up at me. "Then what my baby say?"

"Then 'Rosie' or 'Rosa' or 'Sistah' or something like that."

"That's me!" she exclaims, jabbing her fingers into the bright smocking at her chest.

She climbs up beside me in my berth, sucking her thumb, and calls Tiger. His head reaches my mattress, so his cold nose lies on the berth beside us as she pets him. Restless, she jumps back down and coaxes him into running back and forth with her. Their feet get tangled up, making them tumble, while I laugh. They lie there in a snuggle till she starts crawling over him. He rolls his body with her. I'm grateful for this great Newfoundland dog, so silkily black, so faithful, so protective of Rosetta. And grateful Nicholas made provisions for me to bring him on board.

Sarah has gone into town and delivered a note to Lucy Audubon. I am in great anticipation that she will appear this afternoon. She is such a friend. I am giddy and want to be out of this bed and dressed to receive her. Sarah is adamant that I should not be on my feet. She brings me my soft old shawl and helps me into one of the armchairs from the gentlemen's quarters. By the time I hear light steps coming down the passageway I have nursed Henry and closed my gown. I push the curly fringes of my messy hair away from my face and, much to Sarah's consternation, rise and hurry forward to embrace my guest even as she enters the doorway.

"Lucy!" I clasp her sideways so as not to squeeze the baby.

"Lydia, sweet Lydia, you are really here!" She grasps my shoulders. "On this astonishing vessel. With a new baby! Who could have imagined such a thing?"

As she releases me, I hand Henry to her. She is tickling his chin and cooing to him when right behind her comes little Victor, only slightly older than Rosetta. It takes a few minutes of encouragement for the two toddlers to overcome their initial shyness, but soon enough Bessie has them engaged with some of Rosetta's toys.

My friend is as lovely as always, tall, with wide-set eyes that droop, as if she might at any minute fall asleep. And yet, with such a spritely spirit, dancing with every word. I feel an exceptionally deep bond with her for many reasons: our high level of education, unusual for women, gained mostly from our fathers; our fathers' opposition to the men we love; our commitment to our husbands' passionate quests for something new, out of the range of ordinary life; our lives organized around our husbands' pursuits. Where will she and I be in a few years, I wonder. Will we dedicate our whole lives to our husbands' wanderings? Will we accompany them on those wanderings with our children? For the moment, this is our shared, and welcome, reality.

Lucy sits with the baby, and I scoot a dining chair to seat myself close to her. She is full of news about her travels with John—she calls him only that, though wherever he is known, it is by both his names, John James. She seems truly sad that he sold the store here in town—she does not mention the reason being his complete loss of funds and his failure to attend to the store, and I do not, either, but regardless, she will be glad to reach Pennsylvania and home again. My intuition says this trip home may be to solicit funds from her father. I think for a moment how this is another point we share: our husbands' lack of interest in finances.

"We are riding on horseback," she exclaims. "Can you imagine? A full thousand miles! On horseback?"

"Whatever for, Lucy?" Is this about the lack of money, I wonder. "Surely there is coach service available."

"Oh, to be sure," she says, with a bit of an edge to her voice. Then more lightly, "John has decided against the coach because he would be hampered in sighting the birds!"

Sighting birds is more important than the comfort of his family, I think, but I keep my thoughts reined in.

"And what about little Victor?"

"He rides in front of his father mostly. John points out all the birds to him."

"Does that excite him?"

"Sometimes yes. Sometimes no. As you can imagine with any almost three-year-old. Sometimes his head is slumped in sleep when John sights one. He never hesitates to wake that droopy-headed child."

"Yes, I can well imagine!" I am suddenly grateful, immensely so, for Nicholas, and for Bessie and Sarah and our stash of playthings. Grateful for our berths, however narrow; for the children's beds, safely anchored to the floor. Grateful for our crew, proficient to a man, including the cook and his son. The whole of it, this floating home, however much this compartment differs from the cabin I designed for the sunken flatboat. Never again to have to stay at some filthy inn along the way, though I do believe they are of a better sort farther east.

"What are your plans, Lucy? Do you have help along the way?"

"John has his slaves that accompany us, nine of them, some women. They help with Victor whenever we stop, which is often, as John halts for every bird that flies, and for some that don't—to see the nesting. He's constantly sketching."

She shifts the baby and rearranges her skirt. I reach for him, but she shakes her head and lifts him close to her face.

"We carry books and books of very large paper. And boxes and boxes of pens and pencils and ink, of course."

She shifts in her seat once again. I realize suddenly she must be uncomfortable from the long days on horseback.

"We have one packhorse for nothing but John's supplies," Lucy continues, "and several others for backup, as well as our personal possessions. We make for quite a procession through these woods and trails. No wonder the birds are quick on the wing!"

I laugh. "You make me think of one of my father's stories about trying to find his way through this country. Seems he went some miles on a trail, turned around, totally lost. He came upon a man working a field and asked directions. The man leaned on his shovel and considered. 'Well, sir, seems you've come a ways too far. You have to go back the way you came. Now back the way you came, you'll come upon a road to your right hand—that would be your left hand coming this way. Now, don't take that road. About three miles on, you'll find a road on your left hand—that would be your right hand as you come this way. Now, don't take that one. But about another half a mile on, you'll come upon another road on your right hand—would've been your left as you came. Now, as you came, that one is the one you missed. Take that one.'"

Lucy is laughing with me now. Sarah and Bessie, too, as though they have not heard me tell this story more than once.

"I'll spare you the rest," I say. "It's actually much longer. There were several more roads, all described in the same way."

"Oh, my!" Lucy is still laughing, and Henry is smiling, open lipped, up into her face. At least I want to call it a smile. I realize I'm enamored of my newborn. Lucy shifts, and Sarah comes to take the baby from her arms. She lifts a light satchel Sarah had set beside the chair for her as we embraced.

"This is not quite so entertaining, but I did bring you a preliminary sketch of what you and I would simply call a duck. It is, however, officially the American pied-billed. This sketch," she says, handing it to me, "is a bit odd. It's his style for first impressions—simple, linear, spare, but catching the fast forward motion of the birds. And here are John's first notes on this bird. You will see how entertainingly casual he is in addressing the bird!"

I take the paper and read: *There go the little Dobchicks,*

among the tall rushes and aquatic grasses that border the marsh. They have seen me, and now I watch them as they sink gently backwards into the deep water, in the manner of frightened frogs. Cunning things! "Water-witches," *as they call you, I clearly see your bills, although you have withdrawn all of you save those parts, and sneak off towards yon great bunch of bulrushes. Well, speed on, and may safety attend you!*

"You must be constantly entertained," I say.

"It helps," she replies. "Once we reach home, he'll proceed on his own. I've no idea how far or how long this project will take him. He fully intends to publish."

"Publish? A book?"

She hesitates. "In stages. By subscription for funding. Finalized paintings done in aquatint plates. It's a demanding project."

More demanding than ours in a number of ways, I think, wondering how she will handle such long separations from John James.

"You make this journey of ours seem simple," I say.

Sarah takes Henry, who has fallen asleep in Bessie's arms, lays him in his crib. Startled, he waves his hands as he half wakes and resettles.

"There is nothing simple for either of us," Lucy says as she rises.

We hold each other long and firm as we bid farewell. Indeed, we do ardently hope the other fares well as we accompany our husbands on their passionate journeys, journeys that we have each chosen out of love—and a desire for adventure—as our own. Yet as I watch her steps down the passageway, I am thinking not of her exploits but of her fatigue. A thousand miles on horseback with her child! My gratitude for the relative comfort of my own journey is immense.

I think of the peril of those falls we must pass through any day now. At least we hope to, if the river will only rise enough to allow our transit. The idea makes me restless. But Sarah is assisting me back to bed, sensing, I imagine, that I am overtired from Lucy's visit. Poor Lucy! I'm wondering if there are folks saying, 'Poor Lydia.'"

CHAPTER 12

When morning comes, I am even more restless. Waiting for the river to rise is stressful enough, but I am not fond in the least of this lying-in recovery—wasted days in bed. Though one might die from it, giving birth is not an illness. The sheet is cool as I slide away from the warmth of the area my body has heated. The floor is chilly as my feet settle on it, and my toes search for my slippers, then slip into cozy warmth. Sarah is rushing to assist me, her face concerned.

"You need the necessary, Miss Lydia?"

"Actually, no, Sarah. I want to walk around a bit." I always wish there was no *Miss* in front of my name. Sarah and I have shared more than most sisters.

"That bed get boring?" She laughs and holds my dressing gown wide for me to slip into.

"Indeed, it is, Sarah. I'm wanting some sunshine. This confinement is beside the point. I'm going to make a bit of a foray outside." I fasten the dressing gown, glance at the baby to be sure he's asleep. "You'll come with me?" She wraps me in a warm shawl, looks back to assure herself that Bessie is there and alert.

Nicholas is running almost the minute my head emerges from the passageway, protesting that I must take better care of myself.

"Where are you going? What are you doing?" His voice is slightly frantic.

"Just for a breath of fresh air," I assure him.

Sarah has disappeared. He squeezes past me, takes my elbow, and guides me back again. I defy him and stop.

"Lydia, you must take care! We have two little ones." His gaze is so serious. "Lydia, I need you." He runs his gentle hands up and down my arms. "Please don't take chances. You know how I need you. "

"I know, Nicholas. And I love you so." I lean back, my arm around him, my hand at the nape of his neck. "But childbirth itself is the chance any woman takes, the chance I take with you for these children. That moment is over, done with, at least this time around. I need to get back to life." I stroke his cheek. "Childbirth is not an illness, Nicholas. I don't need to be lying in bed to recover. I need to walk, to have fresh air, to stand on the deck with you. And a pillow to sit on."

His surprise is genuine. Astonishment shows on his face. This birth is so different from Rosetta's more traditional one at the Markses' home. He reaches for the pillow Sarah has brought. "I never heard any woman say such a thing."

"I'm not any woman, Nicholas. That's why you love me." I know the truth of this. "Any woman would never have made that flatboat trip, especially pregnant. Wouldn't have nursed the whole crew—and you—through the fever. Any woman wouldn't have boarded this boat with you on the eve of another birth." My hand caresses his arm. "You love me, Nicholas, primarily because I am not any woman. Now, will you turn back around and walk me to the deck for a bit of sunlight and air? We don't have to stay long."

On the deck, the warm light of the near midday sun lies in a wide swath across the planking. If I could, I would lie down in it. A chilly breeze makes me shiver. Nicholas runs to fetch a warm throw from the cabin and wraps me in it, whirls his own chair round in my direction. Always such noise!. He adjusts the throw, tucking it carefully around me. It takes me a moment to realize what he has wrapped me in—one of the buffalo hides we employed for sleep on the banks of the Mississippi after our flatboat sank. Well, actually, after we abandoned sleeping in the rowboat when an alligator attempted, clawing and scratching, to climb into it, apparently perceiving the boat as a log. I was utterly terrified that night, but I'm laughing now at the memory of Nicholas whanging its head with an oar, even as my fingers trail the supple softness of the hide that is keeping me cozy. I had no idea Nicholas had brought these skins with us. Nostalgia perhaps? I hope not from caution, in case we sink.

"Now is time for us to have a serious discussion," he says.

Ah, now we have it—the lost opportunity to stop in Cincinnati and no sign of the river rising anytime soon. Hitching his wool trouser leg up at the knee, he leans close with a newspaper in hand.

"In town," he says, "I came upon a copy of the Cincinnati *Western Spy*." He pauses, and I am filled with anxiety. He points to a passage for me to read.

> *The Citizens of this place were much disappointed in not having an opportunity of viewing her, only as she passed. She made no stops here. From the rapidity with which she passed this place, it is supposed she went by at the rate of 12 or 14 miles an hour.*

"The river is still quite low," I say. "We have no urgency about attempting the falls." I take his hand. I've been thinking on this one. "This is exactly what we have been waiting for, Nicholas. A chance to return to Cincinnati and prove this vessel can go as well upstream."

"Yes, exactly," he says. "I know it was your suggestion, but are you truly willing for us to take this upriver chance? With Henry only just born and you not entirely on your feet, though you are proving me wrong on that last one. Just look at you!"

I nod, watching the bustle of trade on the wharf, all of it headed downriver eventually, if the river will rise, and virtually none of it up.

"I'm ready," I say.

"Then we shall set off immediately, going north. I will inform Andrew and Baker." He rises, turns his chair again, then sets it down just as noisily as ever.

"Wait, Nicholas," I say. "I have . . ."

"Oh, Lydia. I'm sorry. Let me get you in the cabin again. What am I thinking?"

"No, it isn't that. Would you please just wait for a moment? You mentioned a serious discussion, and we haven't completed that yet."

His chair bangs back into place and he sits down. "Well, yes, going upriver to Cincinnati."

"Yes, that is the idea. Here is my contribution to that discussion. The river is low, and we are in no hurry to leave immediately. I've been thinking, Nicholas. What about having a dinner on board for potential investors . . . ?"

"A dinner?"

"A dinner." I've had time to give this a good bit of thought.

"But what about you, Lydia? You're only barely up. And not yet supposed to be. What about . . . ?"

I take his hand, shush him gently.

"This won't involve me, Nicholas. I'll be invisible. You know these western customs of dinner for only men, so unlike the glittering dinners of Washington. You could do it tomorrow. I won't even need to greet the guests, because, officially, I'm still lying in."

"Tomorrow! Brilliant!" A grin spreads across his face. "At one o'clock. We could well manage that."

"Indeed, we could. We have time to buy fresh supplies in town—root vegetables, apples, corn. And meat from the butcher. There will be freshly butchered pork this time of year. We have ample pickled and potted meats and dried vegetables in store. We even have beaver tails in the larder, quite the delicacy out here on the frontier. We have salted string beans, which we can wash and soak overnight. And plenty of black pepper cake and preserves . . ."

"We can host an impressive feast, Lydia. I'll purchase good ale and shrub in port. Even possibly some applejack. What a way to impress potential investors, as well as passengers for luxury travel! You are brilliant, my dear! Am I repeating myself?"

"Wait, Nicholas. That isn't all." I grab for his hand as he starts to rise. I've another surprise to throw at his feet, one that will erase all my indebtedness for forging ahead to Louisville. "Think of this. What if after feasting and imbibing, the gentlemen on board find themselves unexpectedly moving? Upstream! The very direction they believe we cannot go?"

Nicholas's eyes, blinking at the vibrant sky above us, tell me of his astonishment, his excitement, his sudden vision just as I described it. I grab his chair as it starts to tilt. He leaps to his feet and sprints for the rail, then stares down into the lapping water as its reflections throw dashes of light across his face. Back he rushes, leans over, and throws his arms around me. I'm reminded again how he and my father are equally impetuous, which is why I so love them both. I gather a kiss on both my cheeks, my clasped hands squeezed together in his.

Well, I've earned my freedom from bed, I think.

All is working as planned. The day is thrown into preparation. The cook's son, Gabriel, along with half the crew, are off the boat, roving the town to assemble provisions. Our marvelous cook, Joshua, is scouring our stores below for the finest delicacies. Nicholas is out in search of the best champagne—if applejack is not to be found—and ale, with no worries as to the partners' monetary objections. The prospective prize is too good.

Upon his return, Nicholas makes a list of prestigious businessmen, and together we sit at the table and, sharing the inkwell, write invitations for his potential guests. He has brought fine parchment with us for just this purpose. The sealing wax is an impressive dark blue, to match the boat's hull, and the stamp is an interlocking *TNO* monogram for the name of the boat. Billy, our handsomest crewman, will hand-deliver these and bring us the replies.

When the morning breaks, I am on deck with Rosetta, taking in the glorious peach and rose hues of sunrise. As I relish the sun's first rays over the roof peaks of Louisville, from the kitchen, I hear the clank of pots as Joshua, always extraordinary, is hard at work preparing the final dishes for an elegant three-course dinner. Already the air is filled with the delicious scents of roasting pork and turnips. Bessie comes to take Rosetta and I am momentarily free to inspect the table preparations.

In the gentlemen's quarters yesterday, Sarah covered the tables with white linen cloths. Napkins embroidered with our elaborate interlocking monogram lie beside the ship's molded creamware and sturdy glasses at each place. I can't resist smoothing a fold here and there, rearranging the sugar nippers by a fraction, nudging a glass into a slightly more perfect angle. My excitement ratchets higher and higher. Oh, I must make sure there are a few extra folding knives on the side table, in case one of the gentlemen should forget his. Thank goodness, bringing one's own utensils is customary out here on the frontier. I don't think we could have found an extra inch to store enough. I run my fingers along the tablecloth a last time. Once the gentlemen begin arriving, I will need to disappear. I dislike these western customs where women are not included, but must respect them. They will change as more people arrive from back east. At least I still have a bit of time to indulge myself in the cheery light outside.

The sun is high overhead when Nicholas returns, followed by three young men, each pushing a cart filled with jugs and bottles of various brews. As they rattle across the gangplank, Nicholas is issuing orders and pointing to where the libations must be unloaded. Billy leaps onto the gangplank, then back again onto the deck, and sprints toward Nicholas, hand outheld clutching apparent replies to the invitations. From my seat, I see Nicholas thumbing through them rapidly, the smile on his face intensifying. He looks at me with victory in his eyes, brandishing the fistful of papers aloft. I nod, smiling, then join him in laughter from across the deck. He is on his way toward me when one of the crewmen detains him for specific directions. They turn back toward the gangplank, enmeshed in preparations.

Rising from my chair, I make my way to the ladies' compartment. It is nearly time for the baby to nurse and for Rosetta to eat her spare little midday meal and lie down for her nap. By the end of the hour, I hear the clumping of men's boots on the deck, loud hellos, and other greetings met with raucous guffaws. From the far end of the gentlemen's quarters, the loud tramping of feet resonates from the other door. I can just make out Joshua's voice, calm and level, as he gives low instructions to Gabriel, and then I hear the distinct clatter of various-sized pots and serving dishes, followed by the scrape of chairs across Nicholas's finely finished bare floors. Judging by their voices, the men are heady, impulsive, and a tad rash. Through the wooden partition between the quarters, it is difficult for me to make out quite what is being said, though now and again, I hear a word or two that indicate Nicholas is promoting the idea of investment. Primarily what I hear are objections that the boat, elegant as it is, will never go upstream, against the treacherous river currents. I smile to myself as I tuck little Henry into his well-secured crib and lie down to rest a bit myself.

I must have drifted off. I wake to Sarah's loud whisper. She is standing near our passageway, across from the doors to the gentlemen's quarters. The gathering in the other room must be working on the third course by now. The men's voices, interspersed with chortles of laughter, seem much louder, presumably from the generous libations. There is no cessation in the rumpus when I hear Baker and Andrew begin to fire up the engine and the paddles go into thumping rhythm, slow at first—at least for the time we exit the harbor—then faster as we go up against the current.

My feelings are a rising mixture of excitement and anxiety. What if this surprise doesn't work? It will be my fault. No, not my fault. The fault will be in the paddles, in the concept, in the design somewhere. But I am the one who insisted we come all the way to Louisville. It is I who planted this grand untested scheme of proving ourselves prematurely in my husband's head. If we fail, it will be my responsibility and my shame to see him mortified as he faces potential investors. And I will be the one who fears the response of the partners and my father.

The men are growing quiet. As their loud conversation dissipates, the fiery groaning and banging of the engine increases. Chairs crash to the floor. Frantic cries and the sound of dashing feet reach me through the wooden doors. The men are roaring and screaming.

"What the bloody hell? We're unmoored. Get off the boat!"

"Oh, my God! We're going over the falls. We'll be killed. We're on the falls!"

"We're on the bloody rocks. It's the rocks! The boat is coming apart."

I can't resist a glimpse. Taking Sarah by the hand, I cross the threshold at our end. Peeking out the door, I see the first wild

panic on deck, men running, pushing, shoving in every direction, bashing into one another, knocking each other down, and
scrambling for footing again. One stout gentleman is attempting to throw his hefty leg over the rail, and then I see him stop.
He's staring at the water below, then at the bank, where the
dock and the buildings of Louisville are slipping away behind
us. Nicholas walks toward him, speaking in a low voice, gesturing toward the passing scenery as the town gives way to glorious foliage along the bank. His leg comes back down. The man
turns. I cannot tear myself away. I'm choking on my own
laughter.

Other men begin to surround Nicholas, who is gesticulating
calmly, explaining just how this is all working, his gestures
moving confidently from the passing scenery to the water
under the paddles to the firebox and the stack. He waves to Andrew in the wheelhouse, and the men around him turn to see
our pilot wave back. A new excitement is growing now, a thrill
at realizing that indeed we are progressing upstream, against
the current, at a fair rate. This is what I needed: to see Nicholas's triumph. I duck back into the women's cabin in time to
find Rosetta rousing from her nap. Tiger stretches his big frame,
ambles over, and positions his soft head under my hand before
nudging his nose into my palm to be petted.

CHAPTER 13

Success! We have proven our countercurrent capability. Our excited guests will have much to talk about in Louisville until our return in a week or so. And stories to tell long after that. At last we are on our way back to Cincinnati. The trip is one hundred eighty miles. Andrew, Baker, and Nicholas calculate that it will take somewhere between forty-two and forty-eight hours against the current, given no complications. Nicholas is more charming than ever, smiling and chatting, basking in his triumph in Louisville. The surprise of the upriver dinner trip has won him respect and several possible large investors. We are still absent of passengers. I sense this is a disappointment to Nicholas. But not to me. I'm basking in his contentment and unwilling to share it for the moment. Though I know even a passenger or two would add to the allure of our achievement, I'm grateful to have our privacy and his undivided attention.

The ship has recovered from the grand dinner: all the table-cloths and napkins have been washed and are fluttering on the lines, nearly dry and ready to be ironed, folded, and stored away; the creamware has been carefully stacked in the vertical bin I designed to minimize the danger of breakage; and the glassware has been packed in fresh straw, awaiting its next opportunity to beguile investors and passengers. All these practical things, I had my say-so in, thank goodness. Such things are, after all, women's business!

Meanwhile, we are making ourselves at home with our newborn and Rosetta. I am luxuriating in Nicholas's attentive presence with us, undiverted except by the regular work he must oversee, as always. Henry is as good an infant as one could hope for on such a journey as this: sweet, seldom fretful, sleeping and nursing on a regular schedule. The stationary crib beside our berth is immensely convenient for nighttime feedings. Henry rarely cries, just makes soft tutting sounds that wake me. I often fall back asleep with him still in my arms, one of Nicholas's long muscular ones embracing us both. I love sleeping between these two, the warmth of my husband's body cradling me as I cradle our son at my breast.

At the end of our forty-five-hour trip, Cincinnati is exactly as I expected: astounded, excited, eagerly celebratory over our unforeseen arrival back upriver. The crowds on the dock wave and cheer with wild enthusiasm but, thank goodness, do not mistake our arrival for an attack by the British or for the comet crashing into the river. Nicholas, I know, is impatient to entertain his gentlemen friends, those he was sure might have been offended by our previous passing. As some of them come eagerly, almost too eagerly, across the gangplank to greet us, I must confess that I detect at least two who were seemingly insulted at being our second-choice stop: Dr. Jameson and Reverend Hammond. It hardly seems in keeping with his faith that the Reverend should be miffed, but I forgive him.

Once we are securely settled in dock, Joshua, along with Gabriel and a couple of other crewmen, are off already to find fresh provisions for another fine dinner tomorrow to honor possible investors now that we are actually here, the ability of our vessel proven even more. Sarah is at work making every minute count to be sure the tablecloths are ironed and flawless. The fine monogramed napkins, as well. A few fatty food stains call for boiling water; another requires a bit of powdered hartshorn from the larder. An ash stain from some gentleman's cigar will simply need to be covered by a platter for the first course. After that, the spirits will have been flowing enough that I doubt it will matter.

"Here, Sarah, let me help you with those tablecloths." I reach out and take hold of a corner.

"You don't need to be working now, Miss Lydia."

"It is so much easier for two people to spread the cloths and set the table. And I need something to keep me busy," I say, overriding her protests.

I am often distracted with Henry. He is nursing more frequently now, building the milk supply for a growth spurt, I suppose. Rosetta is unexpectedly needy of me, having difficulty, I presume, learning to share my attentions with her baby brother, in spite of all Bessie can do to entertain her.

"She just got a case of the twos," Bessie claims with authority.

Tiger seems, somehow, to understand, the way dogs mysteriously do. He follows her wherever she goes, nudging her to play or rest, curled over his massive softness on the floor. When she is pulling on me, whimpering, he inserts himself between us and begins gently licking her arm or her ear to make her laugh and throw her arms around him.

I am grateful every day for my huge Tiger. I would have been so hesitant to acquire a dog this large—I believe he weighs more than I do—except that my friend Lucille in Philadelphia had one.

"So wonderful with children," she told me. "Like having an extra nursemaid."

When Nicholas brought me this puppy after Rosetta's birth,

and I held his soft, wiggly, black-furred body in my arms, the connection was instant. Now I watch his careful attention to Rosetta—I suppose it might be called herding—and am grateful for the introduction Lucille gave me to this breed. I can hardly imagine life without him.

We intend our visit here to be brief, in case the water rises at the Falls of the Ohio. We cannot afford to miss a chance to cross those deadly rocks. But we must also be effective in using our time here to recruit investors. We must not insult them again, as we did with our first bypassing. There was even note of it in the October 30 Cincinnati *Liberty Hall*. Someone handed it to Nicholas, who hands it to me.

"Look at this, Lydia!"

> *[T]he steamboat, lately built at Pittsburgh, passed this town at 5 o'clock in the afternoon, in fine stile, going at the rate of about 10 to 12 miles an hour.*

"We are not mentioned until page three," he says as I read. "Something of a footnote, it seems, perhaps a bit of a dismissal, thanks to our having passed by without stopping, but they did seem to notice our speed. I'll settle for that—it's impressive enough on its own."

Nicholas is extending himself to the limit, sure that securing investors not only will appease the partners for any annoyance at his unexpected rerouting of the voyage, but will also secure his place in any future steamboat commercial partnership. His compatriots, Dr. Drake and Jacob Burnet, whom he feared he had insulted by bypassing Cincinnati, seem thoroughly appeased by the grand dinner Nicholas is hosting for an array of gentlemen today. General Harrison, whom I confess I somewhat distrust on account of his sly defiance of President Jefferson when he attempted to slide slavery into the territories via indentured servanthood with no limits, is off with his troops, marching on Prophetstown, the enclave of Tecumseh's brother, Tenskwatawa, also known as The Prophet.

"He has, however," says Nicholas when I voice my criticism, "had a cartload of fine alcohols sent from his plantation for the feast."

The gathering is lively and again rather loud, but this time there is no surprise racket from the engine and paddles as we head upstream. By midafternoon, I can tell from my careful spying that the men, thanks to the absent general, seem thoroughly soothed and in high spirits as they make their way back across the gangplank to the wharf, with Billy and two others carefully monitoring their unbalanced steps onto land, where their carriages await.

We are also hosting some general tours of the boat, though Nicholas has raised the price of admission. The increase does not appear to discourage the jostling queue of visitors in the least. There is easily as great a curiosity about the engine and paddle-wheel mechanics as about the ladies' and gentlemen's quarters. Sometimes we eliminate the ladies' quarters so as not to disturb Rosetta's naptime. If it is time to nurse Henry in the midst of a tour, I take him into my berth and close the privacy drapes. Bessie and Sarah do a wonderful job of showing the ladies around. However, the greatest demand among our sightseers is for the short excursions upriver and back, priced at one dollar per trip. The boat is packed almost beyond capacity at every departure, and the excitement of the crowd is contagious and exhilarating.

I observe from my husband's face, when I manage a brief glimpse of it, that he is happy, both about our success and our extra income, to offset the expense of returning upriver. Nicholas exudes an ecstatic confidence at having accomplished this "impossible" feat. It seems to illumine the very air around him.

Our Cincinnati experiment has proven the capability of this vessel. No one can say now that what we have attempted cannot be done. Nicholas's design of this vessel will make upstream trade viable. Surely, the ingenuity of achieving this goal early in the voyage will assuage the partners' concerns and bring increased harmony among them. As well as appease my father.

Nothing short of our marriage, once my father gave in at Mary Elizabeth's intervention and granted us permission, has made my Nicholas this happy.

Baker is looking pleased himself, standing at the rail in conversation with Bessie. She breaks away to catch Rosetta as she twirls around too fast on the deck. Something seems to be blooming between those two. I catch them often sharing glances. Bessie smiles at me as she takes Rosetta in for bedtime. Baker smiles, as well, as he begins making his last inspections of the wood brought on board as fuel to get us back to Louisville. I'm hoping it is adequate, as the racket from it hitting the bins last evening was more than a bit nerve-racking and kept frightening Rosetta, though Henry slept right through the commotion.

Andrew and Nicholas are reexamining Zadoc Cramer's navigational book, the most trusted comprehensive guide to the Western Waters. I can see their heads bent over it in consultation through the window of the wheelhouse. Nicholas is mentioned repeatedly in the new edition, having supplied crucial information from our flatboat voyage. This morning, when Nicholas took his own copy out, I teased, "Are you sure you are still in it? They may have changed your name to mine!" He laughed, though my teasing words were at least partly true. We were a team then. And there was a fair period on that navigational flatboat voyage when I was the only one well enough, pregnant though I was, to be in charge of the boat. But women's names are rarely, or never, where they might be. Of course, I wasn't taking soundings during that period, either.

At that point, I was just trying to survive.

CHAPTER 14

"Given we are moving with the current now, rather than against," Nicholas says as we lean against the rail, "our return to Cincinnati will take a good deal less time than our trip upriver. Time enough, though, for me to catch up with the books."

Yes, if he sets himself to it.

He'd much rather be discussing some new idea, I know, much like my father, than balancing the finances. Since our marriage, Father has expressed admiration for our—well, for Nicholas's—accomplishments in what we are doing. However, there is always a *but*.... In my last letter from Father, he expressed real appreciation for Nicholas's optimism *but* gently warned that great optimism can get a man into too-shallow waters. Well, Father should know. He's had his own moments of running aground with his ambitions, at least figuratively so.

But—here I am saying it myself—Nicholas does need to develop a discipline for keeping his books. That or to hire someone, for which we don't have enough funds. At least during these hours back to Louisville, he will have uninterrupted time to catch up with himself. It must be an hour since I left him at his desk, counting the cash intake from our little ticketed tours around the boat and the packed spontaneous trips from the port and back for the price of a dollar. Those must have brought in near to a hundred dollars a trip. The boat was packed to the rails for each of them. Nicholas seems quite excited about the unexpected income, but I wonder if he has accounted for our purchases of extra wood and coal, and the costs of the dinners and fine spirits.

Just as I think Nicholas has settled into the accounts, he appears in the doorway, holding a newspaper out to me. The excitement of whatever it is has permeated his very presence.

"Look, Lydia! Just look. We've made news in Cincinnati yet again, but this time—*this* time—with a much more favorable account."

He almost tosses the paper into my lap. I drop my knitting to barely catch the paper. There in the December 4 *Liberty Hall*, I see the article, headlined simply THE STEAM BOAT.

> *Arrived here on Wednesday last, in 45 hours from the falls, a distance of 180 miles, against the current of the Ohio. To the citizens of this place, it is an object of much curiosity.*
>
> *Several short trips have been performed up and down the river from this place, and numbers have gratified themselves by taking passage in these short voyages. On the rise of water, she will sail for her place of destination, it is said, to return to us no more.*

I feel my husband's elation. All has gone as I hoped, which is beneficial for my sake as well as his. What if my daring proposal—my desperate one, truth be told—had ended in some catastrophic failure? What would our future be? What would my father say? I would have failed both men I love best so grievously.

But there is no sense in thinking about that! Happily, I haven't. Just the opposite. In fact, this should also elate the partners, as now we have early proof of the unheard of, unbelieved capabilities of this vessel. Though we have not yet succeeded in gathering any promised investors, this news should put them right into the pockets of Mr. Fulton and Mr. Livingston. And remove their constant argumentative criticism from Nicholas's back.

I take a deep breath as I lay the paper aside on the table and rise to put my arms around my husband's neck. He is striking, even with his hair blown wild out on deck. Perhaps especially so. It suits his spirit. He kisses my cheek and turns to gaze into the crib, where Henry is stirring. Nicholas scoops him onto his shoulder, careful to cradle his little head in his palm. He loves being a father. He was equally tender with Rosetta.

I have an unexpected question. I'm wondering if my father was similarly loving to Henry and me before our mother died. A deep longing to remember more from my early childhood penetrates me. What little I have comes in fragments, like random bits of wood and tree branches on the river, floating there, separated from their origin. It seems that Father joined Henry and me on the floor to play with our blocks, building things, knocking them down, and building again. Certainly, he was glad, once we rejoined him with Mary Elizabeth on this continent, for me to tag around with him, watching him at work, asking questions as fast as they spun out of my head. He never laughed at my outrageous ideas, always laughed with me, treating them seriously as he carefully spun them back down to earth. I am aware how he loved that I understood his explanations and translated them into ideas of my own.

He adored my playing the piano. Sometimes he would sit beside me and finger the keys with me in a duet. He wasn't able to do that when I began playing the organ. How I wish I could have an organ on this vessel—utter impossibility—or even an upright piano! Oh, well, no. Even Father's rancor when Nicholas told him of our love—in addition to his initial disbelief, his brushing it off as a joke—was fueled by his love for me as a father, his wanting the best life possible for me. But I wonder periodically how he could have left us there in England, such little children, with neither mother nor father. I understand the turmoil of his grief. At least I think I do. But wasn't there grief at leaving us, too, when he went a continent away? And what of our grief at his leaving, at being left? Us so young. Adults seem to have a distorted way of thinking children don't remember pain for long, that they adjust so quickly to altered circumstances. Indeed, that last part may hold some truth, but only because they have no choice.

Nicholas hands the baby to me, leans in and gives me a kiss. He runs his hand through his messy hair. "Back to the books," he says and strides to his desk in the gentlemen's quarters.

Bessie approaches to take Henry from me, but I want him in my arms. I want to hold him as if I would never let him go, as if I could never go away from him. I will, I know. I will also have to let him go from me bit by bit as he grows. Certain things are inevitable. The question is when. And how. But that's a long way off at the moment.

"Let's go out on the deck," I say to Bessie. "Sarah, you come, too."

Sarah nods and lays aside her dustcloth to help Rosetta gather an extra doll. Three is more than Rosetta's arms will hold, and she's unwilling to leave one of her babies behind. Ah, just where my thoughts have been drifting. Sarah takes two of them in one hand and Rosetta's hand in the other. Rosetta has her doll in the crook of her arm, just as I have Henry. She gives me a smile as she lifts her foot to take the big step up over the threshold to our quarters. A sense of wholeness pervades my spirit. As Bessie opens the door to the deck, I am hit simultaneously by the chill in the air and the welcome warmth of the bright sun, glowing through the mist.

Sarah halts and disappears back down the passageway, returns with a sweater for Rosetta and a small green wool cape for me. The baby is already warmly swathed, blinking his eyes against the light and sucking on a tight little fist. As I situate myself on the deck, I notice Baker over beyond the furnace, talking earnestly with one of the more experienced hands. Our commotion has attracted his attention. And his attention has attracted a smile and a little nod from Bessie. I smile inside myself. I'm not at all sure a smile can be hidden inside, but the feeling is genuine.

Young love seems so apparent. I can't imagine how my parents failed to notice ours and were so shocked when Nicholas approached my father—except that our age difference had made him more like an uncle to me. I had, in fact, called him uncle early on. I assume such a love as ours would simply never have occurred to them. It was Mary Elizabeth who finally saw the truth of it and took up our plea with Father. And though he had grieved for my mother so, he worshiped Mary Elizabeth. She was dear to me, as well, and I confided in her by mail. She knew of the faithful frequency of Nicholas's correspondence with me. And mine with him. She was almost equally as reliable as he in her exchange of letters, telling me of home, my father—who was not so prone to letter writing—of Henry and all the siblings, their antics and their growing. She wrote me finally to ask if I was sure of my commitment to Nicholas. When I answered with the deepest sincerity of which my pen and words were capable, she initiated her efforts to sway my father in our favor, a feat that was not easy—I was then only seventeen—but, thank goodness, was successful.

I wave my hand at Baker, and he takes it as a signal to come over. He is a kind man and full of good humor, though a tad shy. He stands a bit back from us to bid us good day, waves his hand toward the baby.

"That one's getting mighty handsome, there," he says.

"You're welcome to come closer and see him better."

He looks from one of us to the other, as if he's not quite sure what to do, this utterly competent man at his job. I pull back the soft receiving blankets when he comes and leans over to see the baby. Bessie has moved in a bit closer. He seems not to know what to say.

"Baker," I say, "Sarah and I have this under control. Bessie might like a small tour to give her some understanding of just how this furnace produces the steam to run the paddle wheels so smoothly."

Bessie blushes but turns toward him. "That is, if you can spare the time."

"It would be my pleasure," he says.

So off they go, Rosetta running behind to catch Bessie's hand. Sarah, now holding all three dolls, laughs and sits back in the chair beside me, her face to the sun, which has a strange misty glow about it. The morning chill has given way to a comfortable warmth, in spite of a foggy cloud cover that diffuses the sunlight. It's a lovely day regardless. Nice to be outdoors with no urgent pressures on any of us. I glance back toward the furnace to see Bessie seemingly entranced at the boat's technical workings. Rosetta tugs at her, but her attention is all on Baker's hands, as he gestures to indicate flames shooting up, then points to the boiler.

"An interesting lesson on the mechanics of the steamboat," Sarah says, without moving her head.

"Indeed," I say. "Perhaps better than any I have had myself." I laugh.

"What a day this is. A wonderfully warm sun in spite of this strange fogginess."

"Yes, a respite for all of us after our recent exertions. I'm glad we have time for a bit of leisure."

"Is that how you categorize this steamboat lesson?"

I laugh again, a bit louder than I meant. Bessie turns, mumbles something to Baker, and waves him off as she hurries back toward us with Rosetta.

"I beg your pardon, Mrs. Roosevelt. I didn't mean to stay away so long."

Rosetta is gathering her three dolls from Sarah's lap.

"You weren't away so long, Bessie." I motion for her to sit with us. She does but is not as relaxed as Sarah and I are. She reaches for Henry, but I shake my head. He's sound asleep in my arms, and I don't want to give him up. Rosetta hands her one of the dolls, and Bessie instantly takes on a make-believe role, rocking the doll in her arms. Rosetta is laughing and shaking a doll in Bessie's face, trying to tickle her nose.

CHAPTER 15

In less than two days, we dock once again in Louisville. Our arrival is far less dramatic than the first time, but the docks are bustling. Rivermen are hallooing to our crew, and various tradespeople wave. Here and there a cluster of folks raise a cheer to us. I wave and call back to them, which is perhaps not ladylike. Everyone on board is relieved to be back. Once we are securely docked, Nicholas and some of the crew go into town to gather supplies. On his return, my husband looks less than happy. We had thought the river to be rising ever so slightly, but the soundings today show nothing.

"Do you know what that, that . . . ?" He's spitting his words.

"Who, Nicholas? What?"

"Mr. Saulsbury . . . I don't think you met him, and be glad you didn't." He swipes his hand at the corner of his mouth.

"And what?" I repeat.

"Came right up to me without even so much as a hello. 'Well, seems you may have bitten off more than you can chew, eh, Roosevelt!' Blustering! Right in my face."

"Doesn't he know what we've just accomplished?" I'm astounded.

"Of course he does! But he had to be insulting. 'Getting that monster of a ship of yours through those rapids of the falls is another thing altogether,' he said. 'Unless you want to wait for the spring rains!' And he wasn't the only one, Lydia. One said, 'Well, found you a house yet? Looks like you could be in this dock for a year.' Then his inebriated friend chimed in, saying, 'Seen it with better boats than yours.' Damned wiseacres!"

"Nicholas, you must not let these men get you so riled up." I'm trying to calm myself as I hopefully calm him. "They are simply jealous—of you and your brilliant ingenuity. They know a successful voyage will change this river forever. These waters will be bustling with steamboats. It's inevitable. It's the way of the future and will bring you fame and wealth. They see it and wish they didn't, because it doesn't include them." I stop, take a deep breath. "Though it will certainly bring them greatly increased commerce. They should rather be on your side of the scale."

He's still angry. I see it in his narrowed eyes and the tight lines of his cheeks, the thin, straight pull of his lips. I go to him and put my arms around him, stroke those clenched lips with my fingertip, smile at him until I make him laugh ever so slightly. He shakes his head, running his fingers through his hair.

I need to restore some calm to the scene. I don't want the children to see him like this.

"Let's have us a picnic here on the deck, Nicholas. Let the folks out there see us rejoicing at our success, waving at them gaily. Let's let them talk about that."

"Talk about what a fool I am to be so nonchalant?"

I am trying.

He goes to speak to Andrew Jack about the piloting difficulties of the falls. I believe they are equally concerned over a requirement that all boats engage a licensed local pilot for passage through those rapids once the water rises. Both of them are nervous about this constraint, I know:

Andrew Jack, because he won't be able to employ his superior skills and is anxious about relinquishing control of the boat, and Nicholas, because this will be yet another blow to the coffer. But more than that—I know, for I am anxious myself—we are all on edge at the necessity of putting this vessel in the hands of an unknown person.

I must calm myself as well as my husband. Perhaps this picnic will do us all good. I go to the kitchen to ask Joshua if there is something easy to prepare, and he assures me there is. But then he always assures us that everything we propose is easy. When I return, I find Nicholas settled, sitting in his chair with his long Dutch pipe, blowing smoke into the strangely oppressive air.

I nudge my chair over so that I may sit close beside him, facing him a bit sideways. When I take a seat, he rolls his head toward me, slips the pipe from his lips, and exhales. His half smile reassures me somewhat.

"You are beautiful," he says and lays his hand over mine on the arm of the chair.

"People always love to talk. They will say all sorts of things," I say, ignoring his wish not to discuss these issues. "You know that. I know that. We've heard all of it already—more than once. I hope you won't let that bother you. You've proven them wrong, you know, and they don't like to be wrong."

He pats my hand. "I know. It's that I'm anxious, I suppose."

"Are you?" As if I didn't see his anxiety quite clearly. I turn his hand and trace the lines in his palm.

"I suppose I am." He clicks his pipe between his teeth, takes his time to respond. "It's the falls. And this question of hiring a local licensed pilot for the stint of the rapids." He taps the mouthpiece of his pipe against the wooden arm of his chair, sits up. "No one knows how to pilot this boat, Lydia. No one except Andrew Jack. I'm aware how well the licensed pilots know the falls, but they haven't the foggiest notion of this boat. Yet we're required to hire one." He taps his pipe quite hard. "He'll crash us."

Thoughts come slowly. I wait before I respond, struggle to

put them in some semblance of order. "You have a valid point, Nicholas." I wait again. Where to go next? We are required to hire a licensed pilot. We have no choice. "Have you laid it out to the authorities?"

"Indeed, I have!" His shout is unexpected.

I catch my breath. My stomach tightens. "And?"

"And they will make no exceptions. None." This comes almost as a shout. Then, in a quieter tone, "They say there were too many wrecks before they passed this ordinance. Seems to me it's more about fattening the town's coffers . . . two-dollar fee for each passage. For us, they want to charge three. It's robbery, and I can't give control of my boat to an unknown."

Joshua and Gabriel arrive with a couple of large trays filled with dried fruit, three cheeses, fig preserves, and sliced ham, along with fresh bread from the bakery up the dock. Nicholas and I begin to serve ourselves. I manage to drop a bit of preserves on my sleeve. I'm thinking hard as I try to wipe it off but manage to make a larger stain. A second of anger flashes through me as I think about having to wash it out. At least it's only a spot, not the whole dress.

A thought about the pilot hits me.

"Would you necessarily have to give up control, Nicholas?"

He looks startled.

"What if you hire the man of your choosing? You do have a choice, don't you?"

He nods, takes a bite of his open sandwich. "I can insist upon it, since we are an exceptional vessel."

"You make your choice. You and Andrew Jack. Bring him on board now, well ahead of time. Let Andrew Jack begin showing him the fine tunings of this boat as a precaution. Let him take the wheel under Andrew Jack's supervision. You could pay him, then pay him again for the availability of his expertise, to stand beside Andrew Jack and talk him through the falls. Their combined skills can guide us through. In case of any emergency, he will have at least rudimentary skills with the boat to take over. Is that too far-fetched?"

"You're brilliant, Lydia. Brilliant. Assuming the river doesn't rise too quickly, we can resume conducting our dollar tours for this pilot to familiarize himself with the boat, as well as pay his extra time. He and Andrew Jack should be able to collaborate well by the time we go through." He scratches his head. "What enables you to think so well, Lydia?"

"I'm my father's daughter." I laugh. "That's why you fell in love with me." Now we are both laughing.

Nicholas lays down his napkin and his half-eaten food. "What would I do without you, Lydia?" He leans over to give me a kiss. "I'm off to confer with Jack. I'll need his collaboration on this." He tucks his pipe into his teeth again and steps away toward the pilothouse.

Nicholas is relieved, it seems. I wish I were. We are at our most challenging point of this voyage. But Andrew Jack is as competent a pilot as can be found on these or any waters, and by now, he has managed this boat through its first successes. If Nicholas and Andrew Jack together can find in the unknown pilot a man equally knowledgeable about these rapids, we will have yet another success, regardless of the butterflies in my stomach.

CHAPTER 16

The river fails to rise. That is both good and bad for us. Good in that it gives us greater opportunity for our dollar tours, which are somewhat less packed with passengers this time around but are profitable nonetheless. It also allows time for Andrew and our licensed local pilot, Sam Laughton, to collaborate and hone their skills for the passage through the rapids. Bad in that it delays our voyage significantly. Nicholas is exceptionally tense as we are moving further into winter, and he is fearful that the dreaded ice will begin to form before we can leave Louisville. As his tension rises, so does mine.

I think that during the tours today, I will make a trip into town, will even take the children with me. I could use some yarn. Rosetta would love a new cap or sweater—anything for herself, since her baby brother has his new blanket. Bessie could use a bit of time to rest and, perhaps, converse with Baker in our absence. Sarah should be glad to go ashore and explore the town with me.

"I would be delighted, Miss Lydia," she says when I ask.

An expression of both excitement and relief brings a singular glow to her face. She takes Henry from me and cradles his tiny body against her shoulder. I wrap his blue knit blanket over him, then tuck it under his legs and feet as Sarah snugs it round his head. His little arms are waving, so there is no way to keep them covered. We tuck them in, and out they come again. I have knit little mittens for him. As I slip them on, he promptly puts one in his mouth. Now it is damp and will absorb the chill, but that will have to do for the moment. Bessie has Rosetta buttoned in her plaid wool coat. She is holding her hands in the air for her own mittens. Now for my redingote and warm woolen bonnets for us all. There, we are ready. Off we go.

Louisville has grown considerably in these past two years, the greatest change being the somewhat extravagant new brick homes on the bluff and the commerce that has grown up to accommodate them. There are dry goods and hardware and furniture shops now, as well as the ever-present general store. The town has less of a river frontier aspect, though its social customs reveal its western identity—such as dinners only for men.

I find a current copy of the *Louisville Gazette* in the hardware store and purchase it. Flipping through, I see no mention of the steamboat or our arrival. There seems to be little news, in truth, other than accounts of Tecumseh's forays into the South, in his desperate effort to unite the tribes against American expansion, but the greater headlines concern General Harrison's march on Prophetstown and the battle that followed a sneak attack on his forces early in the morning of the seventh of November, which left many dead, including commanders of units.

I haven't time to read it carefully now, but it seems General Harrison prevailed in spite of the odds, then continued on to find the Prophet's settlement empty except for one elderly woman who was unable to move. Once the soldiers removed the old woman, they burnt the town to the ground. To the ground! I must stop reading this now. I hardly know how to sort my feelings—those for our soldiers whirling with my visions of the ashes of the homes of an entire village. I must get my business done. There will be time to examine this news and its possible repercussions for us once I am back on board, where I am beginning to wish I were this very minute.

Sarah returns with oatmeal and sugar cookies from the bakery. I'm thrilled. I can't wait to have a bite and taste that comforting sweetness on my tongue. But Rosetta is squealing and jumping up and down, so I hand the first one to her. Then get control of myself and insist Sarah have the next. It is just as I am taking the first crunchy bite, its welcome flavor filling my senses, that Elizabeth Macon—amazing that I remember her name—approaches, in the company of a woman I'm sure I've never met.

"Lydia Roosevelt! What a great pleasure to see you while you are here. Let me introduce my friend Sally O'Connor." Elizabeth begins to regale her friend with our exploits. Then turns back to me. "Have you found a place to live here for yourself and the children? Or will you be taking a coach back north to go home?"

Taken aback, I am without words for a moment. Then I say, "No, neither. We will continue on board with my husband to New Orleans."

"Oh, really?" She halts for a moment. "But, of course, you and the children will take a carriage overland around the falls to meet the boat downriver at Shippingport. That is a common procedure with the flatboats and keelboats. Almost always unloading cargo to lighten the boat in the process. But, of course, you know that. You'll have no difficulty at all, I'm sure." She pulls her cape a bit tighter around her shoulders.

Sarah steps closer. I turn and take Henry into my arms. Sarah picks up Rosetta, who is waving her cookie about in delight, as if offering this woman a bite.

"Well, thank you for that information, Elizabeth. However, I intend to accompany my husband through the falls." I turn to Sarah to make my escape, but not quickly enough.

"But, Lydia, it's not just the falls, you know. There is a great deal more danger."

I turn back. "The falls would seem to be the last major challenge, Elizabeth."

"But there are the Indians. Have you not heard about General Harrison and his stunning victory at Tippecanoe? The tribes all along this western bank are in disarray and fighting mode. It will be extremely dangerous, Lydia. You must pay heed. You must surely stay here among us or return to your home."

Home? Home is our boat. Home is my husband.

"My destination is New Orleans," I say, then turn to walk with our tight little group toward the dock. This time I will not be stopped. I am sure they are staring after us. Let them stare.

Once back on the boat, I hand everything and everyone except myself over to Sarah and Bessie, who disappear down the passageway. I have retained only the newspaper and go in search of my husband. I find him behind the boiler in deep conversation with Baker. The tightness on his face, the abrupt, almost pounding gestures of his hands warn me that all is not well. I try to slip away, but Baker glimpses me, twists to see me fully, and nods. Nicholas swivels with a scowl on his face, raises a hand to stop my approach.

Anxiety is rising through me. Prickling with it, I circle back to the chairs, where I sit and read with greater concentration the account of an early morning tribal attack on Harrison's troops, which includes the gruesome number and names of the dead, several of whom I know or have met personally. I feel the pounding of my heart in my hands, in my throat. I pause, clinching my hands, before I can go on. The surprise attack was staged by Tecumseh's brother, the Prophet, not by a military leader. So many dead in Harrison's camp, yet when the troops reached Prophetstown, the Indians had fled, abandoned the village they had worked hard to establish.

War horrifies me. I stop again to breathe. As I read on, I have a dreadful sense of yet another war with Britain coming. They are joining with the Indians, it is rumored, or the Indians are joining with them; whichever, they intend to stop the westward expansion of the United States. And here Nicholas and I are attempting a journey that not only will open trade on the river but will also facilitate that westward development by making the western banks of the Mississippi more accessible. What we are doing is not just progress but also possibly a step closer to the renewed violence of war.

And on our western flank will be nothing but Indian Territory until we reach Louisiana.

A veritable fountain of saliva is rising under my tongue. I swallow hard. I am clasping my belly with one arm, my throat with the other hand, when Nicholas comes up, swings the other chair around, sits and starts talking without so much as a greeting.

"Do you know that barge captain Henry Shreve? The one taking forty hands to pole his barge upstream? He came on board to visit. Or so I thought. He's trying to get to Browns-ville before his wife delivers their baby! At least we had that much in common. I expected glowing acclaim for our boat and our progress, but he pestered me with questions. Like criticism. All sorts of what-ifs about my design. What if this and what if that!" For the first time, Nicholas looks me in the eye. "Are you all right, Lydia? You are very pale."

I nod. His tirade has shifted my attention, and my stomach has begun to settle.

"You're sure?" he says, reaching for my hand. When I nod again, he looks at me very closely. Then says, "I don't trust that man. I think he was mentally stealing my designs, working them over in his head." He drops my hand and stands up. "I have to get my patents. Once we succeed, this river will be filled with steamboats."

Nicholas sits again, seems to examine me with his intense

gaze. He's not giving up. "So, what's been amiss in your day, Miss Lydia?"

I hand him the newspaper from town, watch him scan it rapidly.

"We knew Harrison was going, Lydia. That's why he wasn't here for our arrival."

"I know."

"Then, what?"

"The unrest. The unrest we may encounter downriver."

"I can't imagine that we will be in any danger, Lydia. This is a resounding victory for Harrison, in spite of the alarming death toll. We have no reason to be on the west bank of the river once we pass the Indian Chute of the falls. I can't imagine the tribes downriver attempting to take on a vessel this size. Our very noise and the blasts of embers from our stack would be enough to scare them away from us. Remember our first arrival in Louisville! And if they proved foolish enough to try to confront us, we can outrun a canoe by far."

"It's not only that, Nicholas. It's the involvement of the British with the natives and the thought of another war between our nations."

"That will not happen, my love. We are too far advanced and too well established now as a nation in our own right. If the Brits are foolish enough to take us on, we hold the advantage at this point. Far ahead of where we were during the Revolution. The Indians are too disjointed from Harrison's victory at Tippecanoe to be of much value to the British."

He stops. Only long enough to take a good breath. "Now, let's change the subject for a moment. We have no idea when this river will rise enough for us to dare the rapids. I intend to be prepared. I'm making arrangements now, ahead of time, to be certain of having a carriage on hire for you and the children . . ."

"For me and the children! Whatever are you talking about, Nicholas?" I am aghast. "We are going with you."

"That's taking too much of a chance, Lydia. This is pure experiment. Well informed, to be sure, but still utterly dangerous. We've no guarantee. What if something happens, something that—"

"I'll take that chance, Nicholas. I will be with you. I will not be left behind. This venture is ours together."

"Lydia, you must think rationally!"

"I am thinking, and I am rational, Nicholas. We have never discussed anything different. This was always the plan."

"I didn't want disagreement between us. I thought once the baby was born, you would feel differently." He takes my hand.

"I have not come all this way on this boat to take a carriage around the falls."

He smiles, envelops my hand in both of his. "Then, the children, Lydia. At least the children. Let them go overland with Sarah and Bessie and meet us downstream."

"Without us?"

"Sarah and Bessie will have them. Safely, Lydia. If something should happen in these rapids with this untried boat of ours, you and I can survive it, but the children are too small. Even a successful passage will frighten Rosetta too much. Sarah and Bessie do not need to go through this, let alone while trying to care for Rosetta and the baby. Let me arrange a carriage for them. It's the only safe thing to do."

I let it sink in. I have had no thought of being separated from my children for any reason. Memories of my own childhood fears rush through me. My separation from my father pulls me like an undertow. Here is a reversal: Rosetta being terrified by the water, not by a separation from me. I wait for the sense of it to catch me, and when at last it does, I nod. Nicholas puts his arms around me, rocks me gently.

"It shall all be well," he says.

CHAPTER 17

Days pass. I am tense and anxious. Daily soundings show little to no rise in the water. Though the sky remains overcast and heavy, there is no sign of rain. The air is static over the wide, flat stone tables of the fossil-embedded rapids. Strange smelling, as well. Sulfurous. My good-natured Nicholas is edgy, unlike himself, short with everyone, including me now and then. Ice will begin to form in late December, only a matter of weeks from now, that will force us to wait out the winter. We are equally aware of the difficulties such a delay would entail with the partners. Even the fairly successful dollar tours we are using to correlate the piloting skills of Andrew Jack and the licensed local pilot, Sam Laughton, fail to cheer him. The crewmen seem uneasy and restive, even Billy, whom I depend on more than any of the others.

In the quarters, only Sarah and Henry remain calm. Rosetta is fidgety and agitated. Yesterday she threw one of her dolls across the cabin in a fit of temper. That, of course, has made Bessie impatient with her. Luckily, it was a fabric one, so there was nothing to break. Henry sleeps through most of it, waking only to nurse and when Sarah or I lift him into his blanket, needing to escape outside for some minutes. Murmurs of delight arise from the passenger crowd at the sight of him, but their attention goes right back to the shore, the water, the loud flapping and heaving of the paddles, the speed of the boat. Babies are too common to attract attention for long. The atmosphere gives no relief. It is more oppressive deckside than we can handle for long, the air heavy, a yellowish sun struggling against the sulfur-laden fog. We retreat to the cabin rather quickly, unrefreshed.

As the interminable days pass, we become aware of a slight rise in the water only by the difference in our soundings. The increments are so small we almost disregard them. Then we begin, layer by layer, to see a fraction less of the wide shelves of stone. We experiment with taking note of certain slabs or points of rock to see how their visibility compares from day to day. Changes in the three channels of the rapids seem almost imperceptible. The Kentucky Chute, too narrow for anything other than small canoes, is irrelevant to us. The wider middle chute, where we made our flatboat crossing, is irrelevant, as well, though that is where we watch intently for small changes. The Indian Chute, our only possibility for passage, changes little. Yet it is clear the water is rising. Rain or no rain, the water is rising, if barely. And barely is insufficient.

After anguishing days of questionable depth to the rising water, we look out one morning to see two flatboats making headway toward the middle chute, each guided by a local licensed pilot. Memories assault me of our own flatboat skimming smoothly over the water. I feel now the same clutch of frightening uncertainty as we navigated our way through that middle chute. My stomach seizes as I watch these two boats skidding over the rushing water, oarsmen at the ready to push away from the rock ledges, still highly visible all around them. On each boat, at least two men stand ready with sledgehammers in case fossil and rock protrusions grab at the boat and have to be smashed. The center chute is narrow, but so are flatboats. They have the distinct advantage of moving along on top of the water, with no more than an inch or two in depth that could hit the rock below the surface.

The far narrower Kentucky Chute on our portside is empty. No small boats, not even canoes, are waiting to take that route through this last obstacle in the river. In the same way, only a few barges can be sighted waiting to attempt the route to the west at the very edge of Indian Territory. Only that route, the Indian Chute, which passes dangerously around Goose Island, can possibly accommodate the width and depth of the *New Orleans*—and only if the water continues to rise. And by how much.

On the dock, keelboat crews unload their cargo to lighten waiting vessels to decrease their draft, assuming a continued rise in the river. The port is crowded with assorted boats, all of them needing to be lightened. The number of waiting transport wagons, mules, and horses seems countless. The stench of their manure assaults us in the already sulfurous atmosphere. The din permeates the oppressive air as dockworkers reload that same cargo onto waiting wagons. Chains and hitches jangle as teamsters turn their mules and horses away from the dock to transport the heavy goods overland to Shippingport, at the lower end of the falls. There, dockmen will be obliged to reload the boats, assuming the boats make it through. If not, the cargo will be loaded onto other boats waiting to complete the down-river leg.

We have nothing to off-load to minimize our draft. Licensed pilots are boarding the waiting flatboats. There is a virtual procession of them now. Our own, Sam Laughton, has come aboard and is waiting with us in case the river rises enough for the *New Orleans* to pass through the Indian Chute.

I have returned to our quarters and am in the middle of

changing Henry when Nicholas comes to find me. The depth soundings have grown more promising.

"Lydia, it's time," he says. "The river has risen nearly enough. Do you have everything ready?" He glances around the cabin at Sarah and Bessie, who nod to him. "I'll send for Stanton to bring the carriage." He pauses, takes my hand, while I hold Henry steady with the other. "You can change your mind, you know." He is so serious.

"Nicholas," I say, "you would have to tie me up, toss me in a laundry sack, and throw me in the back of that carriage to make me miss this adventure with you!"

He looks astonished, then laughs. I join him as the two women laugh with us. Even Rosetta, with no idea why, laughs in the gaiety for no other reason than that we are all laughing.

Nicholas comes to say he has the carriage waiting. Sarah and Bessie are still scurrying about, gathering diapers and a change of clothing or two for each of the children. Rosetta sits on the floor next to Henry's crib, rocking her stuffed doll and sucking her thumb. Henry is sleeping even through this hubbub. I must wake him now. Must nurse him again, even though it is too soon since his last feeding. How do we know what the timing will be for our crossing the falls—if, indeed, we manage to cross? Even with this precaution, he well may be crying in hunger during our passage.

Rosetta stands and lets her doll flop on top of Henry. When I try to stop her, she pulls it back to lob it over Henry again.

"Rosetta! No, honey. Let Henry alone now."

"Dolly need eat, too, Mama."

"Then you must feed her, love. She can sit in your lap at the table and eat with you."

"No, Mama." She stomps her foot but goes with Sarah, who comes to the rescue.

Rosetta senses something new is afoot, I know. Something

that might be dangerous. And though she has no idea what, she's picking up the tension all around. Bessie lifts the baby from my arms, while Sarah tries to occupy Rosetta with collecting what her dolly needs for the carriage ride.

"Mama bring it," she insists.

"Mama's not coming in the carriage. She's going with Papa in the boat."

"Me go, too." She stomps both feet, first one, then the other, as if for emphasis, in case we are not paying attention. "Go boat with Papa!"

"No, love." Sarah takes her hand. Rosetta jerks it away and covers her face with her doll. Sarah kneels beside her and peeks behind the yellow yarn hair, trying to make Rosetta laugh. "Baby Henry is going with us, too. He's going to need you to keep him company. You and your dolly."

Rosetta jerks the doll away, goes running. Bessie manages to catch her with one free hand. Finally, Sarah has everything gathered, including Rosetta. Our little party proceeds to the deck, where Nicholas, busy calculating our soundings with Baker, looks up and blows a kiss.

Rosetta jerks loose, drops her doll, and goes skidding across to her father. When he hugs her goodbye, she begins to let out a wail.

"No, Papa. Go with you, Papa."

Nicholas tries to make the carriage sound exciting. "You'll get to pet the horsies," he says. "You can even give them a sugar cube!"

Rosetta is getting more and more upset, clinging to his jacket, as Sarah tries to lift her away.

"Papa, Papa, want Papa," she cries over and over.

My breath comes shallow. I want to cry with her. My stomach ties in knots. I am Rosetta. I want my father, and he is leaving me. No, he is gone. His green chair is empty. His warm lap is not there.

Bessie touches my arm. "Are you all right, Mrs. Roosevelt? You look so pale."

I nod my head, try to shake off the sudden intensity of what I am feeling. I'm disoriented somehow. *Where am I?* I strain my neck to see past Bessie's shoulder. There is the dock, the rows of keelboats, workers, horses, mules, wagons, and endless crates of goods waiting to be loaded for the overland leg to the bottom of the falls. I hear Rosetta crying again.

"Want my papa!" Her arms are stretched wildly behind Sarah's shoulder. Grabbing at the air between her and her father.

Ah, now I see it—myself as a girl. Not just the empty armchair, the absent father, but the empty child. The orphan I was at that moment.

CHAPTER 18

At last the children are securely in their carriage, Rosetta distracted by the snorting horse and jingling chains. They are safely off, and Rosetta is waving to me. We've nothing to do but wait. We calculate three-quarters of an hour to make the passage once we find it possible to embark. I am glued to the sight of two barges, each drawing close to four feet, one after the other beginning the passage through the Indian Chute, the only choice we have for this boat. My head fills with the terrible memory of a barge's total wreckage below this chute as we skimmed over the shallower center of these falls in our flatboat.

My heart is beating faster than it should. I hear it in my own ears over the rumble of the falls. My awareness veers to my breath. Why am I holding it? I inhale deeply, let my breath out slowly as I watch the second barge slide into the path of the first. Too close, too close. Now each breath is both short and fast as a result of my fear for these vessels. My hands grip the rail. Nicholas puts his arm around me, tugs me to him.

"The licensed pilots will steer them," he says, pulling me tight. "They know what they are doing."

Apparently, they do. The distance between the boats remains steady and safe, both vessels plying the eddies and the sharp bows of the chute at equal speed.

Nicholas turns to Billy. "What are our soundings?"

"Five inches to spare, Captain."

"Five inches?"

"Yes, sir."

"You're sure?'

"Yes, sir."

Nicholas looks at me, then stares into the water.

"It's enough," he says. He raises his hand in a signal to Baker and Andrew Jack.

Nicholas turns to me. "It will have to be. We may not get more."

I cannot discern his expression.

We have no choice as to the route; only the Indian Chute will possibly accommodate this massive boat. Why am I using the word *possibly*? I must eliminate that word from my thoughts. This has become a regular passage for barges, but nothing so large as the *New Orleans* has attempted it before. And with only five inches to spare?

People on the dock seem startled but raise a cheer as the whistle blasts, then again, and then three times. The engines are gathering steam.

The clanging and scraping of the tempered shovels, flat edged but bowl shaped to hold the heavy loads, resound above the whoosh of the current as Baker and his crew stoke up the fires. Beside me, Tiger pushes against my leg. I am soothed to have him here and not in the carriage. The river sloshes beneath and alongside us as Andrew Jack maneuvers the boat away from the dock, out of the jam of flatboats, keelboats, barges. Nicholas stands beside me. We are steadily plowing our way upstream, away from the falls. We must gain at least a mile against the river, even as much as two, before we can join the current of the chute up past Goose Island.

Now we are there. I feel unexpected alarm as the boat begins to revolve back toward the coursing water. The current against our side in the turn is swift and deceptively smooth. Its flux is surging past us. The rushing water mesmerizes me. I lean out over the railing, as if I could join it, as if I belong to it—to its mysteries, which my vision cannot penetrate, though its depths pull at something deep in me, unnameable. I am so lost in those depths that crucial moments pass before I feel Tiger lurching. With a start, I realize we are escalating, joining the downstream current. *Join* is not the word! We are shot into it, aimed like an arrow at the passage. Stone slabs lie low on our port side; on our starboard loom massive black stone ridges.

I twist to see Andrew Jack standing in the wheelhouse, pointing, beside Sam Laughton, the hired pilot, whose hands are on the wheel. Why isn't Andrew Jack at the wheel? I thought Sam Laughton would be aiding him, not replacing him. What does this man know of our boat? A shock of fear jolts through me as if we have actually struck rock. Why haven't they exchanged places? Is this near stranger taking us through the rapids? I thought he would be at the wheel only to take us out of port and in case of an emergency.

I tap Nicholas on the shoulder, then point. He turns to see, then leans down to me. "Never fear, Lydia. Andrew and Sam have it under control."

I don't fully understand. But I trust my husband. I trust him to know from our experimental practice trips with this unknown pilot that these two are in full control, whoever is at the wheel. Each of these three men holds my trust. And my life.

My hands and feet are tingling with an urge to run as the current propels us toward the chute. Where would I go? To the stern? To run from where we are going, only to see the heaving wake of where we have been? The great waves we are leaving behind? The waves that, no matter how big, will soon disappear? No, where we are going is why I am here. I put my hand on Tiger's head to steady myself. Here is where I belong, my husband and I together! Here is where I must be.

We are catching a curve. I cannot stand. My feet are slipping. I reach toward the rail to steady myself. Nicholas sees me, recognizes my plight. His strong hand takes firm hold of mine until I stop trembling. Far off now as we rush toward the falls, I make out crowds of spectators on the dock. Nicholas, too, notices and points up to the windows of shops and new brick houses along the banks, where I see faces crammed in every open space to watch. On terraces along the banks and bluffs, townspeople have congregated and are waving and cheering as we gather speed.

Behind me, the crewmen bellow commands as they pile load after load of coal into the furnace. Faster and faster. Its enclosed flames grow more intense. The fire seems too extreme. Alarm engulfs me. What if the engine explodes? Steam engines do explode! Have exploded too often thanks to the new high-pressure boilers of Oliver Evans's design. Over and over! One near the docks while our boat was under construction. I heard it myself. Saw the explosion myself. That sudden blast stunned my nerves, if not my body. Saw the aftermath from a distance. Thank goodness Nicholas insisted on the old Watt low-pressure design. Yet even for this more reliable engine, none has ever been put to such a demanding trial as we are endeavoring. What if we push it too far? What if our Watt engine boiler explodes? Would we survive? If we did, could we survive the channel, the water, the rocks? I turn away. I cannot look at that roaring fire. I have to look ahead, keep my eyes and mind on the chute ahead of us, that narrow channel through which we must go.

How like a birthing, I think. Labor has begun, with no turning back. Only forward now through an impossibly narrow channel to reach the other side. We will have brought new life to the river, to trade, to travel, to the westward movement, to this country itself, enhancing its standing in the world. Once we are there, life will go forward inevitably; yet it will never be the same again.

I turn to my husband, reach up to touch him. He bends his face sideways, holding the back of my hand against his cheek, without moving his eyes from our forward progress. I see his focus. I feel the strength of his hand and turn my own eyes ahead.

There before us lie the falls, that misnamed descent of twenty-six feet over a two-and-a-half-mile stretch, formed by shelf after shelf of ancient rock. We are rapidly approaching. There is no further choice. Our only way is forward. And only through this treacherous chute. The roar of the falls becomes deafening. In the hands of our unfamiliar auxiliary pilot, the boat edges to starboard. Before us rises an intense cloud of mist, like a blinding fog. The long, flat fossil-filled slabs of rock slide out of the mist too near to us on our port. On our starboard side, we are sliding under the curved stone bluffs, carved over time by the mad river and marking the edge of Indian Territory. It is here where we are most in danger from the unforgiving constraints of the channel and the caprices of this unpredictable river.

Thundering water overwhelms other sounds. Behind me the screeching thump of paddle wheels and the abrasive clang of shovels drown out in the roiling din of the rapids. Below us a tempestuous eddy grabs the boat in its violent whirling. Nicholas grabs my arm as the boat shifts sideways, and Tiger tenses, his stance rigid against my leg. The paddles churn forward, the bow and stern of the boat shifting in opposite directions, as we are caught in the opposing sides of the eddy. I gasp as we plow through and shoot out beyond it. In the fog, I can see only those things that are close by. Our bow aims at the cascade rushing between the rocks.

We drop, our stomachs churning, into the chute—fossilized shelves of rock on our port side, a carved arc of limestone at starboard. Waves slap cold against us, and water rushes onto the deck, over my boots, my skirt. I grip the railing tighter. Cringing. I could reach out and touch that rock to starboard. It would rip my hand from my arm. Nicholas pulls me in tighter.

Sam Laughton, who has managed to navigate this passage more times than he can count, with the white hair to prove it, is suddenly beside us. Stout and hardy, he works his hands and arms, making urgent gestures, sending intricate piloting signals to Andrew Jack in the wheelhouse, a sign language understood only by them. Not once does he take his eyes from the water. Neither can I take my own off it. We are flying between walls of stone. Over the roaring water, I hear the faint clanging of coal shovels—harder and faster. The men are stoking the fire for all they are worth. Velocity is our only savior now. We must outrun the currents. The men are feeding coal, then wood, into the ravenous furnace, building steam. Only at a speed faster than the raging fourteen-mile-an-hour current can we maintain control of this boat. Otherwise the river will have its way with us. We have only inches of clearance beside us and five inches below.

Froth from huge waves crashes against the rocks, soaking us. My simple homespun dress is plastered to me. I tug my woolen shawl tighter, glad for an instant that I did not put on my redingote. I am freezing, shivering, but the shawl will dry quickly when hung by the fire in the galley. Not so the redingote. How can I have such thoughts at this moment?

In the chaotic din nothing else exists—nothing but the uproar and velocity of the waves, the roar of the water, the thunder of the engine, the clang of shovels, the slap of the paddles, the rock walls flashing past. Faster and faster. Without warning, the safety valve on the engine shrieks above the din. I jump, spin. A jolt of terror races through me. The boat will blow up. I grab at Nicholas.

He jerks away, lurches round to see. At the furnace, Baker waves him off, lifts another shovelful. Hesitates because Nicholas is still staring, the safety valve screeching. Baker ignores us this time. Dismisses both of us as he dumps in the coal. Nicholas is resolute as we turn back. We are making ourselves vulnerable to an explosion by forcing the engine past its capabilities. If we blow up, my last vision will be of the love in my husband's eyes. And my last thought, of my children left orphaned. But we must outrun this raging current.

Laughton's arms are moving, shifting, in his private language shared with Andrew Jack. Before us is the first, the tightest, of two oxbow turns, bends so sharp they could harness an ox into its yoke. The boat turns barely to port as we glide through the barreling water. It seems as if we have somehow slowed our pace. My breath is ragged in my mouth as the boat heads straight into the shelf of rock ahead before we suddenly veer to starboard. The bow has cleared the shelf. I know the stern will hit it, but it does not. There is no crash. We are in the channel. We have cleared the first of the two great oxbows.

I look up at my husband, take his hand. He pulls me tight against him. My eyes burn, and my cheeks are wet. I must be crying. Or it could be the river. I will say it's the river.

Something slams into the boat with a crack like musket fire. I am thrown to my knees. Nicholas grabs me. I stand. My heart races. My breath stops. I grab at Nicholas, who is pulling free of my hand to go. But go where? A protrusion of limestone has struck us in the narrow chute. How much damage? There is no way to know. We sink or wreck or blast on. There is no choice.

The boat plummets downward. I plunge forward. My stomach rebels at the blow against the rail, and then, more violently, from sudden seasickness. I am reduced to a helpless child again, alone on that ship, propelled into the darkness of my childhood. Time crashes in on itself. We level out, the safety valve shrieking. Someone's hands are holding me. I gag and wipe my mouth. Nicholas helps me upright, looks me in the face, holds me. But only for one moment. I am suddenly on my own again. I grab for the railing.

I dodge Laughton's arm as he signals again to Andrew Jack.

Nicholas grips the rail beside me. The boat shifts to port. Once again, the movement seems to slow mystically. And then another slab of deadly rock is before us, but not so near as the first. A turn to starboard, sliding around the sharp curve of the greater oxbow. Back to port and into the current as violent waves crash against the bank, blasting heavy spray across us.

There is no time to think between one thing and the next, only to feel, yet with an awareness so keen it penetrates the universe, holds my children in my heart as I fly past these rocks.

Ahead is another eddy, a larger one, circling wildly to the right. I feel Andrew Jack holding the wheel steady against the eddy's violence as our bow plunges through, and then the stern shifting to port, as if the boat would be thrown into reverse. The safety valve screeches again as I hear the shovels raise their beat, stoking the fires. The paddles blast against the water, plunging us forward against our reversal, as we fight to exit the eddy. I am spinning.

The boat is still flying through the water when my awareness settles and I register the calm. The stillness is so sudden. The clanging shovels stop. The safety valve stills. The grinding paddles slow. Quiet reigns. We are carried on the water fast and smooth. The banks on either side appear almost immobile. The rocky shore has settled into a forested canopy. Here and there, a house or two. On our port side, a town appears. A dock, filled with flatboats, keelboats, a barge or two. Shippingport.

The falls are behind us.

Chapter 19

A shout from somewhere among the crew. Another. Stomping and cheering all over the boat. Nicholas is shouting now, both arms waving in the air, up at Andrew Jack. Then at Baker. Beside us, the auxiliary pilot extends his bulky hand. Nicholas takes it, then pulls Laughton to him with a slap on the back. He has brought us safely through. How could I have doubted? What would we have done without him? Without each man here? Without my husband's genius for design?

Nicholas turns to me, looks at me for what feels like an eternity, takes me in an embrace that feels as if I'm home. When he lets me go, he stands back, holds my hands again, says, "We did it, Lydia."

I wait. He is not done speaking.

"We succeeded." He gives emphasis to *we*. Then, "Without you, Lydia, I could not have accomplished this undertaking."

His love floods my wet, shivering body.

"Get yourself dry," he says, leading me toward the threshold to the quarters. "We'll be in dock at Shippingport in short order to pick up our children. You will need to be festive."

Wet clothes lie on the floor. I don't know where to put them as I change. I don't want to ruin the chairs or, heaven forbid, the bedding. I must be out on deck for Rosetta to see us as we pull into Shippingport. The more I try to speed my readiness, to get myself back out there, the more I'm getting in my own way. There, at least the white muslin dress is on. Now for my striped spencer, with its red and gold cording and fancy buttons. The jacket I have saved for just this occasion. Oh my, and this hair. *Well, push it back and pull the wool bonnet over it. Tie this bow again, and make it fan out.* There. Now Nicholas will have a presentable wife at his side as we make this historic entrance into port. Yes, historic. I seem to use that word too often, but there it is. What we have done in the past hour—proved that our innovative steamboat is capable of both upcurrent travel and a victorious passage of the Falls of the Ohio—will change this young country in so many ways. And our own lives. Nicholas has proven his capabilities in design and construction. And the potential of steam for the future. Now, let me be careful going over this threshold to the deck. I don't want to ruin this triumph with a clumsy fall!

On deck I see the relaxed facial expressions of Baker and Laughton. They are laughing and slapping their legs. All six of the crew are bustling about in synchronized practice for landing, and punching each other on the shoulder as they toss ropes and clanging chains back and forth with precision. Baker and Laughton situate themselves beside Nicholas, and he throws an arm around the shoulder of each. Laughton shakes hands with various crewmen whenever they have a free hand. Up in the wheelhouse, I see Andrew Jack's concentration as he brings us alongside the immense cheering crowd that has amassed on the dock. After easing in front of my husband and the two pilots, I search the crowd for Bessie and Sarah with my children. I can't find them. I look back at Nicholas, who is grinning in victory, as he should, but where are my children?

The slap of the gangplank startles me. I'm trying for Nicholas's attention, but too much is happening. I need my children. I have to find them. I lift my skirt and put my boot on the gangplank. Three steps down, I notice the nearest spectators in the crowd are quieting at my approach. I nod to a man standing just at the end of the plank, my wool bonnet shifting on my wet hair. He smiles and steps back, tripping on the feet of the fellow behind him. Two more steps and those nearest to me begin to pull back, bumping against those behind them. Once again, I could be parting the Red Sea. An older man steps forward to offer his hand. I take it. It's strength surprises me and calms me inside.

As the space before me opens up, I see Sarah and Bessie, each holding one of my children, struggling toward the front of the crowd. The spectators follow my gaze, their awareness moving toward my little ones. Various arms reach out to hold people at bay to let the women pass. Rosetta sees me, jerks free of Sarah's hand, and bolts toward me, chirping, "Mama, Mama." I stoop to catch her in my embrace. A sure grip on my arm steadies me as I struggle for balance.

"I gotcha, ma'am." I recognize Billy's voice and his wide, hairy hand.

Nicholas is behind him, then pushing past him to reach us. I have Rosetta in my arms, and hers are wrapped round me as tight as she can hold. And I—I am in my father's arms on the dock so long ago. I am not alone. His hands are clasping mine as we walk away from my nightmares on that vessel in which I crossed the sea. This memory, this feeling is like entering the eddy, where forces stronger than I are reversing me in circles as I forge my way to where I need to be. Where I need to be is here. On this dock in Shippingport. Not lost in childhood, which was over long ago. Rosetta's tight embrace anchors and steadies me. Nicholas's arm around us both grounds me here. I am on this dock, in this safe place. I am here. We are here.

"Papa, come Papa!" Rosetta is kicking to get to her father. I hand her to Nicholas. Billy goes back up the gangplank, and Nicholas follows, Rosetta enthroned on his shoulders. Sarah trails behind Bessie, who cradles my precious Henry in her arms. Now Billy is scooting around me, holding out his hand to steady her as she steps hesitantly onto the gangplank.

"Bravo! Well done, well done," a man among the spectators shouts.

Sarah smiles. She has an arm around Bessie as Billy helps them all up the gangplank. Just as I take Henry in my arms, Baker is beside me, Bessie in his immediate embrace. Surely this is not the first. I jiggle Henry, rocking him, as I smile at this first public display of budding romance.

Ah, romance, and not just for Bessie! Nicholas is beside me, with both children in his arms, and is bending down to kiss my cheek over and over.

"We did it, Lydia. Together, you and I," he whispers.

Ah, what we have done! That no one has done before! We have proven the worthiness of Nicholas's new design, the power of the side paddle wheels, the navigational finesse of this steamboat against the worst challenges the Western Waters have to give. The challenges are not over, but none ahead of us will be even close to these we have successfully met. I am here. I am part of this history, this wild adventure. Will anyone remember that I was? Are women never remembered unless they happened to have been a queen?

Nicholas leans back, jostling Rosetta, who is squealing and clapping. He sets her on the deck for Sarah to take her hand. She prances away as fast as she can move her little feet. Pulling Tiger with her, she sprints away, leaving Sarah to catch them both.

"You stayed with me, Lydia," Nicholas says. "I wanted you safe on land, but you wouldn't have it."

His amber-tinted dark eyes seem misty. I must be mistaken. But possibly not.

"No, Nicholas, I wouldn't. I wanted this adventure! As much as you did. Look what you have given me." I kiss him full on the lips, even here in public. Briefly, but yes, full on the lips. I can hardly wait to have him to myself. A great deal remains to be done before that can occur.

The crew are hard at work securing us to the dock, trying to work through and around the milling spectators. Billy holds tight to one of the ropes while reaching for a chain and talking over his shoulder to a fellow bursting with curiosity who simply will not let him get his task completed. Finally, Billy just stops, holding both rope and chain, and turns to answer the swift string of questions.

"Did you manage the eddy all right?"

"Yes, sir, straight through."

"Straight?"

"Well, a bit of righting the curves."

"Speaking of curves, what about the oxbows? Bound to have done some damage there."

Baker sees the problem and runs down to interrupt. For a moment, our two men seem unsure about who should take over which job. At last, the fellow latches onto Baker, who turns him away from the boat and moves a few steps into the crowd, his hand guiding the man away from Billy and his work. Immediately, Baker is surrounded, rapid-fire questions are being thrown at him, and hands are waving to get his attention. Baker raises both of his own hands to calm the chaos and begins to describe our adventure however he wishes while Billy secures the chain to a cleat.

Bessie, smiling, watches Baker control the crowd. He's quite good at this. He glances our way. Bessie nods and waves to him. One of his questioners pulls at his sleeve, demanding his attention again.

Sarah has gone below with the baby, and soon after, Bessie, smiling broadly, turns from the rail to follow her. Bessie holds out her hand to Rosetta, who shakes her head. My wave to Bessie assures her I am watching. Off Rosetta goes, scampering about the deck, managing to interfere with any number of jobs going on: the crew restacking wood, scooping up the coal that was spilled from the frantic feeding of the fire; scraping and clanging to clear embers from the furnace; sweeping piles of re-sulting ash into extra buckets; checking to assure no live ember accidentally slips from the metal underlay onto the wood of the deck. The men have an eye on Rosetta, as well, and halt their work to greet and tease her. I'm watching closely, but I do not stop her adventuring until she gets a bit too close to the fur-nace. I scoop her up. At the rail, I sit her down, holding tight. Tiger situates himself on the other side of Rosetta and nuzzles his head against her. Laughing, she lays her cheek on his soft head.

Baker, having shaken himself loose from the curious crowd, returns to begin a check of the paddles and wheels. Nicholas, whom I lost sight of in the throng, reappears at the gangplank with a small crew of men I don't recognize. Rosetta clamors for her father. When I set her down, she darts to him, Tiger loping beside her. Nicholas leans down and points her back to me, puts his hand firmly on her back. As I pick her up to take her in for a nap, I realize that these men must be part of the construc-tion crew Nicholas has sought out in town to inspect the boat for possible damage sustained when we hit the rock.

All at once I remember the crunching sound, the crash on the rocks as we raced through the chute. If there is substantial damage to the hull, we could be delayed an indefinite amount of time. What if we have to raise the boat out of the water? What if there is water leaking in below? I've been so overwhelmed with the excitement of coming through the chute, I'd forgotten the force with which we hit rock.

I have an impulse to run and check for a leakage in our quar-ters, but some of the men have already gone ahead of Nicholas.

He is holding the doorframe, talking to one of these men and pointing from the boat to the dock, when he sees me. He clearly recognizes my alarm, rotates his hand in a partial wave, motioning me off with a gesture of reassurance, shaking his head for me not to follow. I see him gesturing to one of the men to shush them. There is nothing I can do but be in their way. Panic sets in as I think of the cost of repairs—an expense that the partners, Fulton and Livingston, will blame squarely on Nicholas, an expense we cannot begin to afford. Suddenly our great victory takes on a different aspect.

I stare out over the dwindling crowd and compel myself to make my way to the deck chairs, where I sit. I dare not even go to see about the children. They will be fine. Asleep by now, I hope, if these strangers are not too noisy. Henry is asleep the moment things get still, and sleeps through a good bit when it's noisy. But he will be hungry again soon. Rosetta's adventure going overland by carriage has excited her and certainly worn her out. Surely, Nicholas will keep the men quiet during their inspection should they need to enter our quarters. If my help is required, Bessie will send for me.

Sitting here now, I sense for the first time my own fatigue. My senses have been running on high like our engine, but with no warning shriek that I might explode. Now in my chair on the deck, I lift my hands to see them trembling. My body also feels as if it is trembling, though I know it is not. My feet seem cold, and I realize I failed to change my wet boots in my rush to be on deck when we docked. No matter now. Things will soon settle down, and I will be in my quarters, snuggly garbed for supper—if I can eat—and time with my little ones. The very thought of my infant makes my breasts heavy. How long has it been since I nursed him? I've lost all track of time. And will I have privacy with those men about?

The air is unusually warm for this time in December. And

dense. After the swift descent and the flurried excitement of the chute, when nothing existed but the rush of river, and stone, it is peculiar to experience this stillness. Our life-and-death effort to outrun the current, then the milling crowd of spectators greeting us after our triumph, the heart-pounding triumph itself, then my frantic need for my children—these things have kept my mind and body racing, and now all is still. Mingled with the odors of the dock, I notice again the strange sulfurous smell as when we left Louisville. What is causing that noisome odor? I can't imagine.

I sit back in my chair, still so tense. I want to relax. I'm trying. I desire inner peace the way I sometimes desire pudding before I have half eaten a meal. I don't seem able to let go of my tension or even change my position. Something warm nudges at my elbow. *Ah, Tiger. There you are, sweet one.* He prods his cool nose under my elbow and lays his long face in my lap. How does he know that I need him? Or perhaps he needs calming himself. His fur is soft, comforting in my fingers. I breathe more easily, surprised at an awareness that I had not been breathing easily.

My body settles into the chair; my wet feet relax on the deck. I perceive the clamor all around me: the mixed sounds of loading and unloading flatboats at the far end of the dock, the mooing of cows, the chatter of chickens on the flatboats of farmers bringing stock downriver for trade, animal odors mixing with the odorous air. All but that heavy atmosphere seems so familiar.

Memories flood me of sitting atop our flatboat at this very dock a little more than two years ago, feeling the relief of having gotten through the rapids of the center chute. There had been plenty of depth to spare, far more than today, and not such a great need for it with our flat bottom. But we had no power of our own as this boat has, nothing but some long oars to push ourselves away from dangerous rocks. At the mercy of the currents, which, thankfully, had mercy on us. And on the other flatboats that crowded us, too close for comfort, but all made it safely through. No one wrecked. But other disasters were evident all around us, and more than just that devastated barge, its wreckage still visible. Vestiges of flatboats and keelboats lay strewn on the banks or lodged in protrusions of fossil on the stone tables spiked with what resembled stag horns.

Tiger's long tongue licks the back of my hand. Though my mind is everywhere at once, circling round like an eddy, I am settling down. I am here on this deck in Shippingport harbor, past the falls. If there is damage to the hull, it can be repaired. We will not sink.

The men from the construction crew appear on deck again, Nicholas following them. He signals to one man onshore, who gathers the other two there to come on board. They assemble themselves not far from me, where I am somewhat able to overhear the discussion, but not in great detail. Only enough to reassure me that we have not sustained severe damage. Nicholas shakes each man's hand and waves to them as they descend the gangplank and leave us to ourselves.

Tiger keeps his head beneath my hand as I stand up. With the other, I reach for my husband.

"Only superficial damage, Lydia. No delays for repair."

Tiger is on his own now. I put my arms around Nicholas, lean back in his. I want to see his eyes. I want to watch his lips as he speaks to me in this moment of accomplishment.

"No great damage, Lydia. No delays. We are sound."

Tiger presses up against my hip and raises his head. Nicholas smiles.

"The success of this steamboat is the triumph of a lifetime." He stops, looking at me intently. "No," he says. "The triumph is having you love me. Conquering the falls takes second place, but second place is far better than anything else I can imagine, so just think what a pedestal you are on!" He bends down to kiss me, stopping my laughter. My husband pulls me into an embrace that seems to fit me like my skin, but better than my skin in its warm strength.

I am at home here in his arms, but not in this ominous air around us. The heavy odors of sulfur and dung have not abated. The sun is blocked by yellow fog.

CHAPTER 20

Our stay in Shippingport will last several days. Though the great success of this endeavor is now ours to claim, there is much to be done before we depart for the easier portion of this journey. I have to laugh at myself when I say the "easier" part, though it is. On our flatboat mission, the greatest challenges lay unforeseen in that second leg of the voyage. Specifically, the scourge of fever, through which I was the nurse for all on board. Then safely at Natchez, the snag in the harbor that sank us. Why that makes me laugh, heaven only knows! I suppose because we got to New Orleans in the rowboat regardless, our mission fulfilled. Then the long sail around the tip of Florida and that ship hit with the fever. Fortunately, we were able to land safely at Old Point Comfort, Virginia, and take the coach back to Washington. Oh, that coach ride! It's a wonder Rosetta wasn't shaken right into this world on those roads. And now I think of poor Lucy Audubon riding across the country on horseback! At any rate, it does make me laugh at how little success means in the daily scheme of things.

My thoughts are as out of control as the eddies in this river.

Not so dangerous, I hope. Where was I? Oh, thinking how much there is to be done in the few days before we depart this safe harbor. Replenishing our food supplies is of the utmost importance. As we go downriver, there will be little opportunity for securing provisions—a small settlement or two along the way before Yellow Banks, where we may obtain a few turkeys or hens. Of course, the daily stops to cut and load new wood will also afford opportunity for fresh game. But Shippingport, being the last town of respectable size until Natchez, is the primary source of essentials for the river traffic. There is, of course, New Madrid on the way, but it is not large enough to be thoroughly reliable. We must take advantage of this well-stocked center of trade to load ourselves with flour, bacon, ham, and other such necessary staples for the seven hundred or so miles to reach Natchez.

With regard to our vessel itself, there is also much to do. The crew will need several days to make us secure for the remainder of our journey. The fiercest river is still before us, though none of its challenges match those of the falls. The challenges ahead are of the sort for which we have the piloting skills of Andrew Jack; the kind that, in spite of the best charting available, including our own, have a shifting unpredictability that requires a keen eye like his. Sandbars shift, become submerged, form in new places. Submerged sandbars will ground a vessel. I remember seeing any number of such trapped vessels on our first trip, generally farm or lumber boats in the hands of the inexperienced. Some worse than grounded—abandoned and rotting. More hazardous than sandbars, in my experience, are the snags and sawyers. The river has a mind of its own. Things can happen. Things always will happen.

Bessie and I have Rosetta on deck this morning and have left Henry with Sarah to nap.

"He'll be just fine," she said. "You go on and enjoy your feet on the ground."

It amazes me how much newborns sleep.

I am thinking I will take Rosetta into town and give Bessie some time to herself, a chance to have a bit of time with Baker, perhaps.

"I'll be just fine with her," I assure Bessie. "You take time for yourself." I pause. I resist the urge to wink.

She nods, a bit of a blush suffusing her cheeks. I see that she knows I recognize the attraction between those two and not only approve but also will do what I can to facilitate their interaction. We both glance to where the men are scuttling about. Ah, now I see that Baker is intent on the crew inspecting and scrubbing the boiler and supply pump. He gives us a quick nod, and then his attention is glued to the condenser. Billy and another crewman are at work on the firebox.

"Or, Bessie, join me for a morning adventure in Shippingport. It seems to have grown since I was last here."

"Careful now," she says to Rosetta, who, as usual, is scampering about.

We each grab a little hand, with Rosetta between us, and make our way to the gangplank. Tiger, on his leash, follows with his easy grace.

The docks are full, and the town is crowded. The wharves are stacked full with kegs and boxes and barrels. A variety of goods are everywhere to be seen: cotton, tobacco, rolls of fabric, skins of all sorts. Horses and mules throng the docks, pulling noisy wagons loaded with wooden cages of chickens and turkeys. We watch our every step to avoid being bumped or knocked about and step with care around messes that would leave us cleaning the stink not only from our boots but likely our skirts, as well. I feel a bit unsteady as we walk, as if I were still on board, negotiating the rocking of the boat for balance. I could get just a little seasick even here on land. Rosetta is pulling on me, shrieking in great excitement at seeing other children here and there. A few are chasing each other wildly about on the boardwalk. I'm holding my squealing Rosetta tightly, afraid she'll run right off into the melee. In the midst of it all, I feel distinctly uncomfortable as people turn to stare after us.

"Should I settle her down?" I half whisper over Rosetta's head. "Are we making a scene, Bessie? In the midst of all this uproar?"

"It isn't Rosetta, Mrs. Roosevelt." She laughs. "It's us."

"Us?" For a second, I can't comprehend how we are making a scene.

"They want to see who that lady was that went over those falls for her husband. It's not just the paddleboat that folks are fascinated by, you know."

I laugh right out loud. Bessie is laughing with me. I'm laughing the kind of laughter that doesn't stop, or when it does, it just starts back up again for no good reason. Rosetta is giggling with us. Now more people are staring. The more they stare, the more I laugh. Bessie pulls us around the corner onto a side street, where we clasp at our abdomens and struggle to get our breath.

I feel Rosetta tugging at me and lean down. "Mama, Mama, why we laughin'?" She giggles again.

I scoop her in my arms, knocking my bonnet askew, but I don't even care. She fits my arms in a way nothing else ever has. In my mind I see her beloved face as she came into my view after our wild ride through the falls. Such a short separation. Not more than two hours. An eternity until I caught a glimpse of her again. What if I had lost her? What if she had lost me? How did my father see my face, Henry's face after two years' absence an ocean apart? Such thoughts assail me from nowhere, unforeseen, as if they were waiting under the surface like the snag that sank my cozy flatboat, my first home with Nicholas. My breath comes in a shudder as I set Rosetta down.

Bessie is eying me curiously. How could I ever explain?

"This seems a bit much for me today, Bessie. These crowds—

and the stares—really are a bit too much. Overwhelming, actually." I take Rosetta's hand again. I am unable to let go of her. "If you'd like to do some exploring for yourself, feel free. I'm taking Rosetta home." *Home?* To this fantastical boat? Where she shares her space with four adults and a newborn? Had I really said *home?*

Rosetta is pouting about going back. Bessie doesn't say a word. She simply takes Rosetta's other hand, and we turn toward *home.* In just the same way we left it.

On board once again, I let Rosetta go. She is dancing and spinning and seems to relish being free here on the deck. I watch her joy and life return. So much for fame and its effect on her! On me, as well. But fame is not what I am seeking in this voyage, which is probably a good thing since fame is rarely conveyed to women and is unreliable even for men. No, I'm not even seeking to be in the shadow of my husband's fame, assuming it comes from this voyage. It is the vibrancy of this adventure, this doing something no one has ever done that fascinates me. It is being a part of all this with my husband, with Nicholas.

And yet . . . there is something more. Something that is only me. Only memories. And will never be anything else.

Speaking of my husband, I would like to have some time alone with him. The noise on board is that of men's industry at work. A bit like the noise required of this machinery to match and surpass the speed of the currents through the falls. All that clanging and scraping, only now they come from efforts to return all these mechanisms to a nearly pristine condition. Cleaning, oiling, testing, and testing again. This is reassuring, at least. Even if I would prefer to be out on the river, feeling that this time we wield some control as long as we have the competent piloting skills of Andrew Jack. I seem always to call him by both names; it's as if they truly are one name, without a last name at all.

Now, where is Nicholas?

Ah, I see my husband in the wheelhouse beside Andrew Jack. Their heads are almost touching as they lean over what I infer are the river maps. They are quite intent. Dare I interrupt? Well, perhaps only for a moment. I simply need to touch his arm. Or shoulder. Or hand. I simply need to touch him. He sees me as I lift my skirt to mount the short flight of stairs and turns to the door as I step into the wheelhouse.

"Nicholas," I say. I lean around him to speak to Andrew Jack. Nicholas takes my hand as I let my skirt fall.

"Lydia!" Nicholas is not unhappy at my interruption. "Exploring the town? How was it?"

"Far too crowded for me, Nicholas. Too much commotion. So, we just came back."

"Too much commotion for you? After the falls?"

I laugh. We all laugh. The wind, the water, the strange walls of stone fly by in my mind.

"Too much human commotion," I say. "I prefer the commotion of nature."

"Don't tempt nature too far," Andrew says. "It can outdo us if we don't take care."

"I'm interrupting," I say.

Andrew Jack folds one map section to open out another. Nicholas clasps his hands above his head and stretches his back.

"We needed a little respite," Nicholas says, his arm around my shoulder now.

"Indeed, we did," says Andrew Jack. "We are so deep into all this navigation, you'd think we were actually in the river up to our necks."

"Let's don't tempt this river again!" I say.

We laugh.

"And just what are you up to?" I continue.

"Well," says Andrew Jack, "we have the Zadoc Cramer navigational guide out. This new edition includes a good deal of your own charting from your flatboat journey." I'm grateful to hear him include us both with that pronoun. "We have your own notes open and it is obvious that he failed to include some of the hazards and landmarks you documented. But, in truth of fact, he could issue a new edition every day and never keep up with the Mississippi River. Changes its mind every fifteen minutes, at least."

We all laugh again, but not so heartily. We know the deadly truth of his joke.

The paper crackles as he smooths the map they are studying. It crackles again as he lays Cramer's navigational volume at its edge. The sound makes me want to touch the paper myself. I bring my attention back to Nicholas's voice.

"Andrew has been in town, interviewing rivermen who've poled their way back up. He has the most recent reports we can obtain as to new shifts—eddies, boils, sandbars, chutes dammed off by fallen logs and trees. Those logs and debris this river hurls along are just a nuisance for this boat, thank goodness. Nothing like the danger they present for flatboats. But let that flotsam and jetsam dam up a chute! Hack and saw our way through those trees? It's a pure dead end that we don't want to negotiate! And we won't." Nicholas claps Andrew Jack on the shoulder. "Right, Andrew?"

"Right!"

It's time for me to go. These two men must have truly needed a little break. Both of them are so gracious about my interruption. But I see their need to return to their focused concentration. We may be past the falls, but there are a multitude of challenges ahead as we make our way downriver. Just because they are smaller does not mean they are of less importance. When you live on a boat, there is nothing that is of no importance.

As I go down the passageway, I see that Baker has also taken a break. Bessie is speaking quickly, eagerly at his side while

Rosetta prances around her, dragging one hand around her skirt as she goes. Baker steps back a bit to let Rosetta pass between them, then leans forward as if he might kiss Bessie right there. She turns aside a bit, smiling, and sees me. Then he does also and waves and turns back as if to leave. I motion her to send Rosetta to me, but she says a last word to Baker and comes, almost running, over to me, making it a race with Rosetta, who then throws her arms around my knees.

"Would you like a bit of time for yourself, Bessie?"

She blushes. "No, Mr. Baker is busy with the boat. Mr. Roosevelt wouldn't be happy to see me keeping him from his work."

"You might be surprised what Mr. Roosevelt would be happy to see, Bessie."

"Well, we have to get down this river to New Orleans. Once we are there—" She stops, takes Rosetta in her arms. "Tell Mama we'll see her after naptime."

Rosetta shakes her head in protest but waves her hand at me as they head for the cabin.

I'll be there soon after them to nurse my infant boy. For now, I move to the stern, where things are a bit less noisy, and sit beside the rail. Behind us, the river flows on. The anchorage may be packed, the array of boats loading and off-loading nonstop, the waterfront crowded with folks of all sorts, from plain to fancy, but none of this affects the waters behind us. The river pays us no mind. How many centuries has it simply taken its own course, deciding its own way, cutting its meanders where it wishes? Is that what I wish to do with my life? Go where I will, how I will, with no mind to anything else? Cutting my own course where I wish, how I wish? Is that what I'm doing on this river?

I shield my eyes, though I hardly need to, as I look toward the sun over the water. Day after day we have had this heavy air, this strange, almost smoky mist, through which the sun struggles to shine and manages only a blurred yellow glow. As I ponder this strange weather, to which I gave little notice when I was in anticipation of the falls, I think how strange the atmosphere has been. Once again, now that I am slowing down to the moment, I'm conscious of that odorous scent, like rotten eggs, in the air.

Even if it does not clear, we will soon be south of it, regardless. My thoughts jump to Nicholas and Andrew Jack concentrating on the navigational charts, knowing that, familiar as they may be, the river is always likely to have other plans. *Like life*, I think. Life has a flow of its own—apart from us, separate from us, regardless of us. No matter how familiar it feels to us, the unexpected can always destroy our very foundation. Our plans for life are only that: plans. We are like the boats in this river, trying to navigate the currents with oars and poles and engines. We may succeed. To a point. But life has no plan, any more than this river does. It flows how it will, and we negotiate it with whatever tools we have at hand. But ultimately, life is life, and the river is only itself.

I stretch and sit up. How long have I been reclining here, useless? It is rare that I have time just to think. And when I do, heaven knows, my musing tends to be more than a bit erratic, like the crosscurrents of this river. Let me get downstairs to my son. I suppose I'm not that late, or Sarah would have come to fetch me. Nothing like a hungry babe and heavy breasts to get a mother moving at once.

CHAPTER 21

"Good morning." Nicholas kisses my neck as I turn in his arms, waking.

"Mm-hmm," I mutter in a sigh. "Are we still in Shippingport?"

"We are." He props himself up on an elbow, leans in with a warm kiss on my lips. "Would you care to go into town today? Dare brave the commotion?"

"Hmmm, no, not really."

"No? What would you like, then, beautiful one?"

I stretch a bit lavishly and confess, "Today I would like to go to New Orleans."

"Today? Why today?"

"I'm weary of Shippingport."

"You know, so am I. But today is not a possibility." He looks so serious, then smiles. "Would you settle for tomorrow?"

I'm awake now. And excited. I think he means it. "Tomorrow? Truly?"

"I believe we will have everything in readiness to leave at dawn. Baker and Jack are putting out the word with the crew, in case of any detail we may have overlooked. I'm going in to town to bid farewell to a few gentlemen whom I still might hope could be persuaded to invest now that we've succeeded at the falls. You're welcome to accompany me, you know."

"I know."

Nicholas lifts himself over me. I suddenly wonder why he is sleeping on the inside of the berth, but then my milk lets down. He has already taken Henry from Sarah. Cooing at him and jiggling him, he brings our son to me and lays him in my arms. Tiger follows him, lays his woolly head against my shoulder and nuzzles my cheek, then shuffles off to Rosetta as she jumps onto the floor with bare feet.

I am as fortunate as a woman could desire to be. What more could I wish for?

On our last night here, we are having our supper with everyone on this boat. I thought it only right that we should celebrate our accomplishment together. When I say "our," I mean everyone on board—with the exception of the little ones, of course. This steamboat, with its powerful side paddles and sleek hull, may be Nicholas's design, but without every man here—and every woman—we would not be where we are this evening. Would not have made an upstream trip to Cincinnati, a first for steamboat travel; would not be in Shippingport, below the Falls of the Ohio, another first. We would not be setting off from here for New Orleans, having already proven the capability of this steamboat to commence round-trip trade between Natchez and New Orleans. It is the skills of these men as fully as Nicholas's own that have brought us to this peak of achievement that will open a new era in travel and trade.

The men will want to be off onshore for a bit of last-minute free time, drinking and entertaining themselves as they wish, before we depart tomorrow. So, I am holding this festive supper quite early. I want it to be nearly as lavish as those midday dinners Nicholas has hosted to entice investors. Chef Joshua and Gabriel have spared no efforts since we are in port and have no worry about depleting supplies. Perhaps the supper will entail a bit of extra expense, which the partners would thoroughly disapprove of, but in light of all we have accomplished, how could they possibly object? Perhaps they will hardly even notice in the grand scheme of success!

The table is set for all of us, men and women, in the gentlemen's quarters, where there is adequate room for everyone, plus even a seat for Rosetta, her chair augmented with a storage box high enough for her to reach. She is impatiently tapping her plate with a spoon when Nicholas slides back his chair. I have to hold her still while her father rises, his glass of ale held high.

"A toast! To this crew of men, strong, sure and, most importantly, skilled. It is you, with your courage, your determination, and your unfailing cooperative efforts as one, who have achieved what has been deemed impossible. That has been heckled and derided by those who have no concept as to the possibilities of the future—the future of steam, of travel, of trade. The future, in fact, of this new country. Our country. The United States of America!"

Excitement reigns. The men jump to their feet with loud cheering, glasses raised and clinking. In the minutes it takes for them to reseat themselves, I see the glow of accomplishment on their faces. And the glow of recognition for their accomplishment.

Rosetta has joined their cheering, clapping her little hands and laughing up at me. Then her appetite joins that of the men as Gabriel and Joshua serve up the first dish: a hearty beef stew filled with fresh root vegetables from the local market. The feast begins.

In spite of the festive atmosphere I've endeavored to achieve, once the men are settled again, I sense a certain cloud over the gathering. I am reminded of the strange oppressive mist that casts a pall on the sun. There are unexpected lulls in the talk, muffled voices quickly shushed. At first, I think reluctantly, it may be the result of some restraint of the crewmen in my presence, but this seems to be more than careful manners would account for.

Nicholas and I exchange glances. There is the tiniest shake of his head in acknowledgment. I want these men to enjoy themselves. I stand up to say so.

"Gentlemen," I say, wondering how often they may have been so addressed. "Shippingport has been a respite for us from the perils of the river. It has not been a respite from work, I know. You have all been thoroughly concentrated on the tasks necessary to prepare for the remainder of this journey. This evening is a time of celebration for all of us before we continue downriver. We have overcome the greatest challenges, and there are more to come—smaller ones, to be sure, but challenges, nonetheless."

I pause to gather my thoughts. Just how to convey what I want here? It might as well be straightforward. "There seems to be something amiss. I am eager to move on from Shippingport, to reach our destination, but I'm wondering if, somehow, you feel we are not quite ready, not entirely prepared." I glance at Nicholas, whose expression is one of utter surprise, but with a hint, thank goodness, of admiration. I wonder if he has been thinking the same without expressing it and tried to overcome it with his toast. I recognize that look from him. "If so, gentlemen, I would like to know your observations." I smooth my skirt beneath me and sit down.

Rosetta's hand has been in the gravy, and I wipe it with my napkin as Nicholas stands.

"I can assure you, gentlemen, that when Mrs. Roosevelt speaks, she means it. You are not only free but also highly encouraged to speak of whatever you wish." Nicholas sits.

There is a long silence, broken only by Rosetta banging her

spoon. Sarah stands to take her, leans her to me for a kiss, then heads through the doors to our own compartment. Rosetta disappears, waving exuberantly over Sarah's shoulder and blowing kisses. Bessie follows with Henry but soon returns. I know Sarah has taken charge and sent her back to hear anything Baker may have to say.

The lightsome interruption of the children's departure has broken the somber atmosphere.

Indeed, Baker has something to say. He rises. The crewmen grow still and focus their full attention on his words.

"You men have been hearing lots of things that may have made you uneasy. We are here together in a world of our own, so to speak, on this boat. Now we've spent some time onshore in the larger world. And tomorrow we're back to the one of our own making, so to speak. So, I'm agreeing with Mrs. Roosevelt. If we're together here on board for some time yet to come, we need to all be together to keep this vessel working, especially as we will still have some challenges to face, as Mrs. Roosevelt said. Now, if you've seen something of concern, it's only right for all of us to know that before we leave out of here tomorrow morning. Assuming we do leave out of here tomorrow morning." Baker taps his fingers on the table and sits down. He waits, then says, "Well, men?"

Baker's way of talking delights me, though he doesn't often say much to me. His speech reminds me of my thoughts. There is a fair bit of wandering to both.

Billy, sweet Billy, starts to stand, his chair scraping back, but Nicholas motions him to remain seated. "No need to stand, men. Just be comfortable."

So, Billy looks around and then begins. "The boat is in prime condition, sir. There is no problem with the boat." He stops, as if someone might take him off the spot. No one does. "It's not the boat." He's repeating himself. "It's just all the talk around town that's a bit unsettling. That's all."

"What sort of talk?" Nicholas asks.

"Oh," says Ezra, to Billy's left, "it's just a lot of nonsense. We ought not even pay it any mind. It don't mean anything."

"Well, mostly not," says Jacob, "but then you never know for sure, now do you?"

"Like what?" challenges Oren, at the end of the table.

"Well, like Tecumseh," says Ezra. "All this nonsense about the comet foretelling disaster is just that—nonsense. But there's no nonsense to the Indians. I know Tecumseh's too far south and Tippecanoe is in the other direction, but we don't know what's in the minds of the ones in between. After all, the west shore of the river belongs to them all the way down to the boundary of the Louisiana Purchase."

"It's only just a month since General Harrison defeated Tecumseh's brother, the Prophet, and we don't know if the news has passed to the tribes downriver." Samuel jumps in now, usually so silent. "Hard to anticipate if it has, and now they're preparing for war against the river traffic, or if it hasn't yet and comes along about when we do. Remember the war scene we almost caused in Louisville? No settlers, no Indians on this river are anticipating anything like the noise and fire and smoke shooting out of this stack. Folks thinking we were the Brits attacking? Imagine what the Indians'll think."

Murmurs of assent pass around the table. I've never heard so many words from Samuel's mouth.

"Well, what about this weather?" Oren chimes in, changing a frightening subject.

"Yeah, it's ominous like the comet, folks're saying. Usually lots of thunderstorms in this neck of the woods. Clears the air. Hasn't been one rainstorm here in months," Samuel says.

"But then did you hear the fellow telling about a pillar of blue fire, like lightning coming straight up out of the earth?" Ezra asks. "Lasted—hmm, I can't remember—but longer than lightning should."

The fellow next to him, Jessup, pokes him in the ribs. "You listening to tales like that? You don't believe that, now."

"No, I don't, but all the talk from down the river—"

"Is full of tall tales," Jessup interrupts.

The interruption stops things for a moment.

"There's other odd things, Mr. Roosevelt." Billy takes charge. "Things not so spooky, but strange enough, anyway. Things you hear a lot in the taverns."

"Such as?" Nicholas says.

"Such as strange migrations among the animals, Mr. Roosevelt. Not just the squirrels, which we're already too aware of. Birds . . ."

"Well, birds are to be expected, Billy. It's their migration season, and the Mississippi is generally their migration course."

"Oh, it's not the migration, sir. It should be, and it isn't. They're flying in frantic patterns that are messing up migration. The rivermen tell us of hunting onshore and the animals, especially the deer, not running, just standing there without moving, to be shot. And more squirrels, stinking up the waters. Those don't seem far-fetched. The men are telling their own stories from the river."

"Folks out there are getting spooked, it seems," adds Ezra. "Traveling miles and miles for camp meetings. Thinking the day of reckoning is on the cusp, it seems. There's unpredictable floods on the deltas and the awful set-in of deadly fever after. Comet's the star of warning, seems."

"Well, gentlemen," Nicholas says, "it appears we have a number of things to consider. First, I'm reassured that our vessel is sound, and all the machinery of the engine and paddles is ready to take us to New Orleans. We can all breathe well for that." He waits. "Does everyone agree?"

The men nod and murmur their agreement.

What then, with all these rumors and reports, are realistic concerns for us, I wonder.

"Tecumseh, Tippecanoe, and the Prophet's defeat by General Harrison, who happens to be a friend of mine . . . He sent the spirits for our grand dinner, you remember," Nicholas says. "These events are quite real, and your concerns about the news and reactions downriver are genuine. There is the possibility of Indian aggression, I grant you that. There is also the possibility of passivity in the face of our military superiority. And our speed. There is also the possibility of nothing whatever. How are we to know until something happens or it doesn't? But I agree with you men that we should be prepared. Perhaps we should forge a plan amongst us in case. At least we'll feel ourselves prepared."

The men are paying close attention now. They know Nicholas is taking their concerns seriously.

"As to the weather, who can ever predict? Does it have meaning? Not that I know," Nicholas continues. "And the migration of animals? Squirrels we know take a mind—a slightly insane one, I submit—to traveling en masse, swimming the rivers every few odd years and dying in the process. Again, does it have meaning? Not that I know. Erratic human fears, like erratic flights of birds, come and go, and I don't know why, except that humans have always caught fear from one another. It's contagious. Like the fever."

Nicholas looks at me, then taps the table. "Gentlemen, we will depart as planned. Once we are less occupied downriver, we will initiate a plan in case of trouble with the tribes. I don't expect the squirrels or the birds to attack us." Everyone laughs, and the mood lightens. "Meanwhile, finish your supper, if you haven't already. The taverns are waiting, and this is your last evening free for some time." He smiles at all of them, bows to Baker and Andrew Jack, holds out his hand to me.

"Good evening, gentlemen." I take my husband's hand and walk with him to the door, where he turns.

"Make sure you're on board before daylight, men. We can't do without you."

There is general laughter and the scraping of chairs. The air among us seems to have cleared, even if that outside is still thick and sulfurous.

CHAPTER 22

I wake before Nicholas. I think I have slept, but not well. Nicholas seems to have taken the men's remarks at supper in stride and dismissed all of them, with the exception of the very realistic ones in regard to Tecumseh's journeys south to unite the tribes and General Harrison's torching of the Prophet's town at Tippecanoe. I paid attention to my husband's assessment of a possible tribal threat, and I have tried to take it as an assurance. The situation unsettles me, nonetheless. Probably, I think, because of my children. My responsibility for them weighs heavy.

Then all the spooky stuff. That should trouble me least, yet it unnerves me the most. I have a feeling that is true for most people, even our tough, experienced crewmen. I've been like that since childhood: fearful in the face of the uncanny, yet intrepid in the face of real danger. I suppose with authentic danger, I am able to identify its reality, so I find the right place inside me to confront it. But with the otherworldly, not only the unknown but also the unknowable, there is nothing there to confront. I might as well punch at the oppressive air outside. I will be so glad to get farther south, farther west to escape it and breathe freely again.

"Nicholas." I whisper his name into the dark, and he stirs, mumbles something, pulls me close. "Nicholas," I whisper again, trailing my finger around the edge of his ear, pushing a stray hair behind it. "It's time, my love."

He wakens, raises himself on an elbow, and gives me a kiss, his morning wakening ritual. "What are you doing awake? Did you even sleep at all?"

"Enough," I say.

I roll out of the berth before him for a change. Today I have no concerns about not waking Rosetta. Henry sleeps and wakes to his own rhythm. This is not a day for children's schedules. Today we entrust ourselves to this river—and to excellent piloting—as we make our way to New Orleans. Rosetta will not remember this, but I will remember it for her, and I want her to be at the rail with me when the whistle blows. She might remember the whistle. Who can tell what things lodge in our memories any more than what even now lies buried in the muddy depths of these rivers?

We are all scurrying around the quarters, stepping on one another's toes, reaching across each other in our efforts to get dressed and on deck. And doing it all in the dark! Though Sarah is lighting a lamp or two now. I'm about to put my sleepy girl's dress on her backward when Sarah takes it from me and slips it over her messy little curls. Rosetta falls against my knees, rubbing her eyes. Will I remember this tiny moment with her? This moment more precious than all our wondrous achievements. Sarah has Rosetta's stockings and boots in her hands. She smiles into my eyes, as if reading my thoughts.

Ah, finally. Coats on against the December morning and out we go, though our coats are hardly necessary in this unseasonable foggy warmth. Sarah is holding out the lamp so I don't miss my step. Wait, lamps? Other lanterns, one after another, lining and crowding the wharf, lamps bobbing about in the hands of an otherwise invisible crowd.

"Who are all these people?" I ask of the air.

"Spectators?" Sarah says, surmising. "Folks want to see this historic moment. I guess they'll tell their grandchildren, 'Do you know I was right there on the dock when the *New Orleans* puffed off?' Can't you just hear them now?"

I laugh. "And we'll be telling those next generations, 'Do you know we were on that boat when . . .' Can't you just hear us telling our stories? At least as best we remember them!"

Sarah laughs with me as Bessie arrives at our side with Henry. Nicholas is off on the dock, engaged in a rapid exchange with gentlemen I can't make out in the dull glow of the lanterns. Rosetta pulls on my redingote, and I lift her up to the rail, then point to her father. She claps her hands and throws an arm around me. Nicholas looks up, smiles, and runs for the gangplank. He waves behind him as he takes the plank at a bound. I should think that recklessness of his would frighten me, but it doesn't. I've seen him leap up that plank too many times before, so agile, his balance perfect. Billy and another of the crew pull the plank, then close the rail gate with a metallic clank.

"Do you see all these people who have come to watch us embark, Lydia?" says Nicholas, when he reaches my side.

"No, Papa. Tiger not bark." Rosetta is clapping her hands at my cheeks. She loves to clap those little hands.

It takes a minute, but then I'm laughing at her and at the adult language we take so for granted.

"*Embark.* To see our ship leave the dock, Rosetta." Nicholas chuckles. "Look at the lights out there. They've all come to see us off." He seems more excited by this crowd than by the one that greeted our arrival. "Just look, Lydia. Do you see?"

"Well, yes, I see that they are there, but I can't really see their faces other than . . ."

"Do you know who is here, Lydia?" He's practically danc-ing. "Major Croghan! He was with General Harrison at Tippecanoe, Lydia!" Repeating my name seems to be part of his excitement. "And William Clark! He's seen more of the West—well, he and Meriwether Lewis—than anyone yet. He says emphatically that this boat will be important to westward expansion. Also, that we may encounter Lewis when we arrive at New Madrid. Croghan says not to worry about the tribes. They've seen the strength of our forces and wouldn't dare ag-gression."

As he speaks, Nicholas is jumping from one topic to another as fast as my thoughts tend to do, as fast as these waters can shift direction beneath us. "Did you notice no other boats are departing? They are waiting, leaving late just to watch us. Look up there, Lydia! Our sparks are brighter than the stars. Well, except for the comet, perhaps! If we could even see them for this fog!"

Sarah is beside us now with Henry. I hand Rosetta off to Nicholas, who rubs his face against her cheek, making her gig-gle. He's directing her gaze up to the sparks. As the whistle sounds, a long, tapering screech, she puts her hands over her ears, then over her father's. I cradle Henry, keeping his head a bit elevated, so he can see all this excitement, though I know he will not remember it. His little eyes are blinking fast as the bright cinders shoot into the sky. Out of the corner of my eye, I don't fail to notice Bessie watching Baker and his men at the firebox.

Nicholas hands Rosetta to her, and then he's off. He races past Baker, shouting something while passing him, then up to the wheelhouse, where he slams the door behind him before he takes his place beside Andrew Jack. He wants to see every pos-sible detail of this moment, I know—the dock, the spectators, the paddle wheels, our path in the water—and up there with our pilot, he has the best view.

But the sight I want to see is Nicholas. My eyes are on my husband. He is at the peak of his abilities. This is his crowning moment. The falls were a challenge, yes. A challenge that had to be overcome in order for this moment to be. My husband's vessel has set a new standard for design, construction, and speed. This moment, and the future it portends, belongs to this man whom I love. I am here with him to share it, to see his face there in the dawning light.

A sudden urge overwhelms me. I want to throw the account books in the river! Money, the source of constant bickering between the partners, and even between my father and me, in particular Nicholas's shortcomings when it comes to finance. Any man—or woman, including me, for that matter—can handle financial records and balances, but only this man, my husband, has been able to accomplish such an ambitious undertaking as this. This is the full accomplishment of just one man in the world, a man who belongs to me and I to him—we who are at home in one another.

We can hardly predict the implications of this journey and its effect on the future of this country. If only my father were here to see what Nicholas has accomplished! To see what I have done beside him! Not only am I my husband's wife; I am also my father's daughter. My father, the adventurer and hero, who served in both the Prussian and Austrian armies, overcame injury, made the Grand Tour of Europe, all before I was born. My father, who has traveled this land on horseback, from city to city, who designed some of the greatest architecture yet of this country—but not the greatest boat! Yes, I am his daughter, so like him in many ways. But the man he would have prevented me from marrying because of my age is utterly like him. We are three kindred spirits! And Nicholas and I are soulmates. What bearing has age when two souls are aligned?

The engine fires are roaring now. The steam is building. The paddles begin to rotate slowly, pushing us away from the wharf, where the lamps are bouncing about as folks wave and cheer us off. My hands hold Rosetta tightly at the rail so that she can see. Normally, there would be a considerable number of boats departing now, but we have it all to ourselves. We are the entertainment as our audience recedes in our wake. The water sloshes loudly off the paddles as their grinding rotation increases. We pick up speed and round out the great wide turn into the main current. The lights onshore diminish, like so many fireflies dancing at the wrong time of day.

Andrew Jack is turning us wide now into the current. At the dock the keelboats and flatboats prepare to follow behind us. They will be quite far behind and then farther still. Once they have moved out, the barges will proceed, heavy with their cargos and bound for New Orleans. By the time they arrive, we may have sent this boat on its way back to Natchez. Who knows? They may well pass each other en route.

For now, we are leaving the sunrise behind, heading west, toward our juncture with that great wicked river that will take us to New Orleans.

Onshore the cannon booms in salute as we gain speed.

BOOK TWO

CHAPTER 23

As the day progresses, we encounter groups of flatboats and keelboats that departed Shippingport yesterday. The boats appear to be congregating, maintaining an unusual proximity, which puzzles me. Ah, then I remember the fears of Indian unrest. These boats are seeking to create at least an illusion of security. It is a bit of a revelation that we are moving so much more rapidly than they. The river seems to be filled with them, and though Baker slows us down so that Andrew Jack can steer us through and around them, we pass them with surprising speed. Farmers, wives, children, and rivermen flock to the sides of their boats to see us, some waving and cheering, some staring almost with malice as we pass. The current is their mobility. The river carries them, along with fallen limbs, debris, even pieces of wrecked boats, at its own speed and according to its own whims. We alone have agency. Our thrust is slightly stronger than the current, and we can veer to port or to starboard with Andrew Jack's skilled steering, an impossible feat for those vessels that depend entirely on the river's flow.

In the late afternoon, we encounter a keelboat moving unexpectedly, under power of its own.

"Lydia!" Nicholas shouts as he comes running down from the wheelhouse. "Fetch Rosetta! Where are the women? Come see!"

Is something amiss? No, he would seem more alarmed. This is pure excitement! I run to the door to belowdecks, open it, and call out. Rosetta comes tripping down the passageway as fast as her little feet can manage.

Sarah is close behind. "Bessie's wrapping the baby. What is it?"

"I've no idea, Sarah." I grab Rosetta's hand as she is about to fly past me. "Nicholas is exceptionally excited and shouted to fetch you all to come."

Sarah and I are trying to hold Rosetta back safely and to keep from tripping on our skirts at the same time. Tiger is wagging along beside me. We are laughing at ourselves as we go. Nicholas is at the rail, motioning for Rosetta to come to him. We release her. She can hardly get to him fast enough, and when she does, they both are pointing.

"Horsey, horsey," Rosetta squeals, clapping her hands in that haphazard fashion of little children.

"Horses?" Sarah looks at me, puzzled.

Yes, we have seen flatboats with all varieties of livestock on board, even horses, but none that excited Nicholas like this. We, too, have now reached the railing. There before us is a keelboat coming very slowly upstream—yes, upstream—by means of a horizontal wheel propelled by six horses, not quite evenly matched, hitched to the axel of the wheel, treading round and round in a constant circle on the gallery decking. The small paddles of the wheel drive their boat like ours, only far less powerfully. I know that Nicholas has seen these before. He had hoped fervently that we might catch sight of one on our initial flatboat journey. He described the mechanisms to me one evening as we sat under the awning I had insisted be installed on the roof of our cabin.

"Imagine having horses up here with us," he said, chuckling at himself.

"Imagine having horses on this boat with us at all," I said, wrinkling my nose at the thought of having to constantly shovel manure.

He reached over and pinched my nose, then kissed me. We laughed and made our way down to the cabin. Sarah seemed to catch our mood and simply disappeared to the deck. I didn't see or think of her until I woke the next morning. She was always ultimately discreet.

Rosetta squeals again, calling out to Bessie, who appears with Henry cradled in her arms. "Horsey, Henry! Horsey!" Bessie holds the baby up as if he can see where his sister is pointing, and she claps right in his face. "Meg-go-roun!"

Will she remember this? Unlikely. Certainly, the baby will not. Will I? Perhaps. There is already so much of this voyage to remember. And of the one before. Had we not encountered this horse-driven wheel boat this evening, would I have remembered that evening's conversation under the awning and its loving aftermath? I consistently believe that as things occur, I will never forget certain moments, but then, like items that have sunk to the bottom of the river, it is only when something shakes them loose from their mooring that they rise to my consciousness again.

I leave Rosetta to Nicholas's continued entertainment and retrieve Henry from Bessie's arms. In the corner of my eye, I can see Baker glance at us.

"Why don't you enjoy the evening on the deck?" I ask Bessie. "This weather is so unseasonably warm. It should be enjoyable."

Sarah turns to come inside with me. Henry is making little bubbles with his lips. I'm feeling overfull and am eager to have him at my breast. I think of my own mother, how much joy she must have had with us two, Henry and me, how she was denied this joy when she died with her unnamed baby.

Were her breasts full when they buried her, I wonder. Was her unnamed infant ever in her arms before they laid her in the coffin? And my father . . . Did they place that dead child in his arms? Such thoughts have never before occurred to me. A feeling of shared grief and empathy invades me like waves of the river sweeping me to somewhere I have never been before. No wonder my father fled his grief, fled all that he would never again have without her.

In the cabin, Sarah helps me with my redingote as I shift Henry from arm to arm to free myself from its excessive warmth. I did not need it even in the normal chill of early morning. This weather is bizarre. What date is this? Surely, I should remember that. Ah, December 13. Only twelve days until Christmas. The days have been running together as we go downriver, thanks to this strange weather in the middle of December. Not that I want to be freezing, but this warmth, along with that odorous yellow mist, does make me wish for at least a chill and a good shower of rain to clear the air.

I am still a bit too warm as I settle with Henry in the chair and am glad for the touch of cool cabin air as I open my shawl collar to his rooting lips. His cheek is so soft as he snuggles in against me, his little hand opening and closing against my bare skin like a kitten pawing its bed. How fortunate that the trend for wet nurses in recent years has reversed itself, though I know one or two ladies back in Pittsburgh who still chose that route. They were very careful as to their standing in society and were not my friends. Oh, what those women have missed! Suddenly I'm feeling sorry for them. I could become a wet nurse myself and do this all my life. But what a thought that is! I shall be nursing my own children for years to come. Middle age will have caught up with me before I truly have to give this up.

I gaze down at this sweet infant, asleep now, lips still randomly puckered and sucking at air. Sarah sees, and I nod to her.

She takes him from me so gently. His little arms shoot out as she lays him in his crib. I can't imagine life without a baby in it. That time will come, of course, but perhaps by then Rosetta will have her own for me to love. Indeed, Henry may also have his own.

With the boat moored for the night and our small supper done, the children clean and put to bed, I go out on deck to find Nicholas. The early night air is cooling. I pull my shawl around me. It is nice to have December feel a modicum more like December. Of course, as we join the Mississippi and our westward route turns toward the south, the winter will naturally seem less wintry than I am accustomed to. The murkiness of the air remains, in spite of the chill. A smokiness of sorts. It is blocking out the comet, much as it has dimmed the sun all day. We are so accustomed to seeing the comet, even with the fog, that its absence feels disquieting. I gaze across the deck to where Nicholas and the men are congregated around the embers in the firebox.

I shouldn't be eavesdropping, but . . . it seems the comet concerns them, as well.

"If a comet means something bad's coming on, I guess if it disappears, it don't mean a thing, after all," says Jacob. His voice is a deep bass, and it carries across the night with assurance. I could hardly help but hear him.

Nicholas laughs. I hear the slight metallic echo of Andrew Jack's steps as he comes down from the wheelhouse to join them.

"Nah," says Ezra. His words carry too easily through the night. "Way I heard it, means whatever it's foretelling's about to happen."

Andrew Jack breaks in. "Now, you men know better than tossing around some useless old folktales. Next thing, you'll be telling me there's sunken treasure in this river."

"Now, that one could be true!" Nicholas slaps his knee.

They all laugh. Nicholas sees me next to the rail and beckons me over. The men start to rise, but I wave at them to stay seated. Just as I reach my husband's side, I startle violently as wild, desperate screaming echoes off the shoreline. I am terrified. Some woman is being slaughtered in those woods that spread along the nearest shore. Nicholas steadies me with a strong arm around my shoulder. My heart is racing.

"Panther's out," Billy says, as if the dreadful sound were ordinary. "It ain't nothing, ma'am. Those cats scream like somebody's getting killed. It'll be gone in a minute. Maybe," he murmurs. "Let me fetch you a chair, Mrs. Roosevelt." He starts to rise again.

"No, Billy. Thank you. I'm just going to have a stroll around the deck before retiring." I start to say, "Get a breath of fresh air," but there is no air that is fresh, none that is not dense and murky. "If I can manage not to be terrified by that panther."

They laugh as I bid them all good night and leave to take my turn around the deck. I am barely calm, scarcely recovering, still edgy from the panther's screams, so terribly human, when I'm thrown off again by an owl's high-pitched screeching. Far off in the distance, I hear the baying of hounds on some farm, then the howling of wolves. I am accustomed, or at least I should be, to the disquieting sounds of the night, but these eerie noises have me apprehensive for some reason. I heard them almost nightly as we came farther south on the flatboat, the two of us sitting on its roof in the dark, but something is different tonight.

Perhaps it is the uneasiness of the crew, which is really the uneasiness of the general population, as the rivermen have been spreading rumors through the towns, and the rural settlers think the Day of Judgment is at hand. We did not encounter this apprehension on the flatboat. Perhaps it's all due to the superstitions surrounding the comet. How I wish I could see its bright glow through this troublesome mist! The sounds of the night are wrenching me. I'm turning to retreat belowdecks when Nicholas joins me at the rail.

"Strange night, is it not?" he says as he puts an arm around me.

I shudder slightly. "Yes," I say. "But possibly we are only noticing more since we no longer have our minds on conquering the falls."

"Perhaps, in spite of knowing better, we can't help being influenced by the superstitious rumors the crewmen have regaled us with."

"I was just thinking the same thing. Like children shuddering at ghost stories, knowing they are only stories, but then having bad dreams."

The panther's chilling scream splits the night again. As I shudder, Nicholas takes me full in his arms, his warm lips on mine in the chill.

"What say we go below and make sure your dreams are good tonight?"

I raise myself on tiptoe and kiss him as if I might never stop. In truth, I cannot stop kissing him, even as he guides me to the passageway.

As we enter the quarters, Bessie and Sarah look up from their stitching and say almost in chorus, "Well, we are glad to see you two." They scurry to lay their handwork aside.

"We were wanting a break in the night air before bed," says Bessie. I'm hoping she will use the time to be with Baker.

"The children are soundly asleep," says Sarah. "They shouldn't wake anytime soon."

"Is, um—" Bessie stops short. I know she is wondering and is hesitant to ask.

Nicholas picks up on what she is thinking. "The men are

mostly taking their ease on deck, since we are securely anchored to this island." He looks at Bessie as he adds, "Mr. Baker is on break." He gives her a wink, and she ducks her head, blushing.

The two of them make their exit and close the door quietly, leaving Nicholas and me to ourselves.

CHAPTER 24

Morning dawns with nothing more troublesome than Henry's hunger, and that is no trouble. It is, in truth, a comfort. He is going longer between feedings, but I know that before long, in a month or so perhaps, he will hit that growth spurt that will make him ravenous. Nursing every hour for a few days to build up the supply of milk. But for now, he is such a comfort to me, warm and soft in my arms.

Nicholas is on deck, of course. Has been since very early, when he rolled over me, kissing my neck, my arm, the palm of my hand, nuzzling me like our infant boy. Before he left, he propped himself on his hands, just looked down at me, smiling. "I love you," he whispered before he popped out the door.

Today there will be little of interest to see along the river, though what little there is will be superb. I will have some time to finish knitting this blue sweater for Henry before he outgrows it. Maybe time to get my cards and play a bit of Patience. A day for me to practice patience of my own.

I go on deck to check the weather. There is little change. Still murky and somber. We are moving on beyond the hill country now. The landscape is shifting the color of the banks to a dreary ochre yellow—hence, the name Yellow Banks. The shoreline is not so steep and high, though up ahead, I see the towering cliff I remember from the flatboat journey.

Nicholas comes across the deck to greet me, places an arm around my shoulder with a knowing glance at me, along with his deep chuckle. "Last great landmark before the lowlands."

"Hanging Rock," I say. "Yes, I remember straining my neck to keep my eyes on it as we passed it before. I kept feeling it might fall over on us. Silly, I know, but nevertheless . . ."

"A hundred feet of solid rock, Lydia. How you reckon that came to be?"

"I've no idea. But it makes my stomach quail to think, what if it ever fell?"

"Been there since creation. Expect it to be there till doomsday."

"Well, Nicholas, you know that's all these people are thinking about around here—doomsday. They believe we are the ones bringing it. You've seen settlers hiding behind trees as we pass, now haven't you?"

"Ah, yes. We are the portent of the end-time, you know. Coming down this river with a roar like thunder, smoke and cinders flying in the sky behind us. They can hear us a good ways ahead, you know."

"Yes, and others of them are not afraid at all—just greatly curious, I would say. Then cheering as they see we are just a boat going by. But what a boat, Nicholas. Your boat! Not like they've ever seen before, never imagined could exist. Imagine the tales they will tell, will regale their grandchildren with." I tug at his sleeve, kiss his cheek when he leans down. "For that matter, imagine the tales we will regale our own grandchildren with."

"And the ones we won't." He takes my chin in his palm, kisses me firmly, and laughs.

I'm laughing as he grins at me. Then instantly he's pointing up at Hanging Rock again. We are passing it more rapidly than even I might have imagined from our previous experience. Speaking of sounding like a thunderstorm, I can hardly believe I'm wishing for one. We sorely need a good heavy rain to clear this muggy air.

Now that we have passed that last great cliff, the land flattens out considerably. Wide-open stretches are marked with stands of enormous bare-limbed cottonwood trees twisting their branches against the sky. Behind them tower forests of ever-green pine. Dry grasses, heavily seeded, cover the low undula-tions of earth. Canebrakes, growing what seems to be a good eight to ten feet tall or even more—it's hard for me to judge from here—begin to appear. They are astonishingly dense, like well-made brooms rising up from the banks.

Rosetta runs to me, arms outstretched. Tiger lopes along be-side her, keeping watch, as always. He raises his nose and sniffs repeatedly at the foolish air. Bothers him as much as me, I see. I lift Rosetta in my arms, and Tiger presses himself against my leg.

My little one is pointing, kicking her feet against my hips. "Birdy, birdy, Mama! Birdy!"

I look where she is pointing. Emerging from the murky sky, three vultures wheel their lazy way above the river, then disap-pear again into the sunless sky. Though I know this wilderness is eternally full of dead animals, which draw these birds, I can't help a shudder running through me. From Tiger's throat a low groan sounds, then grows into a deep growl. Holding Rosetta close, I glance down at my great gentle dog to see what is amiss. He looks up at me, a brief glance, then growls again. I follow his gaze to the bank, where I see nothing other than movement in the cane, which could be simply from a breeze. I rest my hand on his head, give him a pat.

"There now, Tiger. It's all right, big boy. Shhh now."

He growls again. Billy apparently hears the commotion and is instantly at our side. He, too, follows Tiger's line of sight, and another, louder growl emerges from his throat.

"It's a bear!" Billy turns to the men at the firebox. "Look here, men. We got us a bear!"

I'm searching the shore, the trees, the canebrakes. There it is. Big, lumbering, and dark. And behind it is another, somewhat smaller bear. Their movement seems too awkward to me to think of them as so dangerous. Yet they are. I shudder again: the comet, the screaming panthers, this murky, warm air, the vultures, and now these bears.

"Mama and an adolescent cub," says Billy. Now he's pointing for Rosetta, but she doesn't seem to spot them, and then they disappear back into the denseness of the cane.

"Don't see that every day." Billy scratches his head.

The crewmen turn back to their sooty work at the firebox.

Tiger goes silent, and Rosetta scrambles over me to get down. When she runs happily off, Tiger follows close behind.

Another story that may or may not be remembered. Another memory told through generations, but never quite as the event occurred. Likely not even by me.

Tonight we will anchor at Island Sixty-Eight, near Yellow Banks. The air seems to fit the sulfurous hue of this fittingly named shore. On our first trip Nicholas discovered there was coal to be had and bought controlling shares in the mines to fuel a boat that did not even yet exist. I love how his mind works on things that don't yet exist and how he follows through to make sure they do. Coal is far more efficient than wood, which requires tediously frequent and necessary stops for the men to cut and chop trees onshore.

The cut wood, of course, is green and needs to be at least partially dried, so it is piled inconveniently on board near the stove in the gentlemen's quarters in order to be made ready for the engine. What a lot of work that is for the crewmen! Cutting trees, chopping wood, hauling it on board and carefully into the quarters, then back outside again to pile it near that ravenous furnace, which devours approximately six cords of wood every twenty-four hours. If the haul is ample enough, of course, and the existing supply is ample enough, the bulk of the new-cut wood can be stacked out near the furnace.

How will this process work when we actually have gentlemen passengers on board, I wonder. Will paying passengers be happy with such disruption? With drying wood piled up in their quarters? I suspect not, but they likely will be glad nonetheless to reach distant destinations in only a matter of days as opposed to weeks, at a speed otherwise unavailable, as well as in elegant luxury, as they imbibe fine ale and gamble at cards at the table.

Our plan is to anchor overnight at the foot of the island, shielded from the river's inevitable flow of driftwood and other debris, ready for the next day's work of urgent digging and loading the coal. At the island, we will be only a handful of miles from the mines Nicholas purchased on our flatboat journey, so the men will have an early start at digging the coal. Tomorrow will be difficult for them, I know. They will be exhausted by the end of the day.

As we near the downriver end of the island, activity speeds up on the deck: crewmen are tamping down the furnace, readying the anchor, gathering the coils of rope to tie us up to trees on the island. Some of the men will go onshore to secure the mooring and gather kindling for the woodstove in the gentlemen's quarters. Our timing seems perfect. Dusk is gathering, at least insofar as we can call it dusk. The light is diminishing, at any rate.

Suddenly, a gleaming orb of veiled sun shines through the

dense yellow haze, casting long stripes of golden light across the barren treetops, the leaf-littered earth, and the deck of the boat. Even the muddy surface of the water shines a reflected gold for a moment. I reach into the warm light, as if I might actually hold it in my cupped hands before it slips away. Then it is gone. The world is ochre gray again.

CHAPTER 25

It's elbows and knees as Nicholas climbs over me and leaps out of bed. What a lot of noise he is making while pulling on his boots and dashing out into the vague early light. It's the coal, I know. He wants to be on deck when we cross downriver to the mines for the men to begin work.

For me, there is not much hurry now. We women will have the day to ourselves, to tend the children and invent distractions to pass the time. I'm hoping not to spend much of it playing Patience—or needing to remind myself just to be patient. I hear Henry's soft whimper. A little early for him, but he's surely been awakened by Nicholas's scurrying. I hear the whisper of Bessie's slippers as she brings my baby to me and lays him in my arms. Eager, he is. Faster than I can unfasten my gown, he is rooting for my nipple. Rosetta tucks her head under the curtain and scrambles up to snuggle against us. We have only gotten comfortable, with Henry suckling, when I hear rowdy commotion and angry shouting from the deck. Rosetta sits up in alarm, her eyes wide with fear as she stares at me. Henry loses his latch and starts to whimper. As I'm struggling to get him reattached, Sarah pulls the curtain back.

"I'm on my way, Miss Lydia. You just wait." She lays a reassuring hand on my arm, then strokes Rosetta's hair. "Don't you worry, child. It's all right." She bends and plants a kiss on Rosetta's brow.

Before Sarah can cross the cabin, Nicholas's boots come stamping in again. He snatches the curtain back.

"Some—" I can tell he has barely stopped himself from uttering some ugly epithet in front of Rosetta. I've been trying not to listen to the shouting on deck, and I hope she hasn't heard it, though she's too young yet to understand any of it. "Some—" he repeats, then gets ahold of himself. "Somebody's stealing my coal!"

Alarm shoots through me. "We've no coal for the voyage?"

"No. No, we have coal. I don't mean we don't have coal. But someone's been stealing my coal!"

Henry has let go now. I close my nightdress and motion to Bessie. Nicholas steps aside, somewhat clumsily, and she takes the baby from my hands. Rosetta is staring wide-eyed at her father.

"How do you know that, Nicholas?" I'm trying to settle him down.

"There's coal all over the bank!" He's shouting now.

"Papa cold?" Rosetta is pulling at his sleeve for attention.

It takes him a moment to orient himself. "No, honey. Coal. Slack stuff. Not cold."

"Coal on the bank?" I say. "You mean, just scattered about? Bits of it?"

"No, no, no!" He's virtually yelling now, waving his hands wildly in the air. "Mounds of it. Mounds! All piled up, ready to load onto some flatboat to haul downriver." He runs his hand through his unkempt hair, making it worse. "Clearly, a lot has already been loaded. It's thievery! Pure and simple! That's one hell of . . . heck of a haul, don't you think? Making off with boatloads from my mines! If I see flatboats downriver here, loaded with coal, I'm running them aground." He slams his fist against the bulkhead.

Sitting up fully now, I swivel my feet onto the floor, bringing Rosetta with me. As I turn, she reaches for Nicholas, a little cry escaping her. He settles down a bit, taking her into his arms. She pulls on his earlobe, as if to make him hear, leans back.

"Papa, I run around flatboat, too?"

He chuckles now, releasing his ire even more. He gives her a kiss and sets her down. Sarah takes her by the hand to get her dressed. I reach for my own clothes on the chair.

"I'll join you in a moment, Nicholas." I turn him toward the door. "I'll be right out."

I scramble to dress, grab my shawl in hopes the abnormal warmth has given way to an early morning chill, and make my way to the deck. The fog has thickened, making it difficult to see the shore. I hurry to the rail, where Nicholas is gesturing wildly, in intense conversation with Baker. Billy is beside them, listening. As I take hold of the rail, I begin to discern high black mounds on the bank. The men are doing their best to make sense of the puzzle and to calm Nicholas, who is quite perturbed again.

"How dare they dig so much!"

"More than they could load, for sure," says Baker.

"Yes, sir. A good bit more," Billy adds. "Interesting, that."

I'm attempting to understand. Nicholas is so rarely angry, but the men seem unable to assuage him. I need some clarification.

"Would one of you gentlemen help me understand what has happened?" I ask.

"Seems someone has been stealing the coal intended for our voyage, Mrs. Roosevelt," Billy says.

"Are you saying we haven't enough now for our fuel?" My alarm is too sudden to hide.

"No. No, ma'am. Just that it appears a lot has been stolen. No one would dig and leave this much unless their boat was full. Lot of labor expended here to go off, unrewarded."

Nicholas is about to begin his protestations again when I lay my hand on his arm and preempt him. "So, Billy, are you saying this coal that was already dug is not only ours by right of ownership but also ours to simply load?"

"Yes, ma'am."

I stare through the fog at the black mounds. "Is this enough for us, then?"

"Oh, no, ma'am. Not by far. It'll take at least double that." Baker pulls his beard through his hand. "Maybe more. We'll be hard at the digging for a good time. Well, I don't exactly mean 'good time'—I mean a good piece of the day." He pulls at his hat brim. "Don't guess you could call digging coal a good time."

I want to respond to Baker's attempt at humor, but I'm looking at Nicholas now. "So, you may have lost some coal, but what an unexpected advantage this turns out to be. You've only to begin loading this coal immediately, while the remainder of the crew dig more." I smile at him. "We'll be on our way again in half the time." Simple logistics, which he already knows, to snap him out of his moral outrage at having been robbed.

"Yes, sir. Someone's done maybe half our labor for us," Billy says.

Nicholas rubs his jaw, shakes his head. I can see my husband's common sense returning.

"And no need to pay them for it. Guess they get their wages in profit downriver," says Andrew Jack, who has been standing there listening. He laughs.

"If they make it far enough without our running them aground." Nicholas laughs back. "Well, let's get to it. I've let myself hold us up long enough."

I squeeze his arm and turn to go back belowdecks.

"Lydia?"

When I stop, he leans in to whisper in my ear. "I love you, Lydia Roosevelt. You know me so well."

I chuckle low and make my way in to our children. This day will not be as long as I'd thought. So much for playing Patience. Such a solitary game. Maybe I'll take the children onshore for a picnic. Rosetta would love some time to play. Tiger would, too.

I enter our quarters in a high mood. "The men will be loading coal for most of the day," I announce. "Why don't we all go ashore for a picnic in the woods?"

"What a grand idea, Miss Lydia," Bessie responds. She lifts Henry, who was just changed, high above her head and jiggles him as his laughter charms us all.

Sarah volunteers to run and ask our cook, Joshua, to prepare a picnic for our outing. Bessie shifts Henry into my arms and begins to gather necessary bits of gear in a woven straw basket: extra diapers, the baby sweater I finally finished knitting, two or three blankets to spread on the ground, and several other items. "Just in case," she mutters to herself as I sit and turn my attention to my hungry boy. It makes me smile to watch him work to find his way, then relax into my arm as the milk begins to flow. I ponder again how many women these days turn their infants over to a wet nurse and wonder at how they will never be aware of what they missed.

Sarah returns to dress Rosetta, who's fussing at having to put on an extra sweater under her red woolen cape. The women are searching for her bonnet in a drawer beneath the berth when the cook's son, Gabriel, knocks to announce that the picnic has been prepared, whenever we are ready. Gabriel will accompany us onshore, since all the other men are busily occupied with the coal—loading, digging, and loading more. I can only imagine what the wash will be like tomorrow! What this deck will look like with all those shirts and pants flapping in the breeze at the same time. We will likely have to install some new lines to accommodate this wash!

At last, we have ourselves thoroughly prepared, overly so, I expect. We parade onto the deck, where the rowboat is waiting to ferry us onshore. Gabriel has it loaded already with two large baskets. Through the cloth corners that peek out from one of the lidded baskets, the scents of ham, bacon, and fresh-baked bread escape and fill our nostrils, overwhelming for a few delicious moments the constant stench of the foggy air. I can sense the quickening of everyone's spirits and appetites as Gabriel assists Sarah and Bessie into the rowboat. Bessie settles my excited little girl onto the wooden seat and turns to me for Henry. Then I take Gabriel's extended hand, remembering suddenly how we were left with only a rowboat such as this to reach New Orleans when our flatboat sank at Natchez. So strange how the past flows forward, never ceasing to be part of the present.

The air is quite strange. Of course, it has been for days. Why am I noticing now? But at least it is still an unusually warm December, and we won't be chilled by the air during our picnic. As we pull away from the steamboat, I cough a bit at the coal dust from the shovels, which has mixed with the sulfurous odor in the air. Gabriel is rowing us competently from the bow of the steamboat toward the shore, well in front of the wide plank and the industrious work of the crewmen hauling coal up and down it. The clanking of their shovels and the rattling of wheelbarrows on the wood are in stark contrast to the quiet dip and pull of the oars as Gabriel guides the rowboat toward a low shore of tranquil woods some distance above the steamboat. He is rowing us upriver in the shallows, where the current is negligible and will easily carry us to the boat when Baker sounds the whistle for us to return.

A slow, reassuring crunch vibrates beneath us as Gabriel pulls the rowboat across the sandy bottom. It fills me somehow with surety. I am going ashore. My feet on the earth. No limitations to my steps, other than tree roots and boulders. I will not arrive at a railing beyond which I can go no farther.

I love the sure sound of Gabriel's boots as he runs to secure us to an old cottonwood just beyond the water's edge. Then the flat clang of a plank he lays on the sandy earth for us to step out. All these solid sounds. Our feet on this plank that unites us to the earth. Gabriel extends his hand to assist Sarah, who carries Rosetta. I watch his steady hold until she reaches the end of the plank. His feet planted wide, he extends the other hand to Bessie, who is holding Henry in her arms. I wait, feeling suddenly awkward and in need of assistance with the basket Bessie has so carefully packed. I am grateful for this plank, grateful to have my dry feet on land for a change. I am unexpectedly aware of the difference. Keenly so. I've become thoroughly adjusted to the snapping clicks of boots on the wooden deck, the constant movement of the boat, so that I pay scant attention to my own body's subtle adjustments to its motion now. I feel a bit dizzy. Our previous stops have been filled with busy errands in the few towns along the way. Here I am struck by the stillness of the natural world, the stability of the ground itself—beyond the wet sand and mud, of course, thanks to Gabriel's plank and steady hand.

Beyond the short incline of the shore, the forest of mostly leafless cottonwoods and oaks opens into a clearing. I step into it, turn around, and around again, feeling the ample forest, the sure ground, the low grasses, leaves, and moss. Gabriel takes the basket and helps me spread our blankets and cloths. He returns to the rowboat to retrieve the picnic baskets. Dish by dish, he lays out our feast. I smell the enticing scents of all that his able father has prepared. An unexpected hunger roils in my stomach. Rosetta is running and jumping, her little feet kicking at the leaves in excitement at the sight of a small cake from Joshua's kitchen.

"Sandwiches first, sweet girl," I say.

Sarah picks her up, both of them laughing, and then both quiet as Sarah steps away and begins pointing at various things for Rosetta to see: the tangle of bare limbs above, a leftover leaf fluttering here and there. "Shhh, listen," Sarah says before the rough caw of a raven breaks the silence.

Rosetta is silent, searching for the source of this strange sound. Not finding it, she swivels toward me, still in Sarah's arms, and mimics the sound. "Caw, caw, caw," she cries at me, then throws her head back, laughing.

After Sarah sets her down, she runs to throw her arms around me. She is as happy for the freedom of solid ground as I am, apparently. I wrap my arms around her, hold her tight for a moment, then turn her loose to run back to Sarah, who is pointing to the colorful parakeets flitting through the trees. I am surprised to see them. What a delight this scene would be to the Audubons! I wish they were here. How rich it would be to share this with Lucy! Rosetta is chasing the colorful birds, her arms in the air, waving about in a frustrated effort to catch one. Much as there is to see from our boat, this solid world is magical in spite of the heavy air.

Without a bright sun, blocked as it is by this persistent mist, it is difficult to estimate the time. We are all hungry, I know, and the smell of ham and bacon overwhelms the odorous air. I am impatient to fill my mouth with the delicious flavors these scents promise.

"Come along now," I say to no one in general, motioning to Rosetta and patting the blanket beside me. "I hope you are all as hungry as I am!"

Bessie leans down to hand me the baby before she settles herself. Rosetta is still dancing in glee beside me, soiling the place on the blanket where she will sit, but no matter. We can clean it, along with the coal-stained work clothes. This moment is too delightful to be spoiled. Seated now, Sarah pulls Rosetta

into her lap, throwing me a knowing smile. Each of us takes a
napkin and reaches for a sandwich. Rosetta is eager for the one
Sarah holds up for her. She opens her little mouth as wide as
possible but manages only to pull a sliver of bacon right out
with her teeth. We are all laughing at the sight of it hanging
against her chin. Sarah manages to grab it as Rosetta opens her
mouth in a gale of laughter, utterly delighted to be the center of
attention.

"Me have beard, Mama!" The words can hardly get out for
the giggles. "Me have long beard!" She waves her hands to il-
lustrate just how long.

Sarah takes the bacon, slides it back into the sandwich, and
flattens the bread with her fingers. Rosetta opens wide to try
again. All of us bite into our lunch at nearly the same moment.
The rich flavor soothes us into quiet concentration on the food.
I motion to Gabriel to sit with us, but he refuses, holding out
the rifle he has retrieved from the boat. He is standing watch in
case of bears, though to my memory, it is alligators that are the
danger to rowboats onshore. I laugh to myself.

"You see something funny?" Sarah laughs with me, not
knowing why.

It's the day and the mood.

"Thinking of alligators," I say and proceed to tell that tale
again to entertain our group. I stop at the point of waking to
loud scratching in the night.

"How many times have I told you this tale?" I ask.

"Enough for me to finish it myself," says Bessie.

"Well, I could tell it my own way," says Sarah. "I was right
there in that rowboat with you, listening to that mad clawing,
too, you remember."

"Papa whack it," Rosetta chimes in. She has heard this tale
enough times to think she remembers. "Whack!" she shouts as
she knocks her sandwich onto the cloth in a make-believe imi-
tation of her father ridding us of that creature.

Laughter fills the gathering. We are relishing our picnic and chattering among ourselves when a deep guttural growl startles us all. Tiger has risen and stands on point toward the woods. Another full growl issues from his throat. *Indians.* I turn and realize that Gabriel has moved toward the edge of the clearing, has planted his feet in a firm stance with the rifle raised.

I hold up my hand, my heart pumping. The group goes silent. Even Rosetta.

CHAPTER 26

Over the racing of my heart, I hear it—a crunching in the woods, the deep fallen leaves rustling under multiple footsteps, men's and women's voices in half-whispered mumblings. I make out a word or two of English, and my anxiety eases some. Indians would not be speaking English.

"Who's there?" cries Gabriel. "Make yourself known, before I shoot you!"

At his cry, the sound of the work downriver ceases. Shovels drop, clanking against coal, before two of the crewmen grab their rifles and head toward us at a run, their feet cracking fallen twigs and stirring up leaves as they come.

"We don't aim no harm!" a gruff voice cries from the woods. "Put ye gun down. We ain't aiming harm."

At the edge of the clearing, I spot the source of the voice—a tattered squatter, old and worn, or perhaps not old, only worn from a life harder than I am used to imagining. He raises his callused hands in the air as he shuffles from between the trees. There are other voices, several of them. Behind him I make out a small group of men and women, equally dirty and ragged, looking equally frightened.

Sarah and Bessie grab the children, and I swivel around to see them running not to the rowboat but back along the shore to the steamboat's main gangplank, where Billy is helping them on board. Where is Nicholas? Where is my husband?

The women and children on board, Billy is sprinting toward us, his rifle swinging beside him as he runs. Out of breath, he arrives beside Gabriel and me, then, catching his breath, walks toward the squatter. The man raises his hands even higher as Billy levels his gun.

"What are you doing here?" Billy asks.

The man looks puzzled, lowers his hands a bit. Raises them again as Billy makes a jerking motion with his gun.

"You heard me. What are you doing here?"

"We's, um, we's wanting to know the same thing," the man stutters in reply. "What you, um, doing here?"

Billy jerks his head back at me, as if to warn me away. Nicholas runs down the plank and heads our way along the shore. I back away, but only slightly, holding Tiger, his ruff raised beneath my hand and his low growls vibrating beneath my fingertips. I struggle to keep him in my grip. He will be on the attack if I fail to keep my hold on him. Wait, I feel the pull against me lessen. Ah, here is Nicholas.

My husband looks at me before he looks at the scruffy gathering. He touches my arm in reassurance and advances on the group. Nicholas has such a commanding presence. The squatter steps back as Nicholas approaches him.

"What are you doing here?" my husband asks. "Is it you who has been stealing my coal?"

"Coal?" The disheveled old man looks thoroughly puzzled. "What'd I do . . . What'd we do with coal?" He throws his hands up in apparent dismay.

"Light a fire?" Nicholas is bordering on rage.

"When we got us wood? Mostly just for the picking up? Already on the ground? We ain't 'bout to be digging," the man retorts. "What you doing here? You digging coal for that Devil Ship?"

Nicholas moves as if to grab the squatter, but Billy intervenes, placing his hand between them.

"Let's just hear them out, sir." He lowers his hand.

"We heared all that fiery rumbling. All that noise and splash and smoke." The man stopped and looked back at the stragglers behind him. "That boat what's making the ground shake?"

Billy intervenes again. "I got this one, Captain. You might help Mrs. Roosevelt to the boat, sir."

"Stop," I say.

The men look at me as if I have lost my senses.

"I would like to offer you this food," I say to the squatter, gesturing at our unfinished picnic. Our men glance at me but keep an eye on the intruders. "Please. I wish you to help yourselves. These men will assist you and bring back our cloths and baskets. The food is all very good. I believe you will enjoy it."

Nicholas stares at me, then at his armed crewmen behind Billy. They are clearly still on guard. Nicholas nods and takes my arm. I'm awkward because of my hold on Tiger. Nicholas takes his collar, speaks to him in a firm voice, then releases his hold. Tiger stands beside us, waiting for us to move. And then we do. Toward the gangplank down the shore, our backs toward the gathering at the edge of the woods. Their appearance has burdened my spirit. I know the men will rescue our picnic gear and the rowboat. I do not look back.

It is evening and the copper sun is fading through the yellow mist when the men have the boat fully loaded with sufficient coal to get us to Natchez, hopefully. Billy has all the picnic debris and the rowboat organized aboard. I am in a fit of curiosity to hear more details as the men begin to gather on the deck. I can hear their muted conversation but cannot make out a thing they are saying.

Rosetta has calmed down from the scary ending to her picnic and is rocking her doll, along with herself, on Sarah's lap. Henry, done with his nursing, is asleep in his crib, smacking his lips intermittently. I am looking at the women, from one face to the other, each clearly wanting so to talk about the events of the day, when I hear boots approaching. Nicholas appears at the door. When I shush him with my finger to my lips, he simply motions for me to come with him. Rosetta opens her eyes and sees her papa, so he tiptoes in, as well as he can in those boots, to give her a kiss and returns to guide me outside.

"I thought you might like to join us on deck to hear the conversation about the rather disturbing events of the day."

"Indeed, I would. Such a bizarre experience, Nicholas. Yet, ultimately, somehow not frightening. I can hardly imagine the dire straits in which these squatters must live."

"Yes. Tugs at you, doesn't it?"

I nod my head as we emerge topside and make our way across the deck. Billy, always thoughtful and dependable, has set out a chair for me. Nicholas must have announced to them that he was off to fetch me to hear the rest of the goings-on around these unexpected events. I seat myself and wait. The men are rather quiet. They're shy, I think, about having me in the group. Though I am with them fairly often, this seems somehow different, more serious. But gradually, the men relax and begin to talk among themselves about the day. Initially, Nicholas vents a continued bit of anger about the poachers and their thievery of his coal.

"Sure did make our work half the task," says Jessup. Interesting that he takes the lead. He's usually so quiet.

"Indeed," chimes in Samuel. "We'd still be digging into the night to get as much on board as we've got now."

"Or maybe still digging tomorrow morning," says Baker. I glance at him, thinking how Bessie should be out here with us, but I dare not make the obvious gesture of getting her.

"Well, we'll remain anchored here for the night," says Andrew Jack. "Don't want any risk of moving in the dark. Such as increased odds of encountering sandbars along this part of the river, now that we're in flatter land. No sense taking any risks."

"Or running over someone's flatboat in the dark," says Nicholas. "Wind up dumping some chickens and cattle in the river!" He laughs. "Or maybe a big load of stolen coal!"

Andrew Jack nods. "Or hitting an eddy and getting thrown sideways in the dark."

"What about those squatters?" asks Jessup. "No danger from them?"

"Oh, they're not going to give us any difficulty," Ezra says. "More scared of us than we would ever be of them. They're scared . . . um, scared of this fire-breathing boat. Scared of their own shadows, truth be—and a little bit crazy, to boot."

"Been sitting through too many camp meetings," says Billy. "All that hellfire and damnation preaching. Thinking that comet's a sure sign the end-time's coming."

"And we're the ones bringing it," Oren says. "They're 'fraid to death of us."

"I was quite shocked and then a bit frightened when they showed up," I say, joining in as casually as possible. "But then they seemed so poor and tattered. I felt more sorry for them than frightened."

"Yes'm," says Jacob. "Squatters' life's a bad one. They're just ahead of the settlers, and then they move on, I reckon. Maybe one or two wind up making a life for themselves. I don't rightly know. Sure does age you fast, though. Hard life."

"Yeah," says Billy. "Hard life."

"But they're not out to hurt us," says Ezra. "They're more afraid of us than we need be of them. Still thinking we're the Devil Ship. And they're not messing with the Devil." The others join his laughter.

I rise and move toward leaving. The men scramble to their feet, leaving the rail and the floor and the makeshift seats of a cut log or two. I motion them to sit back down.

"Gentlemen, I wish you good night. You men deserve your rest. You've put in quite a day. And we've only ten more until Christmas."

"Good night, Mrs. Roosevelt." Their voices merge in a tight chorus.

Nicholas turns with me, nodding and waving his nightly farewell to them. When we reach the door to belowdecks, he calls back, "Get your rest, men! We'll be off at first light."

In the cabin, all is quiet, the children asleep and tucked in, the women turning back the covers on their own berths. Bessie looks at me curiously. I smile and wink at her. She blushes as she smiles back. At some point along the way, I think, perhaps we may even have a betrothal.

My own apprehensions and fears from the day's events have settled down now. Sitting on the berth behind our privacy curtain, I relish the feel of the brush in my hair. The familiarity of the mundane soothes me stroke by stroke. I hope Nicholas, already in bed behind me, stroking my spine with his fingers, is feeling a sense of accomplishment and the resulting peace that I am this night. He has worked so diligently over the past years to come to this moment. We have proven this vessel's capabilities, taken so many people on little paid tours, raised a bit of money doing so, carried them upstream, gone all the way from Louisville to Cincinnati, and conquered the Falls of the Ohio. Now we are loaded with coal, despite the poachers, and actually thanks a bit to their aid, whoever they are. Now we are safely anchored for the night, with the gangplank lifted, with no fear of harm after our bizarre encounter with the poor squatters.

Nicholas's hand moves from my spine to around my waist. I lay my hairbrush on the ledge, twist my hair behind me, and turn into his strong arms.

CHAPTER 27

Something hits us! I'm only half awake, jolted to the edge of the berth, in danger of falling. The boat is wrecked! Another violent lurch!

"Move, Lydia. Move! Let me out!"

An elbow in my ribs jolts me fully awake. The weight of my husband, the hard jab of his knee. Too dark to see. What can be wrong? Fear shoots through me. We were wrong. It's the squatters! They have attacked us!

"Move now!"

Suddenly his weight is gone. His feet hit the floor. Other feet in the cabin. Rosetta screaming. Henry crying.

"What's happening?" My bare feet on the chilly floor, hands jerking at the curtains. I can't get out, for Nicholas is in my way, striking a match to light the candle. I grab at his arm, at the berth frame, losing my balance, the floor convulsing beneath me.

"What is it?" I cry, near screaming myself.

"We've run aground. Must have come unmoored! Get the children!"

Gone! He's gone. Like that! No sound of his feet going out, only this wild, deep racket from beneath the boat, a groaning scrape. I lose my balance again as the boat lifts under me. I'm reaching for a chair. Rosetta is on the floor. Sarah and I crash into each other as we reach for her. In the pitch-black darkness, I must rely on voices and sounds to ascertain where Bessie, Sarah, and the children are. Henry's wail pierces the darkness. Bessie has him. She hands him to me, feeling my arms and fingers to be sure I have him securely.

I'm bouncing him on my shoulder when another blow beneath us throws me off balance yet again. Dear Lord, I could drop him! Bessie grabs me, grabs the table, pulls at a chair and forces me into it, my arms too tight around my baby from fear. The next jolt throws Bessie to the floor. Sarah says something I can't make out, and I realize she, too, is on the floor with Rosetta. At least my girl is only sobbing now instead of screaming. Sarah has her in a firm embrace, I know. I hear her soft murmurs to Rosetta. Henry is hiccoughing from his crying, the rhythm of the small jerks of his body like a descant over the deep rumbling beneath us.

At least now we are seated, whether on a chair or on the floor, safely off our feet. A sudden rolling motion tips me into nausea. I struggle to hand the baby to Bessie, turn away from them in case I vomit. The boat rights itself. I breathe in deep, then take another breath, trying to settle my stomach. The boat is still; the noise subdued.

"Keep the children," I say. "I'm going on deck."

"You won't be safe. Don't go!" That is Bessie's voice.

"I'm going," I say. "Don't move! Keep my children safe."

I fumble for my dressing gown, pull it around me by feel, realize when I try to tie it that I have it on inside out. It doesn't matter. I'm feeling my way to the door, holding the edge of the bulkhead to find my way. I am so afraid and hold on to the bulkheads with both hands in case the boat tips again. *Ah, here is the threshold. Don't trip.* Once on the deck, I am terrified by the close bolts of lightning. Inexplicable lightning, shooting up from the earth instead of down to it. A thunderous rumbling comes from below, the earth itself the source of the thunder.

"Nicholas!" I'm trying to see in the dark. Frantic! "Nicholas!" Even louder.

Above me in the charged night atmosphere, the wild screams and flapping wings of terrified birds fill the air competing with the grinding roar. I make out a figure running toward me . . . not quite running, though. The deck is so unsteady.

"Lydia!" It is Nicholas. "Lydia, hold on!" He pulls himself from one handhold to another, lunging as if intoxicated, until he reaches me. "What are you doing out here?"

"Are we aground, Nicholas? Are we wrecked?"

The intense stink of rotten eggs fills the air. I want to throw up again. The deep breaths I took below to settle my stomach have only made the nausea worse. Nicholas has hold of my arm.

"What's that smell? Are we on fire, Nicholas? Are we?" I am clinging to him desperately.

Onshore another broad streak of fiery blue lightning shoots up out of the ground. I watch it ascend into the black sky. Somewhere in my chaotic thoughts stirs a vague remembrance of a biblical description of lightning and thunder, dire prophecies of danger. The shrieking birds threaten to descend on us, then rise away, slamming into one another in the chaos, so that some fall dead or unconscious on the deck.

"No, Lydia. It's an earthquake." Nicholas has me by my shoulders, as if he needs to shake the truth into me.

"Earthquake? Here? It can't be, Nicholas." I'm stunned.

"But it is, Lydia. It is the earth itself that is shaking, not the boat." His hold on my shoulders tightens.

From the earth itself comes a thunderous rumble, and behind it, two, three strikes of lightning ascend into the night from the other shore. An uncommon terror seizes me, of what I cannot name. I'm trembling, my breath short in the horrid air.

Nicholas has me in his arms, like a child. "It will be over, Lydia. They never last long." How does he know? But he insists. "It's already been some minutes. *Shhh.* It will go quiet any second now."

But it doesn't. Another deafening rumble and shafts of blue lightning ensue.

"Come with me, Lydia. We're going to get the children."

"No, Nicholas. Not out here in this." I struggle against him. "The women have them safe inside."

"It's better out here than inside. The deck is more stable. Nothing to fall on us."

"But the air! It's unbreathable!"

"Gases from the earth. Sulfur. We've been smelling it for days. Leaking up from the earth and now let loose. But we are all safer out here."

I can't think how that could be, but I trust him. Then I realize in horror what Nicholas means—if the boat's hull fails, my children could be crushed. I follow him in the direction of the cabin, holding his hand on one side and the rail on the other. We seem stable. Maybe at last this is over.

Nicholas throws open the door to belowdecks and goes in. As I put my foot over the threshold, the boat rocks hard. I grab for the rail. Nicholas bolts into the cabin, shouting instructions to Bessie and Sarah. They grab for blankets, fighting for their balance.

"Sit back down," I shout. "Only one at a time. Nicholas, take Henry and Bessie. Sarah and I will bring Rosetta."

Slowly, with a bare modicum of calm, we make our way topside, as many blankets as possible tucked in our arms. Rosetta has ceased crying, but her breath is still catching in gulps. At the open door to the deck, she suddenly spins, jerking her hand from mine, fighting the air in front of her nose.

"Mama, so stinky. So bad stinky."

I drop my armful of blankets and lift her into my arms. Her head jerks as she makes a frantic effort to shake off the smell.

"Stinky so bad," she repeats as she buries her head in my neck.

Yes, it is, I think as I pat her back and wait by the porthole for Nicholas to settle the others safely outside and return for us.

"Mama, me scary."

Me too, I think. Nicholas is back. He picks up the blankets, puts his arm around me, and guides me until we reach the little circle huddled on the deck. The unseasonal warmth has given way to piercing cold. The air is raw. Billy appears. He kneels to help Nicholas wrap us in the blankets.

"We'll be back in a minute, Lydia." Nicholas turns, calls out to Andrew Jack on the other side of the boat. Billy rises to follow.

"Billy." Bessie raises her hand to him. "Is—is Mr. Baker all right?"

"He's fine. Checking for any damage to the coal supplies." Billy half smiles before he disappears into the dark.

Off toward the furnace, I hear one of the men muttering, "Damn squatters was right. Comet's a sign of the end."

"Shut your damned mouth, man!" A commanding voice in the night. It's Baker. "I mean, stop that nonsense. Now."

"It's the comet—" Sounds of a slight scuffle reach me after a momentary silence. The muttering stops.

Then, "Yes'r."

"I hear that again and you'll be looking for another job at the next harbor. Poling a keelboat up shore. That what you want?" There is the slap of a hand on something hard, perhaps the bulkhead.

"No, sir."

A shovel clangs against metal; then footsteps sound. Baker is standing over us.

"We're all right, Mrs. Roosevelt. We're doing all right. Boat's holding tight. Quake'll be done in a few seconds, if it's not over already." He leans down to Bessie. In a low voice, says, "You all right, Miss Bessie?"

She nods, looks back down at Henry. I watch Baker's gaze on her and suddenly the image of those two with an infant of their own rises in my mind. He excuses himself and heads back into the dark just as Nicholas reappears.

"I think the boat is undamaged," he says. "As far as we can tell in the dark, at any rate." He leans over Bessie, as Baker just did, and gets sight of her holding Henry. "Warm enough?" he asks, addressing us all. When each of us nods, he sweeps his arm in an arc to include everyone. "We will leave at first light, assuming all is well. If you want some rest—if you can even rest at this point—now would be the time. Henry is almost asleep. And little Rosetta is a sleepyhead." He ruffles his hand through her hair. "Things seem to have calmed, so I think we may be done with this quaking. If by some chance we're not, we'll come and bring you out again."

Nicholas assists us all to our feet and swings his drowsy daughter into his arms. With Sarah holding his elbow for balance, he leads them belowdecks. When he returns a moment later for Bessie, he reaches to take Henry from my arms. I can hardly let go of my boy to hand him off.

"I'm staying with you, Nicholas, if that suits you," I say. I'm relieved that he nods.

And then they are gone.

As I await his return, I feel my way with urgent care to the deck chairs and sit down. I take a deep breath and come near to changing my mind about remaining on deck, but this awful rotten smell may have equally penetrated the cabin by now. At any rate, I must be near my husband; I have no wish to be lying alone in that berth, thinking of him and this awful ordeal we have been through. At least, I pray we are through it.

An earthquake? The reality is difficult to absorb. Earthquakes are only to be read about in history books, and they occur somewhere else entirely, off in some distant part of the world in the distant past. The chill has me rubbing my arms. I have failed to pull my blanket up around me. As I do, I feel my husband's hands wrapping the blanket snugly around my shoulders, then its edge around my neck. How did I not hear him? He sits beside me, holding my hand in his.

"I brought your gloves," he says, holding one open for me to slip in my fingers. Now the other. "Are you all right, Lydia?"

It takes me a moment to respond. "I think so."

"Forgive me, Lydia. I should have insisted you stay in Louisville." He drops his head. "I have put you in danger."

"You have not put me in danger, Nicholas. The responsibility isn't yours. I would not have stayed anywhere without you—not at home, not in Louisville, not anywhere." In spite of my subdued terror, I know this to be true.

"But, Lydia, I—"

"But nothing, Nicholas. No one has put me in danger." I laugh at my own absurdity. "I have put myself in adventure! What would I do without you? Without sharing this?" What would I do somewhere else and alone, as I was as a child? "Nicholas, you lived beside me when I was a bride on that flatboat! Was I ever afraid? Did you ever see me avoid danger? Ever see me less than exhilarated? Well, a time or two, perhaps . . . when everyone was so ill with the fever. I wasn't exhilarated then, but I was courageous. You can't say I was not. And when that alligator tried to claw his way into the rowboat in the middle of the night! I was laughing by morning. I'll be laughing again when this morning dawns."

I cradle his chin in my gloved hand and raise his face to mine. "Look at me, Nicholas. I want to know that you hear me."

"Yes. My intrepid Lydia. What would I do without you near?"

Someone has lit a lamp and is approaching; its soft glow swings back and forth with each step. Another person appears behind him.

"Captain."

I recognize the voice of Andrew Jack, then distinguish Baker's face as he steps up beside my husband.

"We've done as thorough a check as we can in the dark, Captain. No leaks anywhere. May have some dents in a plate or two, a little paint to repair, but nothing to prevent us from traveling on downriver."

"Plenty of fuel," says Baker. "Is, um, everyone all right?"

I know he is trying to ask about Bessie. I nod and smile. "Yes, everyone is quite safe."

"Just need some light," says Andrew Jack, "enough to make out sandbars and shifts in the river. Trees and debris, of course. Quake like this is sure to load the water with lots of such. But we're better off on the river than on land, should there come more tremors. Feel it less with more balance in the water."

I chime in. "More tremors?" I can't help myself. "What do you mean, more tremors?" I'm reeling from the reality of this earthquake.

"Oh, not the first time there've been tremors hereabout, Mrs. Roosevelt. Nothing so bad as the quake we just had, but tremors. Indian tales . . . and now squatters and settlers along this area of the river. You heard those squatters asking if this boat was shaking the earth. Probably tremors leading up to this quake. I've brought a number of keelboats down, and I've heard plenty of stories from different sources, but nothing significant. Heard once this whole Indian Territory round about was called 'earth that trembles.' Somebody else said it was once called 'fearful earth,' but I figured that was just made up."

The night seems endless. I have been pacing the deck for hours, it seems. The quake hit at about two in the morning, Nicholas told me when I was calm enough to ask. I am attending to the wild sloshing of the river, its harsh slaps against the boat, when I become aware of the morning. The first ragged tops of the trees protrude from the heavy mist against a brooding sky. The sun shows itself in a coppery flush through the thick mist. Earlier brief scattered showers forced me to take shelter in the doorway to the gentlemen's quarters, but there was not nearly enough to clear the sulfurous air. And nothing to clear my mind of the anxiety aroused by Nicholas's concerns, especially for our children.

Guilt and fear creep into my thoughts. I should say rather *slam*, the way the quake slammed this ship into the earth beneath us, and me with it, my children, all of us with it. But that slamming elicited pure shock, and a fear I have not known since I was a mere child, sick and afraid in the depths of a dark ship, on my way to my father. So strange how this current experience drags me into that other one so long ago, as if I were in it again or in both at once. The light is increasing, but the visibility is limited. Pieces of dull sky in broken bits emerge between the jagged, leafless branches of the trees.

What is this slow guilt consuming me? My children. Feeling again like the child I was on that sea, assailed by the dark, the nausea, the fear. Now Rosetta. How can I know what she experienced during this quake? How can I ever discern what fears may someday emerge in her life, as life itself hits her with some unforeseen distress? And Henry? Can an infant remember? Nicholas is right. We could have been safely at home. At home? Where is that? Or in Louisville. I could have taken part in this adventure that far, shared that much with my husband. I could have even gone through the falls with him and then simply returned home to Louisville by carriage. Home? What nonsense. A temporary dwelling, like all those other temporary dwellings I have inhabited all my life. Without Nicholas? What if the quake hit even there? But that is not where we are.

We are here. The quake has passed. I have no way to undo what has already been. The choices I made cannot be reversed. Better to concentrate now on what is. We are here. With our children. I must go and find Rosetta. Must hold her in my arms.

Must be with her in the way I needed so much, the way that, after my mother died, was never again possible for me. I must use this fluid history of who I am to be the mother my children need. Here on this boat. Having survived an earthquake, I need them in my arms. As they need me.

Though it has grown lighter, I hold tightly to the handrail, feeling my way toward my children. I am at the door when I feel Tiger's damp nose against my hand, lifting and dropping, lifting and dropping. I kneel beside him and put my arms around his supple neck, feel his cold nose nuzzle my ear, a warm tongue lick my cheek. Though he is a faithful guardian of my children, I am the one to whom he is genuinely bonded. Holding the soft fur of his neck, I rise again and go toward the voices of my children. Bessie lifts my baby toward me, but before I can take him, Rosetta has flown into my arms and is fighting to be lifted up and held. I rock her back and forth, my hand in the curls at the back of her head. Tiger must be satisfied now with pressing his head against my leg as closely as he can. Rosetta settles down. I shift her to one hip and open my other arm for Henry.

How shall I hold them all when I have more? We won't be on a river then. We will be on land somewhere—land that neither shakes nor even trembles, I pray. Where will that be? I wonder. Home? Is home ever to be a place at all? Or merely a concept to carry within?

I am shaken like this earth and cannot still myself. My inner disturbance must show on my face, for Sarah takes my elbow and guides me to a chair, each of my arms holding a beloved child, each of them a comfort I so need.

CHAPTER 28

I am sitting here still, watching the growing light through this vile fog, my children in my arms, when Nicholas comes to check on us.

"I believe the quake has settled now," he says before leaning down to kiss first Rosetta's cheek, then Henry's downy head, and then my forehead. "You might soon feel safe enough in the cabin to breakfast, if you are hungry."

Close behind Nicholas, Sarah approaches. Her step seems lighter, though still careful. She announces breakfast and takes Rosetta by the hand, then leads her toward the table. Nicholas holds out his hand to assist me from the chair. I am half standing when a loud rumble and a fierce blow hit at once. I fall back into the chair, clenching my baby in terror. Nicholas lurches backward. Sarah falls to the floor. Somehow Rosetta maintains her footing and flies back to me. Crying in fear, she grips my skirts in a frantic effort to pull herself back into my lap.

Nicholas regains, then loses, his balance as another blow shakes the boat. Sarah is on hands and knees, crawling toward us.

"Get out of the cabin!" Nicholas yells. "Now! Out! Go!"

In a wild scramble, we are fighting to take care of these children—and with ourselves. Above the rumble, I hear the shouts of the crewmen as they bark out confused commands to one another. Bessie emerges from the cabin, waving her hands, and heads toward Baker, but he motions her away. She stops, seems lost, then makes her way with hesitant steps toward us and holds out one hand, which Nicholas manages to grab. We are all anchored to my deck chair, into which I have fallen with my baby. Nicholas turns and disappears into the fog.

Terror has taken hold of me. Taken hold of all of us. I see it in the faces around me. Tiger puts his head in my lap, between the children, and gives a low growling moan. Have we grounded? Did the earthquake leave us as vulnerable as this? What must we do?

I hear heavy footsteps, boots that can only be Nicholas's. He comes into view as suddenly as he left.

"Another quake!" His voice is uncertain. He seems as disturbed as I am. "We are pulling out into the full river as quickly as we can manage. We are safer away from any land with the water to keep us steadier." He takes a deep breath. "Stay here! Don't move!" he commands.

Why would I move? How would I move on this unstable vessel? The women are clearly with me. I see it on their faces. I motion, and they sit on the deck. We hold on to one another, grasping the children and each other as securely as we can. With only this deck chair to steady us and no assurance it will not fly across the deck with another jolt.

This quake seems as violent as the one that woke us in the night, but with less thrusting and fewer tremors afterward. Gradually, we seem to stabilize. At least our vessel does, if *stabilize* can be used to describe what is happening to us. Perhaps it is that we are fully in the middle of the river now. Along the shore, great swaths of the bank rip free and slide into the water, creating roiling waves, which slap against us on both sides.

Waves like I remember from the sea. I am lost in this bizarre experience, which seems to bear no reality. All I can think is to hold on to my children. What else is there to do? There is no escape.

We are silent. Not one of us has made a sound, other than Rosetta's low whimper and Tiger's continued moaning. The noise of the river and its crashing banks drowns out other sounds. We can do nothing but listen and fear. Faintly over the din of the quake, I make out shouted commands back and forth among the men and the vague slap of the paddles, their repetitive hammering frightful. We are here holding on to one another in some strange mercurial space, holding on to fear as if it has no end, as if it is the only thing in existence on to which we can hold.

The earth is falling all around us, rumbling into the river. Suddenly the word *Monongahela* descends into my consciousness, that name from our point of departure, which I was so glad to leave behind. What else that I thought I left behind still waits to assail me? Will this ever stop? Why have I brought my children into this? Am I insane? All those insulting critics I ignored . . . Were they right? What am I doing here?

The heaving stops. Almost as suddenly as it began. Only the wild sloshing of the waves hitting one another, hitting the sides of the boat, spraying us over the deck. It is cold. When it had been so warm. We must get into the cabin, warm ourselves, warm these children, comfort Rosetta, get her blue bunny. I'm wild to rise, get them all to move, go below.

Behind us, onshore, if it can still be called a shore, a horrendous boom erupts and, with it, a towering shot of water and sand into the sky. The stench of sulfurous gases inhibits my breathing. Rosetta is rubbing her face frantically to wipe the stink away. Farther on, another such eruption of water and sand flies even higher. And a third. I am paralyzed. I must do something. But what? What is there to do?

All of a sudden, Nicholas is here. I startle at his unexpected grip on my upper arm as he lifts me out of my stupor, his other hand extended to Bessie. Sarah stands up on her own. Confused, Tiger is twisting his body underfoot. Nicholas calls to him in a calming voice. I want my husband's arms around me. I want to be belowdecks. I want my children in my lap. I want to be on land. No, the land is falling, shaking. The land is the villain here. My brain will not slow down. I don't know what to do. My head turns, and I watch ancient trees fall into the water. My ears are stunned by noise.

"Lydia!"

I hear him as if in a stupor. I'm turning. Where?

"Lydia!"

He's here. Right here. Beside me. Holding my arm. Reaching for Henry. I can't let go. He's holding me. I cross the threshold. I'm in the cabin. Rosetta is there, holding her bunny, running to me. Sarah and Bessie are sitting on the floor, calling her back, talking to her. At least Sarah is. Bessie puts her face in her hands, sobbing.

Nicholas sits me down with them. And then he sits. My husband sitting on the floor!

"Rosetta, come sit in Papa's lap," he says. And she does, hugging Bunny tight to her neck, hiding her face in its softness.

"Bessie," he says. He waits. "Bessie!" There is a pause before she lifts her head, gulping back her tears. "Baker is all right."

After another frozen moment, she nods. Nods again.

"Lydia." He waits for me to look at him. His face is gaunt but set with determination. "We are going downriver. The water is the safest place to be. I've said that, I know. But I want you to know it, to trust it. The river will soften the effects of the shocks and will balance us. We are floating. Remember." He is holding all of us in his gaze, watching to see if we feel the reassurance he is offering. "Our trajectory downstream should take us beyond the limits of this quake. We will soon be in calmer, safer territory."

He pauses. "Well, I say safer. The territory may not be safer, but I want you all to know that we—you—are safe on this boat. Every inch of this vessel is sturdy. You saw how it was put to the test in the passage through the chute. Our continuing voyage, in the hands of Andrew Jack . . . and Baker, Bessie . . ." He pauses to see if she has heard. "Our voyage will be as steady as this river allows. No matter what the earth around us does, this water is deep. There is a proven channel that remains, and those two men will guide us."

"Rosetta." He gives her a slight hug. "Whose lap would you like to sit in now?"

She lifts her head, wobbles to her feet, and drops herself into Bessie's embrace.

Nicholas rises. He strokes the top of my head, buries his fingers in my wild hair. "I'll be on deck. I pray the worst is over. You should be entirely safe here in the cabin. Nothing is going to collapse. But if we hit another bad shock, you must come out on the deck. Someone will be watching to help you. Otherwise, you are safest here."

Then he is gone.

CHAPTER 29

The day is grim. We try to cheer one another, to keep Rosetta calm and occupied. Our breakfast is cold, has partly spilled. We eat it regardless, clean up the mess, listen to the determined rhythmic pounding of the paddle wheels, chatter incessantly about minutia, boring ourselves in order to avoid speaking of our responses to this experience, which is not yet assuredly over and done. It is clear we are all holding our fear at bay.

I am trying to knit. I'm working on a little sweater for Rosetta. Bessie is tending to Henry, who is fretful. Sarah is on the floor with Rosetta, playing pretend with her dolls. My little girl hasn't let go of the blue bunny. She is holding it tight, giving it a kiss now and then, so the bulk of pretend play is on Sarah. Rosetta, at least, appears comforted. Now and then, Sarah gives me an intense glance. It's an unanswered question: either she's trying to see if I am all right or making sure I see that Rosetta is.

The boat is at last making some uninterrupted progress. Tiger comes over now and then to lay his head in my lap, moaning, as he did during the quakes. I realize that each time he does this, the boat is jarred by another shock soon after. How does he sense it ahead of time? The paddles thump harder in the water, their impact shaking the floor. I feel the river's level rising and dropping. I don't wish to imagine what we are passing outside. At some point, I must move, must go topside to witness the damage of this earthquake. I must find Nicholas. Must know what is happening. I lay down the nearly finished sweater and walk out without speaking to my companions. I wouldn't know what to say.

Out on the deck, the fog seems ever more dense; the odor as intense as before. The deck is awash still from the roiling waves the quake slammed across the boat. Sticks and branches litter the wet decking. I'm holding the door for balance. I dare not walk to the rail, but over it I see uprooted trees floating close to us and slamming into us in the current. Remnants of flatboats, broken apart, swirling in the volatile currents. A brown leather settler's jacket caught in the jagged broken limbs of a half-fallen sycamore. A mewling calf from some farmer's flatboat, its legs mired in the mud of a collapsed bank.

Nicholas crosses the deck. He is at my side before I can take three steps toward him.

"I doubt you should be out here, my love." He bends to kiss my cheek. "Not the best conditions for sightseeing," he jests.

"I needed to move," I say. I make an attempt to jest back at him. "Needed to have an afternoon stroll, see what sights there are to see, find my husband." I finger his collar and fake a chuckle. Then he does. It is enough.

"Sights are slow in passing," he says. "Engine's laboring, and we're working hard to move at all. Almost as if we are going backward."

I must look alarmed, though I certainly do not mean to. I'm leaning over the rail. The current does appear to be flowing backward. It is true. I glance at the banks. We seem to be standing perfectly still, in spite of the men hard at work loading the furnace. What more can happen?

"Backward?" I repeat, almost as if it were a jest. "Backward!"

"Oh, no. Not really," Nicholas says. " Of course not backward. That's an impossibility."

Baker has quietly come up beside us. "What's an impossibility, sir?"

"The river running backward. Can't happen. But look at this water!"

I'm looking at Baker, hungry for some kind of reassurance.

"Andrew Jack says we are fighting the flooding of the river. We're a ways yet, but it's a sign we are nearing the Mississippi, its flooded waters pushing back against us." Baker shakes his head. "But I swear when you study that water, it looks like it's going upriver." He slaps his hands against the rail and backs off a step. "Whatever it is, our difficulty is in consuming so much extra fuel to make so little progress. We are virtually standing still against this."

"Are we in need of more fuel?" My alarm is rising again.

"No, ma'am. We will be fine until we reach Henderson. Then we will replenish not only our cut wood but all our supplies. We should be well equipped, then, to reach New Madrid." Baker turns toward the steps to the pilothouse.

Nicholas turns behind him. Another kiss on the cheek. "I'm off to consult Andrew Jack. Don't stay out too long in this gloomy air!"

He's off in a virtual sprint. I've delayed him. These men need a solution to all this perplexity.

Above us, the murky sky is alive with the chaotic flight of birds of multiple sorts: blackbirds, jays, parakeets, doves, a lone woodpecker, birds I can't name. Where is my friend Lucy? Is she experiencing these quakes on their overland journey by horse? Whatever their names, these birds are screaming in various tones, flying this way and that, hurtling into one another. Something thumps on the planking—a sparrow has crashed onto the deck and lies unconscious. I grapple my way to it, to caress it, to attempt to revive it. I hold it in the cup of my palm. So tiny. So innocent. My fingers feel the still warm softness of its feathers. I wait for its breath, for its movement. There is none. It is dead. The sparrow is dead. I am stroking it in grief, this little creature that is still so warm, so soft, so fragile. As I lift it over the rail, I feel an unexpected movement. The sparrow is alive in my hand. Its struggle eases into a flutter, and I release it into the high wind. It sails in a slow curve through the gale our boat creates, out past the pounding paddles, and over the wild river.

I should go below but find myself unable to. Mesmerized by even these smallest signs of crisis, I wait for the next. Then the next. Ahead, I see what should be a small outpost, what was indeed a minor settlement, its few primitive houses crumbled, chimneys collapsed. A handful of disheveled settlers are holding on to each other as we go by; others are hiding from us where they are able, behind crumpled walls and fallen trees. I see the fear on their faces and know they believe us a part of this terror. Or the cause of it. All I can think is that at least the earth beneath them has not collapsed, the banks have not fallen into the river.

Along the remaining shore, great bare trees—oak and cottonwood, birch and maple and hickory—are bending and flailing as if from the great force of a wind. I can feel the gust of our own speed, but there is no wind. Is there a wind? No, there is no wind but our own. It is the earth! The earth itself is moving, the ground shifting, rising, and falling in great waves, as if it were water. The trees are riding the waves of the earth like a farmer breaking a colt.

This cannot be real. *No more, Lydia. Give this up and go inside. Hold your children in your lap. Sing nursery rhymes with*

Rosetta. Sing hymns with Bessie and Sarah. Play patty-cake. Take off your wet boots, so you will not be tempted to come out here again. At least not so easily. Smile when you turn back. Do not let your face reveal what you are seeing. Inside you do not need to see it. You can choose to see your children. Choose to be with them. Choose for them that they not be without you. Turn around now, Lydia. Hold on. Don't fall. Do not injure yourself. Just turn and go below.

CHAPTER 30

I wake, though I do not believe I have slept. At some point, I must have. "Nicholas?"

"I'm here, Lydia." His voice is a whisper. He caresses my forehead and leans over to kiss me. He tucks the loosened tresses of my hair behind my ear.

"Have you been up long?" I'm mumbling. "I couldn't sleep. I thought . . ."

"No, you were asleep, my love—finally. I know how hard this has been. I was awake myself. Hard to sleep with the constant noise of uprooted trees slamming against us. It's frightening even for me, though I'm certain the boat's hull will withstand blows such as that. It's the noise that startles me so, like someone yelling, *Boo!*'" He chuckles, tucks my hair back again. "When you finally fell asleep, I was fearful I'd wake you as I was climbing out of the berth. I'm glad to see I didn't."

"What time is it, Nicholas? I must see to the children." I'm struggling with the covers, my left foot twisted in the sheets.

"No one is awake yet. Not to worry. It's early. I wanted a moment to talk before the world comes alive again and you and

I both are in high demand." He untangles my foot and helps me slip from the berth. "Let's go across to the gentlemen's quarters."

The floor is chilly under my feet. I wish for my slippers but follow him. With the greatest care, he closes the door silently behind us and takes me in his arms. His ardent kiss awakens me fully. I lean back in his arms and smile. But his face is serious. Too serious. Several chairs have tumbled over and slidden across the floor. Nicholas helps me to a seat, rights a tumbled chair nearby, and pulls it close.

"I need to know how you are, Lydia."

In all this, he is asking about me? How can I possibly tell him? How can I say I'm afraid, that a great sense of guilt has risen in me for bringing my children into this terror?

"Nicholas." I'm working to find the words to assuage his concern. "You must not fret about me. We are all doing fine. Well, that is, everyone except Tiger. He's constantly with his head in my lap, moaning, as if . . . Well, actually, he seems prescient, Nicholas. He seems to sense ahead of every shock what is coming." I take both his hands and announce, "We have a prophet for a dog!"

Ah, yes! I manage to make my husband laugh, divert his attention for the moment from the grimmer subject of our fears.

"The river is in a different state, Lydia. Our careful notations from our flatboat expedition are nothing but moot at this point. Every landmark seems to have changed. The banks are so flooded, the forest has become swamp. Andrew Jack proclaims himself lost."

"Lost? Nicholas!" I half rise, then sit again, working to keep myself calm for his sake.

"We are all right, Lydia. We will be fine." His hand on my shoulder is firm, assuring. "Andrew is the finest pilot I know. He sees the river as no one else does. His eyes note every nuance of color and the slightest shifts of current. He and Baker will see us through."

This chair is stiff, masculine, and my feet are tingling against the chill floor.

"He knows the river, Lydia. As do you and I, of course. But he knows it far better and in a different way. We have the Zadoc Cramer, though it is hardly worth much at the moment. And our own drafts and records. But even if most of the landmarks have disappeared, we can somewhat calculate where they should be, where you and I marked them, and make a reasonable guess how to go next."

Calculate where our landmarks should be? And aren't? Every navigational aid we depend on of no use anymore? What have I done? Bringing my children here! Myself! To be with my husband! For them to be with their father, and he with them! To avoid all separation! Now we are lost in this wicked river, at its mercy, this river that has no mercy. I'm immobilized.

"Lydia?"

I'm working to muster my courage, to say anything that will have some sense to it.

"Lydia, I'm sorry. I shouldn't have told you all this. I should have protected you. Forgive me. I don't know what . . ."

Something in me awakens.

"Nicholas, there is nothing to forgive. You have trusted me. Trusted me as you did on the flatboat. Forgive you for trusting me? For including me as a fellow adult in all that is happening?"

"But, Lydia, I should have—"

"You should have done exactly as you have." I take both his hands, raise them to my lips, then bring them firmly to my lap. "And you have done exactly as you should."

He reaches for me, and we rise together, our arms around each other, holding one another in firm reassurance.

"We will pass out of the worst destruction as we find our

way downriver. Things will become more normal as we pass out of this hard-hit area. There are very few settlers along this stretch as we pass the Kentucky side. We will stop at Henderson, where we should be well out of range of the quakes. We'll get ourselves resupplied. Who knows? We may even be able to show off the boat, make enough tour dollars to fund the supplies."

From across the passageway come sounds of stirring and low voices, then the high chirping of Rosetta's morning greetings, a whimper and then a wail from a hungry little boy. I turn to the door, to the necessities of motherhood, which defy the vagaries of this river and of this shaken earth.

Not until later in the day do I venture onto the deck. I do not want to see more of yesterday's destruction, bluffs collapsed into the water, forest transformed into swamp, houses destroyed—though we should hardly see any settlements along this section of the river, with the exception of Henderson, and that we will gratefully see some distance ahead thanks to a long straight stretch in the river.

The river sweeps out hard at the last bend before Henderson and then straightens. We are clearly in the channel now, and the town is visible some miles away. Nearer. Nearer now. The paddles are actually making progress. We will have relief and a replenishment of fuel and food. The town is coming into view. As it should be. I make out crowds of people on the bluff, which has thankfully not collapsed. But it is solid mountainous rock. Someone is on horseback, heading this way. We have friends in town from the flatboat voyage. Friends to welcome us, to hear our tales of terror.

The boat is slowing now, moving out to curve its way in. But no, there is a raft of torn-up trees blocking the landing. I'm looking at faces now, searching for friends, but I see none that are familiar. Every face there is haggard from fear and despair.

The chimneys have all fallen and have taken down walls in their toppling. Figures are running away, into the woods. Afraid of this boat? In fear of us when the earth itself cannot be trusted?

We cannot land. Billy and Nicholas lower two of the rowboats into the water and fight their way around the blockage onto the muddy shore. I can see them talking, but not to whom. See them rushing about, loading bits of things into the boats, and paddling out to us again. The crew reach for the tossed ropes and raise the now heavier boats to the deck. I have to find Nicholas. I'm tearing through our men to reach him.

"What is it?" I say when I find Nicholas. "What's happened here?"

"Same as elsewhere, Lydia. Now, make room for these men." He's pointing, silently instructing the men to unload the meager cargo. "We have a scant amount of sausage and ham there. And wet kindling and small fresh-cut wood. At great expense, I might add. We'll have to make do with this for now."

I back away as the men scurry to put us right again, reversing the paddles out into the churning waters.

Morning breaks, and I must attend to the seemingly ordinary domestic chores of housekeeping and caring for my little ones. We have little to show for our stop at Henderson yesterday, enough perhaps to tide us over stingily until we reach New Madrid. Little lies before us other than Shawnee Town, just into the Territory of Illinois, a generally lively spot to stop for all the boats going south, a sort of anchor for the hunting grounds shared, in keeping with a truce, among the tribes of the Chickasaw, Choctaw, and Cherokee. But today there are fewer and fewer boats on the water and certainly no mirth. As we round into sight of the small town, a huge tree blocks our access. Beyond it we see fallen chimneys and broken houses, shops, and taverns and a handful of tattered residents clustered far from the ruined buildings. I cannot bear the hopelessness of

all this. Will it never ease? Has the whole earth been shaken? I
need to see my children.

Bessie has Rosetta thoroughly immersed in make-believe
with her dolls and her bunny. She is on her knees, crawling in
and out under the table and chairs, the dolls visiting for tea in
fine pretend houses. Henry is still soundly napping. Sarah is
mending a little tear in one of Rosetta's pantaloons, her needle
sliding competently in and out of the fabric as she forms the
fine stitches I see her make habitually. I pick up my playing
cards, shuffle them, lay them aside again. I'm entirely too restless. Done with Patience and most thoroughly out of my own
patience at being cooped up belowdecks. I stand and stretch,
motion to Sarah that I am going back out to the deck.

At the bow I see, as best I am able, that we seem to be in the
channel. The river is implausibly wide, perhaps as much as two
miles. Entirely flooded. Little of it can be deep. I detect what
should be sandbars only by lighter shifts in color in the shallow
water. Ahead there are tree trunks and bare branches entangled
against the fog where I sense islands should be and are not. The
damage seems not to be lessening but distinctly increasing.
How far have these quakes spread their destruction? Surely, we
must soon pass out of their range.

I wave to the men hard at work shoveling coal as I make my
way to the stern. The boat, at least, seems to be maintaining stability. That in itself is reassuring. Nothing endangers my balance, and we seem to be making some headway. From visible
tremors onshore, I can tell that minor shocks are continuing,
though we do not feel them so much on the water. A good sign,
I think, that we may be moving beyond the bounds and the
damage of the worst of the quakes. Yet something prevents my
letting go of anxiety.

I am staring at the banks. Or the stands of trees where the banks
should be. Something seems to be moving among these half-
flooded trees. Maybe nothing? Difficult to make out. Branches?

Broken trees? Flatboat wreckage? I wonder. The fog is thicker away from the boat. The motion seems unusual. All these erratic crosscurrents. Logs? They are constant companions in these deadly currents and make me jump with their wild banging against the hull. I turn to see where the men are, where Nicholas may be. Why do I feel so uneasy? Alarmed, in truth. Where is Nicholas? I am strangely troubled. Is this how Tiger feels when, moaning, he puts his head into my lap, presaging a heavy shock? How he senses some deep alarm, warning him something isn't as it should be?

I glance again at the odd movement among the trees, and I am turning to find Nicholas when I see Baker striding toward me.

"Mrs. Roosevelt, should you be out here, ma'am?" He's invariably polite, doesn't want to tell me that this smelly fog is not the place for me.

"Good day, Mr. Baker. I was just about to go below, but I was studying something there." I point. "At the shore, among the trees. I can't quite make out what it is. It has me feeling quite perturbed. Perhaps you could put my mind at ease."

"Happy to, if I can." He stands beside me at the rail, and when I point again, his hand is across his forehead.

There is only our mutual silence and the slapping of the paddles against the water. Then he grabs me by the arm, jerks me away from the rail, and pulls me, running, toward the cabin. He is screaming out to the other men as we go.

"Indians! War canoes hiding in the trees! Up the steam! Now!"

CHAPTER 31

We are running. I'm tripping on my skirt. Loud slamming of shovels and the loud whistle of rising steam overwhelm the sound of the river. The slap of the paddles hits a faster note. Baker is pulling me hard to the threshold. I stumble across it. He prevents my falling, then releases me.

"Stay there!" he exclaims. He slams the door and is gone.

"What on earth?" cries Bessie as I right myself. She has seen Baker's panic.

I must calm her. And myself. I race down the passageway, Bessie on my heels. I examine the cabin, locate Sarah and Rosetta, still at play beneath the table, and see that my sleeping baby is securely in his crib. Sarah looks up at Bessie's cry. I shake my head, hold up my hand in reassurance that I do not feel, my insides in a knot. What can I possibly do? What can I say?

"All is well, Bessie." I take her by the shoulders and guide her back to her chair. On the floor is the sewing she dropped in her fright. I bend to retrieve it, hold it up, as if to examine her fine stitching, return it to her. "Beautifully done. You have a way with the needle, Bessie."

"What is the matter out there?" she asks, her voice tight. She is not giving up. "What is all that noise? Have we hit something? Is there another quake?" She lays the sewing aside. Starts to stand, but I hold my hand on her shoulder, shake my head emphatically.

"I'm not quite sure," I say to the women, running my eye from one to the other. "Not a quake. No, not a quake. Something in the river. Something we have to avoid."

"But the noise!" Bessie is young and not so easily calmed.

"Yes. Yes, I know. They need more steam to avoid whatever it is. Like when we were going through the falls," I say, forgetting for a moment that neither of these women went through the chute. They safely transported my children by carriage around the falls to Shippingport. "Yes," I say, "we had to force the engine to full speed for that. Very noisy. Yes, very noisy."

I stop to get my breath and clear my wits. What else can I say? I see in Sarah's face she knows there is more. She has traveled this river with me already. Not until she catches my eye, her gaze reinforcing my courage, does she resume her play with Rosetta as if nothing were amiss.

Bessie is less easy to settle.

"What is it we are trying not to hit? Did you see it?" She's trying to stand again, so I sit, motion her down beside me. "Not trees. Rocks fallen in from the bluffs?"

"I'm not sure, Bessie. I wasn't able to see just what it was. But I know it isn't a quake. They wouldn't want us below if it were. We are safe here. We simply need to be calm and wait."

"Wait how long? Is . . . is Mr. Baker all right?"

I remember she saw his alarm. "He's quite fine, Bessie. He just wanted to hurry me in so I would not be getting in the way of their work out there." I'm trying to make our situation sound as ordinary as I am able. "They are shoveling very hard to get our speed up so that we outrun whatever it is."

"But doesn't the speed put us in more danger of hitting things we can't . . . I mean, Mr. Jack can't see?" Her voice takes on a tone of urgency.

"Mr. Jack is the best pilot on the river. He has the keenest eye for things no one else is able to see. We are safe in his hands, rest assured." I fight to control the tenor of my voice. Still trying to pretend it is nothing more than logs or uprooted trees. Trying to pretend I am not equally—no, more—frantic myself.

Sarah knows me too well. "Rosetta, I think your dolls need more friends. They need a little settlement of their own. Let's give a doll to Mama and one to Bessie. You keep Bunny, and I'll take your wooden doll. We can have a real village, then, a settlement. Look, let's turn this chair on its side and hang a cloth over it to make a place where there can be a store for the ladies to come and buy their supplies." She's already on the floor, arranging the cloth over the upended chair. "Now then! How's that, little miss?"

Rosetta squeals and bounces her bunny into the make-believe supply store.

"Have carrots?" she pipes. "Need carrots."

Like the paddles outside, my heart is pounding. I feel it below my breastbone, in my throat, below my clavicles, even out toward my shoulder joints. My breathing is erratic and heavy. I take the doll Sarah offers me, her fingers warm and steady around my trembling hand.

"Why, yes," I manage to say, then cannot continue.

"Where carrots?" Rosetta looks put upon to have to ask.

"Oh, dear. Right here under the counter." I manage to speak again, a bit better this time. "Seems I forgot to put them out this morning. That's how fresh they are."

"I take one now, one later." Rosetta is bouncing her rabbit in great excitement.

"Here you are." I pretend to give her the carrots, handing her a handful of air.

The game of make-believe goes on and on, Bessie playing her part as a seamstress, fitting Bunny for a new outfit. There is no game for me and no pretend. I am terrified. More so because I cannot go see what is happening. The unknown of it all is as fearsome as knowing that there are Indians.

Yet perhaps they are harmless. It's possible. Maybe they just want to see *Penelore*, the fire canoe, as we've been told they call the boat. The Indians have been subdued, defeated even. General Harrison won the battle at Tippecanoe. Why am I so afraid? And why am I even here to be afraid, with my precious children? Why did I fail to heed the warnings of all those critics before this voyage? They were right and well intentioned. And I held them in hidden contempt as prudes and cowards, unwilling to face any challenge, too secure in their well-established homes. What would they think of me now, cowering here in this cabin with my toddler and my newborn?

Stop it, Lydia. Cease this now! I must. I must stop myself before I go berserk and truly lose my composure in front of everyone. In front of Nicholas, to whom I insisted I must come, must not be left behind. How must he be feeling out there? He must be terrified for us, for his family. How have I thought only of myself? Suddenly I can't conceive of what this must be like for him. What must he be feeling not only to be in danger but also to have allowed his family to be?

I lean over with my doll. "Dear Bunny, would you help me carry my packages, please?"

As I turn my head away, I'm aware of the portholes. I normally pay no attention to them. There is nothing to see through them except perhaps the rails and a bit of water beyond. Hardly scenic. But there they are. Perhaps I can manage a glimpse of what is happening through one of them. Sarah takes the doll from my hand as I reach toward her, and climb to my knees to stand. Her eyes take in the shift in my focus, and I see she understands.

I run to the first porthole at starboard, where the commotion is greatest. The view is too limited. I go to the next. Playtime has paused, with everyone staring at me. I am too frantic to urge them back to their play. There is motion on deck: running, figures moving back and forth too fast for me to identify them. Then Billy. Yes, it's him. I'm sure. He has a musket, but he holds it loosely, without aiming it. Is that a hopeful sign? Where is Nicholas? I hear his voice above the clamor.

"Stoke the fire! Harder!"

Beyond the rail, I barely make out the outlines of a canoe, long, filled with warriors, who are paddling hard. Another close behind. I hear their voices, strange and unfamiliar, pulsing in time with their paddles.

"Harder!" Nicholas again. "Harder! We are winning. We have the speed. We will outrun them! Baker, are we clear in front? Jack, are we clear? You have the channel sure?"

What about my husband's voice so calms my nerves? Nothing is different. Except that I have a sense of his presence, a sense of the power of this vessel. I want to run on deck. I know not to do so. I would only divert the men's attention from their desperate work to outrun these war canoes. How many others are there that I cannot see?

"Mama?" Rosetta is pulling on my skirt. "Mama, play dollies!"

Her urgent pulling arrests my attention. This is my child. She is more important than anything outside. Or in my head. And my sleeping infant boy. I must protect them. I must protect Rosetta from fear. I must take my doll and make another trip to the settlement store underneath the toppled chair.

"Bessie, could I have three yards of that blue calico, please? That will match Bunny's fur and make such a nice outfit. Could you help me sew it then? Your stitches are always so nice."

I pretend to hold up fabric to Bunny, and Rosetta twitters with delight.

*   *   *

Rosetta is in her bed, napping, with Bunny snug beneath her chin. Henry is awake with a satisfied tummy, his warm brown eyes blinking up at me. Sarah has righted the chair, and Bessie has folded the cloth. The paddles, the clanging of shovels, the shrill escape of the steam have slowed. All of us inside the cabin are acting as if life is normal when Nicholas walks unsteadily over the threshold.

"All is well," he says. "We have safely outrun them. You may rest easy. They can do us no harm."

I am in his arms before he can finish speaking.

"Who? What?" Bessie is suddenly frantic. "Do us harm?"

Over my shoulder, he says to her, "Mr. Baker has done us proud." He straightens his arms, moves me aside so that he may address Sarah and Bessie, as well. "Our strong vessel has been proven yet again. We have outrun the Indians. No human being can hold up against our power. Be assured, we are all safe."

"Indians?" Bessie's face has blanched. I did well to cover up our crisis.

Baker walks in the door behind Nicholas. Bessie jumps to her feet, heads toward him, then stops short. Propriety wins.

I take her hand and guide her into Baker's waiting arms. There is a small round of applause from the other three of us in the cabin. She lays her head against his chest.

Exhaustion rules. The men have pushed themselves to their physical limits, their efforts made more urgent by fear. I am exhausted from holding my own fears at bay. Joshua, the cook, bless him, has managed to assemble a small supper of ham, bread, and a bit of cheese, in spite of the day's commotion. I fear our larder is more in need of replenishing than I imagined. We've had no hunting opportunities ashore because of the quakes. Our great stash of coal is becoming depleted. Our supply of firewood has gone quite low, as well. There has been little opportunity to restock fuel, and what we have has been fiercely put to use outrunning the Indian canoes.

"Don't you fret, my dear," Nicholas assures me. How is it that he always reads my mind? "We will be in New Madrid soon enough and will restock there—both food and fuel. We should be well out of the range of the quakes at that point."

"What of fuel between here and there, Nicholas?" I ask.

"We've enough, Lydia. I'll confess, we used up most of our dry wood in this race today. We have a fair supply of dry, but not that most recently cut. We can dry smaller pieces well enough in the larger cabin overnight. Wood is not our primary problem at the moment. Rest is our greatest need. The men have been almost overwhelmed today. No one will have to take a long shift. With the crewmen standing watches of two hours on duty and six off, they will have ample time to sleep. That should leave us well prepared to continue on in the morning."

"Is it safe to stop for the night, Nicholas? You are sure it is safe?" I realize I am biting at my lips, and force myself to stop.

"We are well beyond the main Indian Territory, Lydia. There are far fewer of them dwelling along this stretch, and by and large, they are peaceful." He pauses, looks me straight in the eye. "I'm not even sure those who chased us meant to be threatening. There is no way to know. I am aware many of them attribute the quakes to our steam and cinders. Perhaps they were only curious. We will never know, but we could not chance an attack. Tippecanoe is only recently behind us. It could be construed as a defeat, or it could rile them up, so that they unleash more violent attacks." He holds me by both shoulders. "The point is, my love, we are safe now, and you must rest."

Indeed, every one of us must rest. This difficult journey will not be less so tomorrow.

CHAPTER 32

Darkness. Knees and elbows in my thigh, my side, my ankle. Pain shoots up my leg. Noise, like thudding steps, running. Voices in the night, yelling, urgent, chaotic. Nicholas jumping from the berth, across the cabin. Rough clanking as he tries to open the doors to the passageway, to the other cabin. And in the dark I see the blazing light of ascending flames!

I leap from the berth, grab my infant son, try to lift Rosetta into my other arm. So clumsy. I'm struggling. Sarah has me, has Rosetta. She's wailing now.

"Bessie, Bessie!" Where is she?

"Here. I'm here."

"Go to the deck. Run now! Run!"

"The baby—"

"I have him. Go! We're right behind you."

Tiger is beside me, moving like my shadow, if one could have a shadow in this darkness.

Outside the night is brighter; the comet is high above; the fog less dense. The men are running, running, buckets in hand, and line up to pass buckets from one man to the next. But still they must run short sprints. Not enough men for a continuous line.

"Here!" I hand the baby to Bessie, point Sarah to the stern. "Go. Go, Tiger. Keep them safe." I point, and he follows them, as close to Rosetta as he can get.

I leap into the line and grab the next full bucket, pass it on to Jacob, take an empty one from him, hand it to Baker. Bucket after bucket, one to another, back and forth, full and empty. Endless. Too occupied to feel the terror of the moment. Too occupied for anything but the next bucket. And the next. And the next.

My feet are freezing on the bare wood; my nightdress is clinging to me from spill after spill of cold river water. Suddenly Nicholas is running from the gentlemen's cabin, his nightclothes as soaked as mine. Out of breath, he props his hands against his thighs. Behind him the yellow flickers of light have dimmed and disappeared.

"It's out!" He stands, runs his hand through the shambles of his hair. "We think it's out, at least."

No one in the line speaks. The buckets spill or rattle, empty at our feet.

Nicholas rubs his hand over his forehead, down his face. I see in him a gesture I might make before I weep. He turns to look down the river. I want to go to him. I know not to do that. Not now.

"We need water still," he says more quietly, "to be certain nothing rekindles. Let's keep it coming until I tell you to stop. But you can work more slowly now."

He seems just now to notice me. "What are you doing, Lydia?"

"Hauling water."

"Where are the children?"

"At the stern. Safe with Bessie and Sarah."

"You don't have to do this, Lydia. Do you know that? Go to the children."

"I know I don't have to do this." I pause. "I need to do this. Do you know that?"

He takes a bit of time to answer. "Yes, I know that." He turns back through the threshold toward the gentlemen's burnt cabin.

I have no sense of time. No idea how long we have been passing the buckets. No sense of how much longer we go on passing them without the panicked urgency and with a growing fatigue, which makes me want to stop and lie down on the cold deck. My hands and arms ache as if they, too, were on fire. I'm afraid I may simply drop a bucket, when Baker takes a full one from my hands and sets it on the deck.

"Enough now," he says, taking me by the arm and leading me aft to my children. "Bessie, will you get Mrs. Roosevelt below now, please? She's soaked. And you can take the children, as well, Sarah. You'll need to get everyone warmed up. The fire is out."

"You are sure of that?" Sarah says.

"The men will guard against any rekindling. You will be safe." He looks at Bessie, who is holding my wailing and hiccoughing infant boy in her arms. I want to take him from her, but I cannot. My arms have nothing left in them.

Our cabin is filled with the smell of smoke. It is less offensive than the gaseous fog of the quakes, and somehow it ironically imparts the same sense of reassurance as the hearth at home. Henry is still crying, though less intensely. I can hardly move, but I feel my milk responding. Sarah has already dropped my wet nightdress to the floor and is slipping a dry one over my head, telling me gently to lift one arm and then the other. She guides me to my berth and helps me in. Bessie has my baby in my arms as soon as I lie down. I hear Rosetta clamoring for her mama. Sarah lifts her in on my other side, where she snuggles against me.

"Mama, I scary."

"I know, baby girl. I scary, too." I squeeze her as best I can.

Morning comes, but the usual activity is slow to follow. The night has taken too much from all of us. What little we had to give after the previous day is gone into deficit. Activity in the cabin and even out on the deck is sluggish. We have yet to un-hitch from the island and trust ourselves again to the current. Gabriel brings in the tea and biscuits Joshua has prepared, along with a few slices of ham. Rosetta has gone back to sleep in the berth, where she has been with me all night. Nicholas did not return to bed, and I've no inkling where he may be now that the day has come. What did he do about his wet clothes, I wonder, worrying. We cannot afford for him to get sick.

Henry is cooing contentedly in my arm as I drink my tea when Nicholas appears. His face is gaunt and haggard. He motions me to remain at the table as I rise to go to him.

"No, no. I'll have some tea with you," he says, "before I get back to work." He pulls out a chair and sits facing me.

Sarah is busy getting his tea. She lays a spoon beside his clenched hand.

"Sit down with us," he says to her. "You, too, Bessie." He motions her over.

"We had a fire," he says. Then laughs at himself.

We laugh with him at the absurdity of his announcement.

"Here is the story. We took on wet wood, as you know, and needed it dry in a hurry. Jacob and Oren laid it out near the stove in the other cabin, where we kept a fire going with small kindling and stove wood. They were to alternate short shifts." His agitation is obvious now. "That Jacob—damned negligent fool!" He stumbles on his words. "Fell asleep! Logs too close to the stove. And he fell asleep! It all caught fire!" The teacups rattle as his fist hits the table. I jump for fear they may break. His voice has reached a volume that is hard to bear. "I should throw him off the damned boat! Everything, everything I worked for is ruined now!"

There is a heavy silence around the table, except for the soft baby sounds Henry is making. Their bubbly rhythms do not lighten the atmosphere.

Nicholas began speaking with such composure. His distress will only increase. Conflict will not serve us. We cannot afford to alienate our crew. My poor husband! I absorb his despair and his rage. And yet we are still afloat. We are not sinking. Our men need to be supported in this chaos, as well. We must get to New Orleans. Without them, we cannot do that. Everything is not ruined. This vessel has already proven more than even its supporters believed possible. A cooperative spirit, among and with our crew, is essential to the remaining leg of the voyage, to overcome this crisis or to overcome another—Lord, help us—should there be one.

Not willing to hear the angry words he may utter next, I jump to my feet, hand Henry off to Sarah, and beckon my husband to come with me.

"Nicholas," I say, taking his arm and guiding him out into the passageway. These women do not need to see him like this. Rosetta does not need to be wakened by this turmoil. She does not need to see her father in this state.

Once out of their earshot, I attempt to calm him. "Everyone is exhausted, truly." I stop to assure myself he is hearing me. "Almost beyond endurance, Nicholas—as you know too well. You and I are equally depleted." I caress his cheek. "You are a competent captain, Nicholas. You were so wise to set up short shifts, back and forth, so the men could rest without falling asleep. It was a wise intervention, but the exhaustion was too much. Jacob was the one at the end of our line, lowering the empty buckets, filling them, and raising full buckets over the side all night. We owe the water in those buckets to him. He was simply overcome."

"Overcome? On duty?" Nicholas stamps his fist against the bulkhead. "Damned fool laid the wood too close to the stove. Fatigue is no excuse for idiocy!"

"Nicholas . . ." I touch his arm, feeling his own exhaustion and grief. Dare I ask? How would I handle another sinking boat? I wait a moment. "Are we safe?"

He hesitates, shakes his head in a kind of defeat, raises his eyes to mine.

I repeat my question.

"We are safe," he says. I hear in his tone that he is including us all. "No structural damage. The boat is still sound. Only cosmetic."

"What do you mean, cosmetic?"

"Floors. Carpentry in the forward cabin. No structural damage beyond that."

My stomach is in a knot. For a moment, I can say nothing. I am understanding his fury.

"All the beautiful carved woodwork?" I say, finding my voice at last.

"The bulk of it, I'm afraid. My great enticement for passengers!" The anger in his voice is moving back into rage. "If I could get that man off this boat, I'd throw . . ."

My husband's beautiful carved woodwork, his means to impress other men so that they join us on this boat. I run down the smoky passageway and through the doors to the other cabin, where the air is so dense, I am instantly coughing. Charred firewood is scattered across the floor. Odd buckets are strewn here and there. At the end near the stove, there is only black, half-burnt wood from floor to ceiling. The beautiful damask privacy drapes are gone, only scorched shreds remaining here and there. The bedding on those berths is black and seared, the ends of burnt feathers protruding from the soaked remains. And around and above, where beautifully designed and carved woodwork should be, there is only charred wood. Some is in place; some is burnt through and has turned to ash, which now covers the planks of the floor. The brass spittoons are scattered about or lodged beneath a fine chair or two, their leather blistered and eaten away by the fire.

Beyond weeping, I look about the cabin as if I'm lost. From behind me, Nicholas takes hold of my arms, turns me to him. We hold one another, immobile, for countless minutes before my tears make their way slowly onto his jacket. But no, it's not his jacket. I pull back. Whose jacket is this? I'm so confused. Then I remember. I see him in his wet nightdress, smudged with ash. My husband has not been back to our cabin till now. One of the men has lent him dry clothes. I look at his feet. A pair of worn leather slippers, too small by a size, cover his toes and most of his feet, his heels hanging out the back. For the first time, I laugh.

My husband looks down, laughs with me. Then he goes silent.

"It will never be the same. There are no repairs we can make. We will get it clean and at least tolerably presentable by the time we need to have a passenger or two," he says, with a great sigh. "And we'll have an entertaining tale to tell them, as well. Or an entertaining tale that will assure they never want to become passengers."

Now Nicholas laughs, and I laugh with him. What else is there?

CHAPTER 33

"Sixty miles yet to New Madrid," Nicholas announces over breakfast. Henry is falling asleep in his arm, while he tickles Rosetta under her chin with his free hand, making her laugh, milk sliding out the corner of her mouth and dripping down her chin. Sarah grabs a napkin to wipe it away. "Our plan has been to restock there for the remaining seven hundred miles to Natchez. I keep saying with every destination that we should surely be past the limits of the earthquake's devastation. It is inconceivable that the quakes have done such destruction even this far."

"But you believe we are moving past it?" Sarah asks.

"I hope so, Sarah. Though we have not seen any diminishment in the damage. But there has to be a limit. Destruction this far reaching is almost beyond comprehension."

Rosetta goes off in another gale of laughter as he tickles her chin once more. Sarah is quick with the napkin this time. Nicholas rises and leans over the crib to lay Henry down. The baby gives a little jerk, rubs his eyes, and settles as Nicholas tucks the blanket around him.

"So far, the day appears to be as good a one as we are likely to get with this air, so you may want to be out to observe for yourselves. We'll be passing Iron Banks and Wolf Island today. Sarah, you remember that island, a good forty square miles, timbered and prairied, where Mr. Hunter raises livestock in the middle of the river." He steps over the cabin's threshold. "Or again, you may simply wish for some rest at this point. Lord knows, we all could use some." And he's gone.

We occupy ourselves with housekeeping chores, taking turns at specific tasks so that each of us has a chance for a good stroll about the deck. The table is cleared, and the dishes are cleaned.

"Bessie, would you please take the dishpan and throw out the water?" I'm hoping to give her even a brief moment with Baker while the demands of the boat seem at a bit of a lull. Sarah is reading Rosetta the same little book she has read her every day since we embarked. I'm smiling at Rosetta's unbroken attention as I dry and carefully replace each plate in the secure vertical cabinet I designed to prevent breakage.

Bessie returns more quickly than I had hoped, carrying a shirt, and organizes what mending she has into a neatly folded pile. There is more than she can handle, even with her quick needle, given our seemingly endless disasters. She takes up the shirt, which I now see is one of Baker's, and begins working on it. There is a small rip in the sleeve. I stop for a moment to watch, picturing her at a hearth of her own, caring for him, far into the future.

From the door to the deck, I hear Nicholas calling my name. "Lydia! Come quick!"

I'm running, my whole body on fire from fear of another dire emergency, when he stops me at the door. "It's all right, Lydia." He puts his arms around me. "Nothing wrong. But I wanted you to see this as we pass."

"Iron Bank?" I say as we step out on deck. Things are looking familiar, then not so familiar.

"Look at the eddy." He points across the water toward the shore. "I've never seen one so large or quite so violent."

From our apparent safety far out in the midst of the swollen river, I see beneath the high bluffs an utterly horrific eddy. Roiling water at its edge is coursing round massive fallen stones from the cliffs, then back onto itself against the treacherous current. Just as Sarah joins us, we are stunned by the deafening cracking of a giant slab of rock as it peels from the bluffs and crashes into the water. Great waves from its impact slam into the boat and wash over the rails. We are suddenly drenched and laughing, our hands waving in astonishment, like children at play rather than our adult selves here in what has become this deadly endeavor.

How grateful I am for my simple homespun dresses, which are easily washed and quickly dried on the clotheslines running along the port side, designed to benefit from the wafting heat of the engine. So fortunate that none were hanging when we had to push that engine to its limits. The air has warmed again, so I have on only my shawl, and not a soaking wet redingote. Rosetta is quite giddy when Sarah and I enter the cabin with our dripping clothes and hair.

"Mama wet!"

"All right, little miss, you just got wet, too!" I pull her up into my arms and shake my wet hair at her.

Now I'm grateful our carefully stretched extra clothesline is tight enough to hold this new laundry!

By the time we've finished changing—and seen that the clothesline will indeed hold—Nicholas is at the door to the deck again, calling for all of us to come, even Bessie with baby Henry, who is awake now, sucking on the corner of his blanket. I'm a bit puzzled, but I lay down my knitting and take Rosetta by the hand. When we reach the deck, Nicholas heads forward and we follow. We make quite a little procession up to the bow.

There before us in the distance lie the remains of what must surely have been the largest island in the river. While Wolf Island's fifteen thousand acres of farmland had at one time parted the waters, visible to us now are only the crowns of bare trees, entangled with logs, pieces of wrecked boats, and debris from the floodwaters. At the far center, where only the remnant of a small plain remains unflooded, are gathered all the living livestock of the place. All the farm animals are uncharacteristically silent, save for random mooing or high neighing. The water is muddy brown from swirling sediment. Of the house and the stables once there, nothing can be seen.

Rosetta is giggling at the farm animal sounds, as if this were one of the games we play with her. I raise my face to Nicholas. He clearly sees my concern.

"Never fear, Lydia. I'm sure Mr. Hunter and his people were able to leave safely in their boats. They had quite a few, I remember." Something has occurred to him, I see by his brightening expression. "Else they would all be right there, milking the cows." He's waving his hand as he laughs. So contagious! We find ourselves laughing with him.

We are dry, and the chill has disappeared. How strange for the weather to continue to be so warm late in December! But, still, we are farther south, approaching Island Twenty-Five. At least it is pleasant to be out of doors. Even if the sights along the shore are disturbing, at least they are fascinating. Who knew the earth could be so devastating to itself? For a heartbeat, I think how devastating people can be to themselves—and to one another.

I keep hoping that we will pass the boundaries of the destruction, and I pray for signs that the effects of the quakes are lessening. But that is only a hope. In fact, as I see, and as Nicholas points out somberly, all signs indicate that hundreds, perhaps thousands, of acres of shore have fallen into the river, changing its course entirely and repeatedly. Neither what we charted in our flatboat nor Zadoc Cramer's reliable guide serves us now. Only Andrew Jack's uncanny vision and keen instincts about water levels, courses, and the vagaries of the water's color keep us safely in the channel. The farther along we go, the more we encounter uprooted trees, branches, unmanned boats and parts of boats, and other debris obstructing our passage.

In the late morning hours, we suddenly hit upon an area of the river where, instead of uprooted trees, we face a virtual forest that was long submerged, now shaken once more upright, the barren tops rising above the surface of the water. Our way seems nigh blocked off. Then the force of the river pushes the jam across to the side, and a way opens for us. With the paddles moving as slowly as is possible, the boat still makes progress. I jump as a paddle slams against a piece of debris. This happens regularly now, and I fret about one breaking from the force. What would we possibly do? Proceed with a broken paddle, of course. There would be no place to stop, let alone any means to make a repair.

The children are safely in the cabin with Sarah and Bessie. I am sitting in my chair at the stern, watching the crumbling banks for miles on one side and on the other, a vast thickening of barren trees in every direction, upright, uprooted, upside down, when I feel the paddle wheels suddenly stop and reverse. What have we hit? What now? I'm unequipped for another emergency. No inner resources remain.

The engine stops as I hurry to the bow. The obstruction is clear. And dire. Before us is a full blowdown—a dam of trees, driftwood, and debris, trapped and matted together so as to make our progress impossible. Nothing will give and float away this time to offer us an opening. Crew members hang over the rails, staring in defeated astonishment. I turn to see Nicholas, Baker, and Andrew Jack in pressing deliberation below the pilothouse.

Concerned, I dash toward them and stop short when I am within earshot. I manage to pick up pieces of their decision-making debate.

"Can we reverse ourselves out of this trap and find another channel?" asks Baker.

"No." Andrew Jack's response is instant. "There is no assurance of an open course elsewhere. It would be a useless waste of fuel. We've no idea how far back we might need to go or if an open course exists with deep enough water to pass."

"We will have to cut ourselves free." Nicholas sounds adamant. "There's no way to know how much time that may take. Or how far the blockage continues ahead. But it is the only alternative."

"Billy and I can go out and take stock!" Oren raises himself onto the rail. Clinging to a heavy rope, he disappears impulsively over the side and drops onto the logs.

"You have your balance?" Nicholas asks, leaning over to see.

"I do." Oren sounds so certain of his skills that I trust him.

"Then get to it," Nicholas says, the command unhesitating. "Get the axes and saws," he shouts to the crew standing by. Then to Billy, he says, "See just how far this thing extends."

Billy flips his leg over the rail, gets his bearings, and jumps onto the logs. He struggles for balance, and he and Oren reach out to support one another, going from tree to tree, log to ragged roots.

"Two more men and a rowboat," Billy yells. "Lower a boat full of saws and axes. There's wreckage of some boats in here. Don't see any people. But lots of wreckage."

Are those Hunter's boats? Where are the passengers? Or did the river tear the empty boats loose and smash them up here?

Nicholas rights himself and comes over to me. "Lydia, this will take a while . . . for reconnaissance and for cutting our way free. The deck needs to be open. The men will need the entire space. There will be a great deal of activity. You must stay in the cabin. Will you feel safe to witness the work?"

My husband recognized my fear of the unknown when the Indians chased us. I want more than I know how to voice to witness this work, to see how it is done, but I nod and move toward the door to belowdecks. Nicholas knows me almost as well as I know myself. He follows me and takes my elbow.

"Lydia, I know you want to be part of everything. I know it's hard to hold back. Once we get some solid information and a firm decision is made, I'll come and tell you. If it's deemed safe, you may even wish, no, *want*—I know you, you see—to observe some of the cutting process. Will that do?"

"Indeed, it will, Nicholas." I cock my head. "I'll be eagerly awaiting your next fulfillment of my wants." There is an intimate little gaze between us before we both laugh. I kiss his cheek and go my separate way.

As the day progresses, I hear the voices of the men, the rasping of saws, and the hacking of axes fast at work. I'm waiting for Nicholas. I want to be topside, where I can see the process, understand the work that hopefully will set us free to be on our way. I'm wondering if we might rescue some of this wood they are cutting for fuel when I hear a violent explosion.

The boat! The boat! I grab Henry from his crib and hand him to Sarah. Rosetta is clinging to my skirts. I free myself from her little hands as Bessie reaches for her. The fear on all their faces almost halts me. But I run. Down the passageway, out the door, onto the deck. I turn in every direction to find my husband. I reach out for balance. Something blazing hot hits the back of my hand. The pain is searing. Water, sand, stones, pieces of wood blast toward the sky! I back away, look up to see a towering geyser raging up beside us. Vile gases fill my nose and lungs. I gag. My hand is throbbing. I cannot move.

Someone grips me hard and pushes me into the door.

"You must stay belowdecks!" It is my husband. "Nothing is damaged. Do not come out! It is not safe out here."

I hold out my hand, where a blister is beginning to form.

This is a moment when everything seems to stop, and then he hands me off to Sarah.

"Take care of her," he says. And then he's gone.

Once in the cabin, I am shaking all over. Sarah is running for lard, I know. When she returns, she lays the grease carefully, lightly, thoroughly over the blister. Bessie, who is holding Henry tight, has retrieved a scrap of muslin from a drawer and hands it to us, Rosetta clinging to her.

"Mama hurt! Want Mama!" She is crying and struggling. Bessie holds her up close by me so she can see. I lean to the side and kiss her cheek, blow my breath against her skin as Sarah wraps the bandage around my hand and tucks the end under to secure it. I take Rosetta in my other arm, and she lays her head against my neck, sucking her thumb.

"Mama's all right," I say, running my good hand up and down her arm in reassurance.

"Yes, she is," says Sarah, stroking this little head and taking Rosetta from me. "See? Mama's just had a great adventure."

"I did!" It takes my whole concentration to pretend I am fine, but I do. "I just saw a huge fountain of hot water spraying straight up out of the river! And I got too close. Imagine that!" I tickle her tummy with my free fingers.

"Me want see, Mama! Want go see!" She's reaching for me.

Sarah saves the day, whirls Rosetta around. "Not right now," she says. "That fountain's too hot for you. Too hot for any of us. See how it hurt Mama's hand? We don't want Rosetta hurt. Or Bunny, either! Now, where is Bunny, I wonder. I think he's hiding. Let's go see if we can find him." Off she goes with Rosetta in her arms, playing a new game of hide-and-seek with Bunny and the dolls. What would I do without Sarah?

The explosive noise of the geyser and the scramble of boots on the deck diminish fairly quickly, more quickly than I might have expected. Nicholas appears at the cabin door and comes straight to me, reaching out for my hand.

"How bad is it?"

"Nothing to worry much about. Just a small blister. It will heal in a matter of days."

"That explosion—"

"Terrified me," I interrupt. "I thought . . . I thought the boat had exploded."

"Not the boat, Lydia. No harm done. But so close to us! Thank God, it did not blast up through that raft of trees where the men are working. No one got hurt except you, Lydia." He stops to look around the cabin, to include Sarah and Bessie, to take Rosetta into his arms.

"We've seen these erupt onshore." He seems to need to explain. "Sudden great geysers shooting up from the ground, water, gases, debris. You've seen them, I know." He waits for the women to nod. "This was the same thing, except close to the boat, here beside us in the water." He stops, seeming unsure of what else to say. "Lots of cleaning to do on the deck, but the real task remains to hack our way free through this blockage of trees. You ladies must occupy yourselves safely in the cabin. I am emphasizing *inside*!"

By midafternoon Nicholas comes to find me and we go topside. The men have worked themselves beyond their physical limits yet again, and they collapse onto the deck after the rowboat is raised. Nicholas fetches a bottle of whiskey to pass around. By turns, the men gulp from it. Their arms, I think, will be sorer than mine were from the buckets. They have cut and lifted all the day long. Wet, but not especially muddy, they must surely be cold, though the air is fairly warm.

"Did you hear it, Mrs. Roosevelt?" Oren asks as he swipes his mouth with his wet sleeve and passes the bottle on. "I bet you sure did. God-awful noise!"

"I thought the engine exploded, Oren. It terrified me."

"Yes, Oren, so she ran right outside and has her proof of seeing the geyser." Nicholas frowns. "Show them your hand," he says to me, pointing at the bandage.

"This is nothing," I say, "given the scratches and slashes you surely got while cutting us out of this maze of trees."

"We're all right," says Billy. "Just tuckered out again."

"All right," says Andrew Jack, who appears from the pilot-house. "Let's see if we can do this now. It's tight."

"All you men, off the rails." Baker is in charge now. He will be our eyes for Andrew Jack, using his arms in an intense silent language only the two of them decipher, but fascinating for us to watch.

Our hacked-out narrow opening snakes its way through the matted obstruction of trees and debris. I can only watch silently as Andrew Jack and Baker communicate and navigate the boat through the dense logjam. The opening is as narrow as the Indian Chute but, thank goodness, is not winding. Yet it's so narrow that I hear, over the thunderous rumbling of the earth below, the scrape of cut wood against the metal of the hull.

Overhead birds streak about in a continuing wild commotion, their cries unearthly. At the water's edge, where the entangled wood meets the sunken shore, I glimpse small corpses ensnared in the knotted limbs: squirrels, which we once saw en masse, rabbits, even a raccoon. The smell of death mixes with the noxious gases from the rifts in the earth. A piece of debris from some flatboat makes me wonder who rode on that boat. Workmen, a farmer, a family? And who survived. Whom might this boat be passing over? My stomach goes heavy within me.

A buzzard circles overhead. Then suddenly we are free, the entangled raft of trees and debris behind us. Free to chance our fate on this deadly river, for which we have no guide.

My thoughts are floating round again, like the foam that seethes on the surface of this chaotic water. My mind tends to go in that direction—or in the lack thereof—when I'm not physically in action. Much like this wild river we negotiate, my awareness refuses to still itself. And fate . . . Why am I thinking of fate and of surviving it? Is it possible we may not? No! We have managed every challenge, those we knew lay ahead and those we could never have imagined—Indians and geysers and fire. Earthquakes? No. No one could have imagined such a thing. Lasting for days, not minutes! Stretching for hundreds, perhaps thousands of miles! So violent! Yet fate has somehow brought us through, closer and closer to the goal we set long ago—going on three years, to be exact. Not counting the years before, when Nicholas was turning these ideas in his head like the sidewheels on this boat. Fate has been with us. What worse challenge could face us now? A question I know I should not ask.

Soon we will arrive at New Madrid, beyond the boundaries of all this violence.

CHAPTER 34

Daylight comes, and with it, new reasons for dismay as we churn our way downriver. Whereas in past miles, we witnessed banks that had fallen, slid, or crashed into the river, now we spot strange cracks in the earth, fissures wide and narrow, which grow more alarming as we go. Great jagged gaps in the earth's surface run parallel to one another, sink deeper than we can tell in many places, as if the earth has been torn apart in huge serrated strips that stretch endlessly across the land. Here and there a cow, a dog, a pig is stranded in the midst of a yawning cavernous stretch. Its cries of distress chill my bones. I want to cry out with it. I want this all to end. No more horrors, no more angst.

I wanted to be with my husband. Wanted adventure, discovery, something new. I have all three, but none in the way I foresaw. We expected danger, of course, especially while traversing the Falls of the Ohio. Other dangers along the way. Small ones, of course. How else would there be adventure? But how could we have imagined this? The earth shaking itself apart, tearing itself into fathomless canyons. The river we spent six months charting, raging itself into an unrecognizable and deadly torrent—as if it had not already been treacherous enough.

"Lydia, what are you doing out here?" Nicholas has come from the pilothouse.

He realizes I am trembling, puts his arms around me. I lay my head against him, put my arms around his waist, hold him until I can let him go without shedding tears.

"What are these rifts in the earth, Nicholas?"

"I don't have a name for them. Something from the violence of the quakes."

"This seems far worse than where we started with the quakes, Nicholas. I thought we would be coming into territory that would be less affected, not more." I'm holding his arm, as if to keep myself upright. "How wide are those tears in the earth? Can you tell?"

"Thirty or forty feet wide." Billy's voice comes from behind me.

"And deep?" I turn to see his face.

"No possibility of knowing that, Mrs. Roosevelt. Most likely, even if we were on land."

"If one of these opened under a settler's house . . . ?" I ask.

"The house would be gone," Nicholas answers. "Barns would be gone. It is fortunate, I suppose, that this land is as yet so sparsely settled."

Along the shore, the rifts are growing in magnitude. I am holding my stomach from increasing fear of what we may find downriver "What of New Madrid, Nicholas? Our fuel supplies? Food supplies?"

"We're bound to have seen the worst of it, I'd think. We'll be all right." Billy has coiled some rope and laid it to the side. His very presence is reassuring. "I don't know much about earthquakes but can't imagine this much more widespread. Already been days and days passing damage just here on the river." He stands up. "That's one hell of a quake!" Then immediately corrects himself. "Beg pardon, Mrs. Roosevelt. Not thinking."

"Billy, there is no pardon necessary. You've simply stated the truth."

He blushes. "Well. I'm off to tend the engine now. Thank you, Mrs. Roosevelt."

What a shame that men cannot simply be themselves in front of women! Well, what am I thinking? There is a limit, of course, but there is more than a hint of hell to this earthquake!

"Where are the children?" Nicholas seems distracted even as he asks.

"With Sarah and Bessie. In the cabin. Henry fed and asleep, Rosetta playing."

He is watching the shores, made distant by the flooding, looking like anything but natural shores. Out across what should have been a plain there stretches a lake. On the other side, the broken chasms of twisted earth. I know we should be reaching New Madrid today. We were so sure the conditions would be better here, but for now, they appear even worse. Anxiety is rising in my chest, affecting my breathing. The sight of these jagged, bottomless rifts makes me want to run, to hide, to escape, where there is no escape. There is only this endless unknowable river, with nowhere else to be. There is only here.

But here on the water is, at least, a place of greater safety, I remind myself. The river keeps us afloat and somewhat steady. We are not shaken to our bones. We do not have walls and chimneys collapsing on us. We are not in danger of plunging into one of these jagged, boundless chasms. Here on the water we are safe, if that is not an illusion. Even if it's an illusion, I will hold to the belief that we are safe. Here on the water, I am with my Nicholas, with my children, my trusted and cherished nurses, our trusty staff and crew, even our cook and his son. Here on this water, I should be nothing but grateful, and yet I am fearful beyond measure. But fearful of what? Of the unknown. Yes, the unforeseen, for which I am not prepared.

* * *

"We will put in at Chepousa Creek, above New Madrid," Nicholas announces.

Normally, the mouth of the creek should offer us safe harbor, even if there is damage to New Madrid. We should also find other rivercraft there, who may have news as to the conditions farther on. Andrew Jack and Baker are hard at work determining our route through a sunken forest of leafless cottonwoods and willows angled upstream, as if some great current had forced them in the opposite direction, against the flow of the river. The boat lurches sideways as a raft of matted trees and logs slams into us. Andrew Jack has us steady in a matter of minutes. I begin to relax, but I use that word loosely—I'm just a bit less nervous than at the peak of my anxiety.

"We'll be there soon, Lydia. Everything will be better." My husband knows me so well, even without my saying a word.

I lay my hand on his arm. We are near to rounding the great bend that will bring us into sight of New Madrid, high on its magnificent bluff.

"Stop the engine!" cries Baker.

The shock of his command flies across the boat. The crew bolt to obey it. The released steam hisses through the air. Our motion grinds down to a bare turn of the paddles.

In the distance New Madrid lies almost in the water, its bluffs broken and fallen, its houses collapsed. Instead of ragged fissures, huge eruptions of earth and sand have opened yawning holes across the landscape. Logs, pieces of board, parts of houses and fences float in the water. Upturned boats and a stable door. A lake that had not existed before stretches almost into the town. Livestock wander helplessly through the rubble in a din of agonized discord. More horrifying yet, a graveyard has been torn open—uprooted coffins and partially decomposed dead lay on the broken ground or swirl aimlessly in the foaming water. I gag and vomit over the rail.

High on the remaining bluff, beyond the collapsed town, is a cluster of makeshift tents with people moving about. Some have spotted or heard us. They stare down at this unknown fiery thing on the water. Beneath us, with the engine stilled, I hear ominous rumbling deep in the earth. At the edges of the shattered town, I make out a gathering of people, staring, waving, and calling madly. The boat draws slowly closer. I make out individual faces now, haggard and terrified. Does this boat terrify them? Or is it the quakes?

Nothing we have seen compares to this destruction. But then, nothing we have seen has been such a town as this, only scattered settlements and villages, but here is a town of nearly four hundred residents or more. Thank goodness, many seem to have found refuge on the remaining bluffs, but there must be near a hundred, possibly more, at the water's edge. There are overturned and untethered boats floating around among the coffins and debris. A group of men are struggling at the landing to secure a rowboat. In the commotion, a man reaches out to help a woman into the boat. She has an infant in her arms! In minutes the boat is loaded, then overloaded, water sloshing over its edges, impeding a man's attempts to row it toward us. Behind it, another equally overloaded boat pushes away from the landing. They are coming to us for rescue!

Nothing in my previous terror touches what I feel as I realize the truth of our situation. I can barely breathe. I am beyond tears. Immobilized as I apprehend the horror of what is taking place. I see the faces. I see the woman with her infant. I see other children, clinging to parents, crying. I see men struggling to row these encumbered boats. I see the grim faces of these men. I cannot turn my eyes away.

There is a tug at my skirt. "Mama, who that?" She is pointing at the boats. "Playmates, Mama?" Tiger is close behind her, as if guarding her.

Her tug, her voice, her presence rouse me from my paralysis. Onshore, yet another overloaded boat is attempting to push off. If we take on the passengers of one of these boats, we must take on the passengers of all of them. We cannot choose. If we take on all these passengers, we all are lost. They are trying desperately to survive. If we take them on, we cannot care for them; we haven't food enough, supplies enough. We haven't fuel enough to navigate with such a load. We may not have enough to save ourselves. If we take on the passengers of even one boat, we are lost. We all are lost. No one will survive.

"Take her below," I say to Sarah, who comes running behind Rosetta. I see by her face that she has already assessed the situation and understands the impossibility of the choice to be made. She grips my arm momentarily as I lean down to say, "No, no playmates this time, love. You and Tiger run inside now and get Bunny. I think I heard him calling for you to come back."

I stand up straight to see that Nicholas has been watching. His eyes glue themselves to mine. Neither of us speaks. He turns, steps across to Baker, signals to Andrew Jack, and I hear the engine engage, the predictable clank of shovels in what little coal remains. Instead of rounding to, the boat moves forward, in danger of swamping the rowboat closest to us now. When I take my hand from the rail, it is shaking like that of an old woman suffering from the palsy. I know I dare not try to walk. From this spot where I am rooted, I see nothing but the faces of those left in our wake.

CHAPTER 35

The hush that envelopes the boat for the remainder of the day is broken only by the continuing desolate cries of the birds overhead, circling aimlessly, seeming lost in every direction. Birds of untold species, some colliding in the air, none finding a place to land safely: ducks, crows, pigeons, birds of a brilliant color and drabbest gray, birds with a wide wingspan and others tiny. But not one living sparrow falls to the deck. The sky is full: a flock of swans caught in their migration, a great blue heron gliding and flapping, gliding and flapping. Even an eagle high above. And vultures, waiting.

Below, on land, more numerous huge crevasses, blowholes, surrounded by piles of sand and blackened rock. Around a bend we see a geyser of sand, water, and stones shooting out of the ground, spouting perhaps as high as thirty feet or higher. More bluffs crumple into the river. Sandbars emerge where there had been none, and islands that are landmarks disappear. Other islands form where the violent current has created chutes between collapsed land and the remaining shore. Around us are threatening snags and new eddies. Rafts of matted wood. Empty canoes and upturned rowboats. Barrels, holding anything from whiskey to flour, if they are still holding anything at all, bobbing in the current.

Baker and Andrew Jack carry on their silent communication. Now and then, there is a low-voiced command near the engine and a quick reply from one of the crew. I have recovered myself enough to go below, nurse Henry, and rock Rosetta to sleep for her nap. As I try to sing her a lullaby, my voice cracks.

"Sing, Mama." She runs her finger across my lips.

After a moment, I say, "I must be coming down with a bit of a sore throat, my sweet." I try to hum a little. Then there is only the sound of the chair rocking.

With both of my children asleep, I pace the deck, watching the wreckage of the land and the forest, unsure now if we will ever see the end of it. My thoughts turn, unwanted, to the dire predictions of fearful squatters far back upriver before this all began—that we are the Devil Ship, that our appearance and that of the comet are signs of the end-times. What I see and feel is indeed apocalyptic.

At dusk we approach the village of Little Prairie, or what little is left of it. The town has disappeared, sunken into the earth or devoured by the mass of broken and uprooted trees. What ruins remain are deserted. Far in the distance I glimpse a small group of stragglers moving away from the river. There is no one else to be seen.

It is no longer possible to determine exactly where we are in the river. The quakes have deformed and reformed the land and water to the extent that nothing we depend on for guidance has any meaning. Our coal has dwindled to almost nothing, and it is essential that the men cut new supplies of wood. Ahead of us, fortunately, is a large island, still wooded.

"What island is this?" Nicholas yells up to Andrew Jack in the pilothouse.

"Not rightly sure, but I'm figuring it's Thirty-Two. We should be thereabouts, at any rate."

"Ah, yes," Nicholas says to me. "We will round to and tie up at the lower end. The island is large enough to shield us from the masses of trees and the debris of boats coursing past us in this violent current. Well, not always past us. Sometimes it doesn't miss." Nicholas chuckles at himself, and I try to join him. "But we should be well protected if anchored and unmoving. The island will shield us."

Here where the island divides the river, its forces and all its deadly flotsam swerve out to each side, leaving us in a relatively tranquil space at the end of the island. The men row out with axes and saws, tie us up as distant from the trees as feasible. The remainder of the day is spent cutting wood and ferrying it to the steamboat in the rowboats. By evening we have a fair supply on board to get us downriver to the next possible stopping point.

Everyone on board must rest. There is no danger here for which to stand watch, though three of the men are sleeping, or at least resting, while stationed on deck at the bow and stern. If there is some unexpected need, they will be quick to rouse from their slumber. Nicholas falls into the berth and instantly begins to snore lightly. Exhausted. As am I, though I cannot fall asleep. Not because of the faint noise from my husband, which soon resolves when he readjusts his head a notch. No, tired as I may be, faces from those in the rowboats at New Madrid materialize behind my closed lids, which fly open again with the pounding of my heart.

Sometime in the middle of the night, Henry stirs and whimpers. I am instantly at his crib. Holding him to me, I can think only of the mother and infant at the landing. I enfold my own beside me, cherishing his warmth, listening to his quiet breathing, counting each breath as they come, his little hand opening and closing on my skin as he nurses.

I count the noisy banging of driftwood as it slams against the sides, sometimes hard enough for the boat to tremble at the impact. Yet not enough to wake my sleeping husband or, fortunately, my children, though I hear movement in the women's berths and suspect they are no more asleep than I. These blows are hard enough to make me grateful that we secured ourselves in the shelter of the island.

Somewhere toward morning, I hear a series of low rumbles, not so thunderous and threatening as I have heard before, but disturbing, nonetheless. A sudden swing of the boat alarms me. A strange tugging. I half raise myself on my elbow, taking care not to awaken Henry. I'm expecting Nicholas to leap over me at any second, but he does not wake. Whatever the disturbance, it is over as quickly as it came, and the boat is still. In the dark, I hear the crewmen's feet on the deck, back and forth, for several minutes, then Billy's subdued voice. The words are unintelligible, but his tone is level. Quiet prevails for a moment; then the air is filled with the wild cries of lost birds in the dark. Animals, too, are so distressed I have difficulty differentiating their howling and shrieks. I recognize only the screams of a panther, so human, so horrifying.

Nicholas is still sleeping as light creeps through the portholes. I have resisted every temptation to wake him. I have managed to contain myself through the long night. No longer able to subdue my restlessness, I lay my baby on the berth, then rise and don my heavy robe. After taking Henry in my arms, I make my way topside to determine if the dawn is visible in the foggy atmosphere. The men are up, commencing their tasks, when I hear a loud cry from Oren, another from Jacob. Chaos ensues.

Baker runs toward the cabin, sees me near the door, and with urgency says, "We need Mr. Roosevelt!" He does not stop or even slow down. "We've come unmoored. Where is Jack?" he demands, as if I would know.

I haven't moved when Nicholas shoots past me and out the door, with Baker trailing him. Inside, I hear the stirring of Rosetta and the women, their voices mingling indiscernibly.

"What is it?" I call out behind the running men.

No one answers.

"We've lost our mooring!" Nicholas is yelling at no one, trying to orient himself in this dire situation after just waking from a heavy sleep. "We're drifting out of control."

Andrew Jack appears. "We are not moving, sir. Thank God, the hawser's caught on a snag." He reaches out to pull on the heavy rope. It does not give.

Billy repeats the action. "Yep, caught on something."

The men crowd at the rail, yelling. I see the wild flailing of arms. I'm out on deck with my baby. What else can happen to us? My alarm is overwhelming. I sense an instability of the boat. The deck is at an angle. Have we fallen on a snag, not just caught one with the hawser? Are we sinking?

The men are too clustered together for me to see the difficulty. I lean against the rail some distance from them, holding my baby. They do not realize I am here. My alarm and my caution are equal. I am instinctively protecting Henry and myself from being unknowingly run over by one of them.

"Get the saws!" Whose voice this is, I cannot distinguish.

Jacob separates from the group, dashing for a saw. I turn back to the rail, and then I see. The river is vast around us. We are unmoored. We have been floating for who knows how long during the night. Where are we? Andrew Jack will know. At least we are caught on a snag and not wrecked or grounded on some sandbar that has risen, unknown, from the bed of the river.

"I don't know where we are!" Andrew Jack, our competent pilot, is distraught. "I have nothing to guide me," he says. His voice is flat and defeated. "We are lost."

In the disquiet that follows, Billy notes my presence and points my husband toward me. I am weak with fear as he comes to me. He puts his arms around me in an embrace that holds our baby with us.

"It will be all right, Lydia. I promise you, it will be all right."
Still holding us, he turns to watch Andrew Jack's surveillance
of our position.

Andrew Jack has quieted himself, taken control. He is scan-
ning the water, noting any differentiation in color, the raw
limbs and tops of trees behind us, the shores on each side. All at
once his face takes on an expression of shocked disbelief. He is
pointing toward a wrecked boat caught in the mangled
branches of a half-uprooted cottonwood.

"Look! Do you see that? I noted that last night, when we
tied up," he says. There is a long pause, as if he's working to be
sure what he says is true. "We have not moved. We are exactly
where we were. Still right in position!"

Moored to the island! But where is the island? There is only
water and treetops. The island is gone. Sunken! How can an entire island sink out of sight? A whole island, covered with trees,
hiding wildlife! An island with which we had shielded ourselves from battering river debris! Our shield is gone. No wonder the night was so noisy. Trees and debris slamming into us.
Here we are, near the very tree to which we tied up last night.
And it is sinking. Slowly pulling us with it into this deadly
river!

The saws arrive. Billy and Ezra grab the handles and are
abruptly at work, the saws rasping against the cords of the
rope, severing our hawser from the sinking tree. One last saw-
ing motion against the cords and the rope breaks free. The boat
jerks, then again, and comes level. We are liberated. And untethered.

Andrew Jack watches the men heave in the severed hawser,
then examine its raveled end, shaking their heads, pointing at the
disappearing tree. As they become aware of the pilot in their
midst, the men move back to give him space. He studies the situation with perplexed concentration. He is holding the Zadoc
Cramer and a hand-drawn map of the river made from our

charting notes. He glances at it and at the river, stretched wide on either side of us and flowing on seemingly forever in front. On the banks are only the riven earth and the fallen shoreline far away. Behind us the water covers a sunken island, one that vanished on us in the night, leaving only bare crests of empty trees, except the lone mangled cottonwood holding the wreckage of a boat.

CHAPTER 36

"If I am right," says Andrew Jack, "we are entering a length of the river noted for numerous bends and meanders, though with the quakes and flooding, who can predict what we may find?" He lays his hand-drawn map on the table. "That does not mean that I am not still presently lost." He lifts his hand and offers us a bewildered smile.

Bessie and I are in the pilothouse, listening to potential plans, while Sarah sits with the napping children in the cabin. I want Bessie with me, as she has had so little time to even have a glimpse of Baker during all our recent crises. A glimpse is all she has at the moment, but it is better than none. I note her lowered face, the faint curve of her lips.

"How shall we determine the channel, then?" Nicholas's apprehension is clear, but the tone of his question expresses his unfailing trust in our pilot.

"As we have been doing," Andrew Jack says. "By keeping ourselves with the fastest-moving water."

"We will be hitting blockages in those bends. And in the sharpest turns, the deep water will bring us nearest the far bank and the treachery of falling trees." Baker has joined in, at last. Bessie's eyes are nowhere but on him.

"The men cut us through those rafts of wood and debris once already. Upcoming ones can hardly be worse." I'm stunned at myself for entering this discussion, as if I belonged in it. I would like to step back, but I do not. It is done.

"You are correct, Mrs. Roosevelt." Andrew Jack nods his head politely. No, more than politely. As if my input was simply appropriate. "We've a long way to go still, something more than four hundred miles to Natchez, possibly six hundred to New Orleans, but our progress now should be a good bit faster, if my sense of the river is correct. I believe we should be at a safe mooring at the mouth of the St. Francis by December twenty-third. I'm thinking we are likely to find any number of refugee vessels there, seeking safe harbor, and we may well find useful news from other parts. In any case, we must plan on a stoppage there to clean out the boiler and make any necessary repairs. That boiler is full of silt—mud, in fact. Miracle it's still working."

"It's all due to the fine design," my husband announces. He waits a moment to let his comment sink in, then throws his head back, and everyone joins in his laughter.

Baker winks at Bessie and their intimate laughter is disguised by that of the rest of us.

Andrew Jack's predictions are on target. We have found our way through the challenging meanders and cut a narrow path through an endless series of tangled rafts of wood. Now that we are past the sharpest bends and into a relatively straight-forward stretch of the river, our steady progress is impeded only by unexpected sandbars that did not exist before. Many are just below the surface and virtually invisible to me, but Andrew Jack's talent for spotting danger eases my tension. We are maintaining a fair rate of approximately nine miles an hour.

The noise has lessened, other than that from the endless slamming of the paddles into floating pieces of wood. The sudden explosions of noise still make me jump, which makes Rosetta laugh!

The air is less noxious, so I take the children onto the deck and let Rosetta play with Tiger, who is so gentle and entertaining to her. The weather is warm, but less strangely so, since we are farther south. Along the banks, there are still caved-in bluffs and wide empty spaces where areas full of great canebrakes have crumpled into the river, which is ever congested with uprooted trees and snags. Rosetta notices these things, pointing them out like it is a game, but she is not disturbed. For her, they are simply novelties that pique her curiosity. Her little mind is far more absorbed with Bunny and her guardian, Tiger. I sit on the deck once more, as I did at the beginning of our voyage, a time in which I could never have conceived of the violent terrors we have survived. I thought then that the Indian Chute at the Falls of the Ohio would be the greatest challenge Nicholas and I could possibly face, one that I knew and expected to face.

As we progress downriver, there are trappers and fishermen along the way, from whom we happily purchase replenishment of our food supplies. All of them have their own tales of the quaking earth, disoriented birds and other wildlife, the destruction of settlements, and of their individual fears as they made their way through. Now along the remaining shore, we begin to see camps of fugitives from the quakes, refugees from the terrible devastation upriver. Their faces show the haggard anguish I hold in my mind of those seeking to escape in New Madrid, those whom we could not save and still survive ourselves. I begin to have nightmares again, their faces appearing in my slumber, dashing hopes of sleep.

"Lydia," Nicholas says to me, "would it have been better that we sacrificed ourselves? You do understand that is what would have occurred? Our children, ourselves, Bessie, Sarah, our men. And to no avail. Do I need to say it again?"

"No, Nicholas. No. Understanding is not the problem. Knowing is not the problem. My guilt at our incapacity to give them aid, my emotional state is the problem." I shake my head, and he takes my face in his hands.

"You are guilty of nothing, Lydia."

"I see their faces every time I close my eyes, Nicholas."

"Perhaps, Lydia," he murmurs, "it is not so much guilt as grief. This unprecedented quaking of the earth has thrown more grief upon this land than we can imagine. How should you and I escape that grief, even though we have survived this well?"

My eyes fill, and then I weep. I cannot stop myself. My husband holds me as I sob. He does not try to help me stop. He does not attempt to comfort me. He lets the storm run through me until it is done. Only then does he let me go.

Natchez is not now so distant. The river and the shores seem progressively more stable. The tremors continue, but with less ferocity. The rumblings from deep in the earth seem deeper still, farther into the depths. There are random camps of refugees, but fewer now. I recognize this as a result of the constraints of travel and of the refugees being farther from the origins of their flight. Now more often we note people onshore who are bearing shovels and hoes. Like Rosetta, they exude excitement and curiosity. Waving enthusiastically, these folks exhibit no fear of our fiery trail of smoke. Or of the slapping rhythm of our paddle wheels.

The trees and the landscape are not only less damaged, but have been transformed by farmers. Beyond the randomly wooded banks stretch what seem to be wide fields of fertile farmland. Other shores are so thickly forested with willows that, from a distance, the woods appear to be dense fields of grass, with no possible way through them. Farther along, giant live oaks appear, stretching their moss-hung branches so far out that the trees are wider than they are tall, wider than I might believe if someone simply described them to me. Or if I had not seen them before from the awning-covered roof of our flatboat. These trees seem as old as the earth itself somehow, with pale-colored beards waving to and fro in the breeze.

A longer time on the deck, fresher air, room to run and play with Tiger have energized Rosetta, as if she needed to be invigorated. Her innocence and verve have enlivened me. Bessie, bless her, runs and plays along with her, then sits on the decking with Rosetta in her lap and Tiger lying as close as he can manage, his head in Rosetta's lap if he can manage. Henry is smiling and laughing now. Is there anything more endearing than an infant's laughter? He stays in my arms most days, cooing, waving his arms. I am only indoors to nurse him, as long as weather allows us to be out. The river is rapid in its course but rarely so wicked now. We feel safe enough to make a pallet for Henry on the floor and give him some freedom of movement. It will be a month or two yet before he rolls over, but the waving arms and feet are pure joy to me—until the woman with the infant on the New Madrid landing drifts into my consciousness.

Sadness presses downward through my chest and back, and I am without means to release it. In those difficult moments, I find I must rise, must walk, must speak to Nicholas, or anyone, about some trivial matter. Shall I carry this desolation all my life? I cannot imagine any way to let it go. I can only pray each time that the people of New Madrid have succeeded or will succeed in caring for themselves, rebuilding their town as they built it at the beginning, sowing and reaping their crops in spite of the torn earth of their fields, obtaining ammunition for the hunt, and in simple caring for one another.

Returning to my children and Bessie, I am aware that Baker

seems to have a moment of respite from his piloting duties as we navigate this relatively even course. Sarah has come out after cleaning the table and sits in the chair beside my little family, Sarah who is virtually family to me. We have shared such experiences from the moment of my marriage, and even before, when I was such a girl, determined to have my way. I think about all the people on this boat, what we have survived together, about the certain intimacy that has developed in our dependence on one another, our trust in each other. We are like family at this point, far more so than any family I have ever experienced.

I'm lost in considering this thought when Baker turns toward us. His smile lights up the atmosphere, and I see Bessie responding, lifting Rosetta out of her lap to rise. I reach over and receive my daughter into my lap. She flings her arms around my neck, kisses and kisses my cheek. Baker holds out a hand to assist Bessie's standing. When she glances at me for permission, I nod. Of course.

Sarah and I have barely had time to turn Henry over and retrieve Bunny for Rosetta when Bessie leaves Baker smiling at the rail. She is dancing her way to us. He is close behind her, smiling.

"I'm to be married!" she announces. Her joy is contagious. Of course.

Baker has caught up with her now. "I asked permission of Mr. Roosevelt, and Bessie has given me her consent. I hope this is welcome news for you, Mrs. Roosevelt." So polite and proper!

"Indeed, it is, Mr. Baker." I stand and put my arms around Bessie. She is barely younger than I. "There is a requirement, however." I put my hands on his arms. "You must make this young lady a happy woman!"

"Exactly my intent, Mrs. Roosevelt!"

Bessie's happiness is contagious, as is Baker's. When Nicholas comes to affirm that I have heard the announcement, he is even a bit flirtatious with me. I imagine that Henry will sleep in his crib tonight.

"Would we give them the gentlemen's quarters, now thoroughly cleaned, even though charred, if I can obtain the consent of a clergyman at Natchez to come and perform the wedding rites here on the deck? You don't expect passengers for this last leg of the journey, do you, Nicholas?" I'm conversing almost in a whisper with only Nicholas, planning a surprise.

"What an idea, Lydia! Only you, my love! Only you!" His lips are warm on mine before he continues to speak. "Of course. If there should be paying passengers, we would be obligated to take them—for the finances of the project. You know that, of course. In spite of the damage. And in that case, Andrew Jack could move into the cabin with the passengers. I'm sure he would not mind for the end of the journey. The bridal couple could have that private small cabin space. Yes, that would work. Jack is such a gentleman himself. But yes, if the gentlemen's quarters are not occupied, they shall be yours. I mean theirs." He gives me another kiss.

Well, now I have a joyous project to occupy me, to entertain my mind and keep me busy in the little time we have before Natchez. I'm trying to remember anything at all about the Natchez church and clergy. The clergy hereabout are almost all itinerate preachers, traveling widespread multiple territories, often sleeping on the ground. Hopefully, there is one in town. I'll inquire from ladies who are certain to be gathered for our landing and send Billy off with an inquiry as soon as the docking procedures are finished. Sarah and I occupy ourselves with the children, giving Bessie time to take advantage of small breaks with Baker. Their faces as they come together near the rail make me remember my excitement each time I came near Nicholas as he and my father worked on one project or another. I remember the overwhelming love I felt in his presence when at last my father surrendered and granted permission for our marriage. My gratitude for my husband grows, for his understanding of my essential need to be with him, to face discomfort and inconvenience, to share his life and his journeys, despite the treacherous unexpected dangers.

CHAPTER 37

My mind floats back to our previous approach to Natchez, the three crewmen and Sarah barely recovered from the fever, Nicholas still too ill to go ashore, the men off in the saloons — and perhaps elsewhere along the infamous stretch of misconduct in "Natchez-Under-the-Hill." Will those high bluffs still be in place when we arrive? Will I recognize the town? Well, it may seem the same to me from a distance, since I never went onto the shore. That is, until the river dropped us on a snag and the boat sank. Oh, those hours of bailing out the boat before Sarah and I finally gave up and let it sink. I think how sore my arms were then from lifting water out of the boat, how sore they were only days ago from lifting water into this boat to extinguish the fire.

If the town is ripe for it, I wonder if Nicholas will have the courage to show off the boat in spite of the damage. He was so proud of his handsome hand-carved woodwork. There will be grief to pay with the partners, especially Fulton, for that expense, I know. Fulton is not a favorite of mine, and I wish both Nicholas and my father would free themselves of him. So ostentatious! He's even at work with the czar of Russia to obtain the rights to operate his steamboats out of Saint Petersburg! He blamed Nicholas for every expense. Most of which we could not avoid. However, the partners will never see the actual damage from the fire. They will see only the damning columns of figures on a sheet of accounting paper. They think only with their pocketbooks and never with their hearts.

The boat will be repaired, though perhaps not so grandly. It will carry passengers on future trips, even though we had none this time. And I hope we have none in Natchez, which we will soon approach.

The dock is crammed with spectators. By my quick estimation, there must be hundreds bustling about to see our steamboat. The noise of our engine has alerted the entire population of our arrival. Indeed, this town has grown and changed immensely since our disastrous first docking here, though it is clear that the area "under the hill" still carries a salacious reputation. I am exhilarated at the crowd. Much the size of the one in Pittsburgh, only celebratory this time! I make out the faces of some friends. There appear to be planters and slaves. Oh, my! I see Zadoc Cramer himself! That will be quite a conversation! And Indians! An entire assemblage of them with native instruments serenading us in. My heart is racing as I lift Rosetta onto the rail to see the festive welcome awaiting us. Nicholas arrives, so handsome in his finest attire, and reaches out to steady her in her excitement. I pull at my finely corded spencer jacket and straighten Rosetta's bow in her hair. Everyone is at their best. Along the rail, Sarah with baby Henry, Bessie with Baker beside her, and Billy are all waving back to the hallooing crowd.

The engine is quieter now, and Andrew Jack has us rounding out to come into this dock, where an unexpected and astounding welcome awaits us. Billy glances back, nods, and returns to the engine, where the men are slowing the loads as we make ready to approach. Something is wrong. I'm feeling disoriented, perplexed, as if we are drifting downriver, past the dock, instead of heading straight in. The current has us in its grip. At the dock there is a shift in the mood of the spectators as, indeed, we float farther and farther away from them. They are confounded to see us slipping past.

My heart is still racing, but now from fear. What can be wrong with the boat? After all we have been through, survived, we are unable to dock? Do we have undetected damage to the boat? The paddles? The rudder? What is it? Nicholas is swearing like a pirate. I know I will cry. Am I crying already?

I lower Rosetta into Sarah's hands. Bessie has baby Henry now. They are making their way belowdecks. I want to go with them and can't. There are tears on my face. We have succeeded at too much to be disgraced now. I'm watching my husband's face as he watches the crowd, watches the river, watches the dock and the shoreline as we pass by at the whim of the river. I want to hold him, want him to hold me, but all I have is this railing.

Voices yelling behind me turn less frantic. The crew are loading the furnace as rapidly as they can. Smoke and fire belch from the stack. The engine is shut to build up steam. A shriek escapes from the top of the stack as it is opened again, and the engine picks up power. The paddles work faster and faster. We are going upriver, back to the shore we just passed, coming into the sight of the crowd. We are there. Pulling in. The crowd is cheering madly.

Billy and Oren leap over the rail onto the solid dock, then pull the ropes and wind them fast around the cleats. Done! Secured! They turn and raise their arms in victory to the roar of the onlookers.

We are here. We are docked. Safe yet again. Safe. Again.

Nicholas stands beside me and wraps his arm around my

waist, his fingers gripping my side under my short spencer. The only fitting response is for me to smile up into his drawn face, frozen in a rigid smile for the benefit of the crowd. The indignation over whatever error we combatted has hold of him still. He can hide his anger from others, but not from me.

The town is elated! Men reaching out for a handshake with Nicholas. Firm congratulatory slaps on his back and his shoulders. I am jostled wildly due to the eagerness of this dock full of people, all wanting to greet my husband, the man who has achieved the impossible. They are also wanting to go on board. I see them herding up the gangplank and fear someone will fall, but Andrew Jack has come down from the pilothouse to speak to the would-be intruders and explains with the politest simplicity that tours will be available tomorrow, after the boat has been examined, cleaned, and deemed ready for visitors. He handles all this like a master. His firm voice is effective, and I am grateful.

On the deck, Bessie stands beside Baker, my baby securely in her arms. They are betrothed. Soon to be wed, if my plan works without a hitch. I visualize them in the near future, holding a child of their own so snugly.

As to my plan, I must make some immediate inquiries. There are ladies I know in this crowd. In fact, I am being encircled by them. Their gathering round me offers a shield from the crowd. Ah, relief from the jostle of the spectators trying to get to Nicholas and the boat.

"Lydia!" It's a lady I should know and don't.

Why can't I remember her name? But others gather closer, calling my name, bombarding me with curious questions, and even quiet admiring comments about having my baby on board. At the periphery, I detect a glance or two of disapproval, but what does that matter to me? I'm answering questions as fast as I can, turning from one lady to another. The speed of the discourse makes knowing their names superfluous. I am saved from humiliation by their very enthusiasm. Now is the time.

"Ladies," I say, raising my hands to quiet them. "Are any of the clergy available in town at the moment? Or has a church possibly been built? I need the services of a preacher."

"Has something happened?" one of the ladies asks in grave concern.

"No. At least nothing bad," I answer. Now how untrue is that? "Something very exciting! We have a betrothal on board and would like to offer them a very special wedding this day."

Murmurs of excitement run through the group. The woman who first called out to me—I must remember her name—steps forward.

"Reverend Oscar Guston is here. He arrived only yesterday. Shall I send someone for him?"

"First let me confer with the betrothed," I say and dart to the gangplank. Andrew Jack sees my difficulty coming aboard with the curious folk already on it and comes down to clear the way for me.

On deck I walk with solid, confident steps across the bow to Bessie and Baker, present them with my surprise. I'm thinking they will need a moment to confer with one another, but Baker nods, his face filled with happiness. Bessie envelops me with a hug. I lean over the rail and raise my hand to Mrs. Brown, whose name I have finally remembered. She nods, and off goes a servant standing beside her.

The men make steady progress with organizing and cleaning the deck. Truly, it is only the deck that makes a difference to us at present. The grungy job of cleaning the boiler can wait. Reverend Guston arrives perhaps an hour and a half later, a solid man with little hair and rather thick spectacles. His demeanor is comfortable and warm. I have no doubts as to how we are proceeding. I introduce the bridal couple, who move with him into the gentlemen's quarters to converse about the seriousness of their commitment, while the crew complete their work on deck.

It is December 30. There are no flowers, but one of the ladies arrives with a wreath of woven greenery for Bessie's head. I go belowdecks and knock on the door to fetch Bessie. She will want to put on her best attire and spruce her hair, I know, for this once-in-a-lifetime moment. She is radiant when I adjust the wreath on her head. I take a small sprig of green from it and put it in her hand.

The wedding is everything it should be, with our intimate group gathered on board, in view of the grand crowd of enthusiastic spectators on the dock. Baker kisses his bride, and she waves her little sprig of green at a cheering crowd. I suddenly imagine generations to come, regaling one another with their tales of being present this day. I wonder how much those tales may vary over time. In truth, over days.

After the joy of the marriage, I am apprehensive to inquire about our almost disastrous docking, or non-docking, as it might have been. Nicholas comes down below after a conference with the crew to plan the schedule for our stop in Natchez. Joshua and Gabriel will be out tomorrow replenishing the larder with whatever foods they find available. Oren, Jessup, and Samuel will be cleaning the boiler, or at least they will have the first shift of this arduous task. Jacob and Ezra will be out with Billy, scouting for already cut wood—at a price, of course— to replenish our fuel supplies. Any trees they might cut themselves are too far away from the boat to make this less expensive option practical.

We calculate it will take a good ten to twelve days, traveling at possibly ten to twelve miles an hour, to make our way to New Orleans, given good conditions. *Good conditions*? I have to laugh at that phrase. It has, so far, had no application to this voyage. However, the two hundred or so miles left to go on this river are generally less hazardous, somewhat more straight-forward than those we have traveled thus far. We did, after all, previously cover those miles from Natchez to New Orleans with seven of us in one rowboat! That does not mean, however, that this river is no longer treacherous. Its way to the sea is per-ilous at every turn.

"We have our first cargo!" Nicholas announces the next day. "Mr. Samuel Davis has charged us with transporting a bale of his cotton to New Orleans. It is only the first of many! Many, I say!"

His delight is infectious, and I am grateful to observe the shift in his mood. Of course, I know this about him—that any discouragement on his part tends to be short lived given his op-timistic temperament. Yet I'm amazed that anything as major as the humiliation of our possible failure at docking could be turned aside by one bale of cotton. Well, perhaps a wedding and a bale of cotton.

"Our docking has turned out to be quite a show," he an-nounces. "A good majority of those gentlemen out there be-lieve it was done on purpose to show off a bit of our power against the current. I haven't corrected them."

"Do you know what the problem might actually have been, Nicholas?" I'm still a bit leery, afraid of undetected damage to the boat.

"Indeed, I do!" He's laughing now. "Our good engineer, Mr. Baker, had his mind so distracted by his beautiful bride that he allowed the fire to go down prematurely. How's that for what love will do?"

His arms are around me, and I'm laughing with him. I love this man.

The final days to New Orleans pass uneventfully. Bessie is glowing as she joins Sarah and me each morning to care for the children and manage our little housekeeping. We are out on the deck in the clear air much of the time. Thank goodness, we seem to be past the disastrous effects of the quakes, though now and then I wonder if I detect a slight tremor. Rosetta is calm but happy, playing pretend with her dolls and blue bunny. Tiger is ever at her side. She pretends he can pretend with her. I join in whenever I can, as do the other women. I think again how like family this feels—or family as I envision it. Nicholas roams the deck and the pilothouse, repeating himself again and again, as I often overhear his conversation with the men. He is replete with a sense of accomplishment. So am I, I must confess.

The river enters New Orleans in a wide curving bow, as if embracing the city. The waterfront runs the length of the bow. Hundreds of vessels line the waterfront, docked in orderly fashion according to size and type. We are not the largest, though certainly the most impressive. There are sailing ships built to cross the seas. I notice sailors high in the riggings staring down as we ply our way around the bow. Over the levee I see the welcome spires of the cathedral piercing the blue sky. Imagine! After all this, we have clear air and a blue sky to greet us. As well as another huge crowd of curious and enthusiastic spectators. People of all ranks and dress, even another group of Indians, in full tribal costume. To greet us here, I believe, will also be the governor of the territory, Governor Claiborne. He and his legislature are petitioning for statehood, I overheard someone say in Natchez. There will be a redesign of the flag, then, if that should pass, as it should. The one with fifteen stars and stripes I waved at Louisville will no longer be valid. Ah, but how it served its purpose in that fearful moment!

We are rounding to, no downriver floating as in Natchez. The paddles are slowing. Smoke and steam drift up, as if to meet the cathedral spires. We are pulling into the dock. Roustabouts run to catch the ropes Billy and Ezra throw out. I assume those men are competing to be part of this history. They are pulling us vigorously into the dock. Again, I wonder what their stories to their grandchildren may be.

A thump of the boat tells me we are secure. I am standing on the bow with Nicholas. He takes my hand and squeezes it between both of his. As I look up, I see in his face that he is basking in this momentous accomplishment, one in which I am innately included. I do not feel the elation that I expected, such as overwhelmed me in Natchez. Possibly because I know this is the end of our adventure, perhaps of this part of my life.

Nicholas drops my hand and walks down the plank to meet the governor.

CHAPTER 38

Memory has let me be for a while. So deep has been my angst at these terrible quakes that there has been no looking back, other than at the faces of those left behind in New Madrid. The *New Orleans* will become a packet boat to enable steady trade between Natchez and New Orleans, just as intended. Other steamboats will soon be built to simulate it. This river will become busier and more effective as a trade route. Our one bale of cotton will become myriad. Passengers, now assured of upriver travel, of the ability of vessels to defy the currents of the river, will choose the rapid pace of the paddleboat over long, wearisome trips by carriage. Steam will change the nature of both travel and commerce. This journey, in spite of the devastation we endured, will transform the nature of this new nation, ease the difficulty of westward expansion. We have made not only memories; we have made history itself. The world will remember us, of that I am certain. We are the first not only to conquer this unconquerable river, but to do it in the midst of earthquakes that may have few equals.

I am wandering again, as I am so prone to do, like this wandering river going where it will. I am gazing not only into the past, searching among my memories, but also into the future, of which I can know nothing, projecting my hopes onto the days to come. Not only my own days, but also the days of those around me whom I love. Will I be raising a family on this boat? Hostessing passengers up and down the river? Balancing expenses with the income to make our partners, especially Fulton, and my father happy with our outcomes? Watching the river shift, changing its mind continually as to where it will take its course? Where it will take us? None of our charts are valid anymore. Will I be regaling my children and passengers with stories of how these shores looked at different times under varying circumstances? With stories of those unprecedented earthquakes? Using my memories to entertain them? And will those stories change, veer and meander, as stories are prone to do?

I hear bootsteps in the passageway. Nicholas comes into the cabin and watches as I lay our sleeping son in his crib for a nap. He takes me in his arms and rocks me back and forth.

"We are here, Lydia."

"Yes. In New Orleans. And with a wedding to celebrate."

"There are so many prospects to see, so much to do. I will continue to be extraordinarily busy for days to come, Lydia."

"I know." I hold his hand in both of mine, raise it to my lips.

"I have no idea what comes next."

"Nor I, Nicholas."

"What would you like to do, Lydia?'

"I'd like to go home." I kiss his hand again, look up into his face to see if he has understood.

He steps back, pauses a moment. "Home?" he says. "Where would that be? We have no home to go to."

"Then let us make one."

Author's Note

People who do not know the Mississippi may think of it as just a river, like many rivers, only longer. Those of us who grew up along that river were warned from early childhood about its treacheries and heard far too often of drownings and the loss of boats near us. The Mississippi, over a mile wide where I grew up, looks rather placid as it flows through relatively level lands. In fact, the river moves at such a speed and carries such a large volume of water that it could fill the Superdome in a matter of seconds: two and a half million gallons per second below Memphis, where I grew up, increasing to four and a half million as it reaches New Orleans. In addition, beneath that deceptively peaceful surface is an invisible plethora of ever-shifting eddies, whirlpools, crosscurrents and reverse currents.

Before the *New Orleans*, the first steamboat to defy the river, made upstream travel possible, flatboats and keelboats carried cargo to destinations downriver, then were broken apart, the wood used to build houses or, if not in good condition, burned as firewood. Return north was generally by horse or even on foot. The few who could afford it might return by sailboat around the tip of Florida and up the East Coast. Keelboats allowed for poling upriver in the shallows along the shore, demanding work that required months to accomplish. Steam changed history, yet the story of the maiden voyage of Nicholas Roosevelt's *New Orleans*, a voyage on which Roosevelt was accompanied by his intrepid young wife, Lydia Latrobe Roosevelt—who was eight months pregnant when they set out with a toddler in tow—has been all but forgotten. It is the later paddleboats of the Mark Twain era that get the attention.

The most violent earthquakes ever to hit the North American continent are also virtually unknown. The New Madrid earthquakes of 1811–12 lasted approximately four months, and at least three quakes are estimated to have exceeded seven to eight on today's Richter scale. Earthquakes on the scale of the New Madrid quakes, which evidence indicates occur every three to five hundred years, seem to be known only by those who live in the general area or by geologists.

This novel is based on thoroughly researched factual history. The following is an abbreviated list of some of the many rich resources used in my research.

Latrobe, J. H. B. *The First Steamboat Voyage on the Western Waters.* Baltimore: The Maryland Historical Society, 1871. John H. B. Latrobe, Lydia's younger half brother, heard the story of this voyage from her. Many thanks to the University of Michigan Library for its online resources.

Rivers Institute at Hanover College. n.d. "Steamboat Adventure: Down the Ohio and Mississippi Rivers with Nicholas and Lydia Roosevelt, 1811–1812." Accessed November 11, 2023. https://history.hanover.edu/texts/1811/Web/Topic-Roosevelt.html. With thanks to the Rivers Institute at Hanover College for the numerous primary sources in its collection, including day-to-day information and news articles from stops along the Roosevelts' journey.

Feldman, Jay. *When the Mississippi Ran Backwards: Empire, Intrigue, Murder, and the New Madrid Earthquakes.* New York: Free Press, 2012. An invaluable repository of well-documented material.

Gillespie, Michael. *Come Hell or High Water: A Lively History of Steamboating on the Mississippi and Ohio Rivers.* Heritage Press, 2002. A very useful overview of the history of river steamboating.

Dohan, Mary Helen. *Mr. Roosevelt's Steamboat: The First Steamboat to Travel the Mississippi.* New Orleans: Pelican Publishing, 2004. An excellent compilation of available research regarding the maiden voyage of Nicholas Roosevelt's steamboat on the Mississippi.

Buck, Rinker. *Life on the Mississippi: An Epic American Adventure.* New York: Avid Reader Press, 2022. A gripping adventure story chronicling the author's construction of a wooden flatboat like those at the turn of the nineteenth century and his boat journey down the Mississippi.

Galicki, Stan, and Darrel Schmitz. *Roadside Geology of Mississippi.* Missoula, Montana: Mountain Press, 2016. A fascinating exploration of plate tectonics and the geologic history and present-day geography of the lower Mississippi River.

Bagnall, Norma Hayes. *On Shaky Ground: The New Madrid Earthquakes of 1811–1812.* Columbia: University of Missouri Press, 1996. An invaluable book that includes reports from the few eyewitness residents who lived in the area at the time of the New Madrid earthquakes.

Penick, Jr., James Lal. *The New Madrid Earthquakes.* Rev. ed. Columbia: University of Missouri, 1981. A critically acclaimed work that explores contemporaneous accounts of the New Madrid earthquakes and discusses their effects on the region's topography, people, and animals.

A READING GROUP GUIDE

FOLLOW THE STARS HOME

ABOUT THIS GUIDE

The suggested questions are included to enhance your group's reading of Diane C. McPhail's *Follow the Stars Home*!

1. When we look back into history, we are sometimes shocked at variations in culture that we would not find acceptable in today's world. Lydia Latrobe was an intrepid girl who fell in love with and married a man one year more than twice her own age. Though marriage between older husbands and younger wives was fairly common in the early days of our nation, the love between Lydia and Nicholas tested even those looser boundaries. They appear to have enjoyed a long, solid, and loving marriage. What are your thoughts on this reality?

2. This story takes place in the earliest period of our nation. President Thomas Jefferson assigned the architect Benjamin Latrobe the principal duty of redesigning and completing the US Capitol Building in Washington, DC, and Latrobe also designed the White House porticos. He is considered one of the primary architects of the young nation. The novel's telling of Latrobe's flight from grief, his arrival in America, his second marriage, and the reestablishment of his family here is all factual. What are your thoughts on Latrobe as a character in both history and in this novel?

3. Most of us consider Robert Fulton the inventor of the steamboat. However, the story is far more complex than that. During the early years of the invention of steam to power boats, Nicholas Roosevelt presented his idea of employing dual-side paddle wheels, rather than a single rear wheel, to propel a steamboat to Chancellor Robert Livingston. Livingston, who was working with Fulton at the time, rejected the idea, only to present it later to Fulton as his own. Nicholas Roosevelt seems to have been a man who simply brushed the dust from his hands and went on with the next project, which in this case was the

"impossible" steamboat, the *New Orleans*. How does this moment in history seem either unusual or familiar? How do you view Nicholas Roosevelt as a man of invention and as a character?

4. Lydia is, indeed, intrepid. There are hardly other words to define her. She married Nicholas Roosevelt at age seventeen and boarded a flatboat, on which she spent her six-month "honeymoon" with him, floating down the Mississippi River to take soundings and compile information to determine if a steamboat was viable as a means of traveling upriver. She put her design skills learned from her father to use, designing living quarters for the flatboat, a novel concept for such a vessel. That voyage involved numerous unforeseen challenges, including fever, which afflicted all on board except her and, ultimately, the sinking of the vessel and the use of only a rowboat to travel the remainder of the river from Natchez to New Orleans. Eight months pregnant, with her toddler and her great black dog beside her, Lydia refuses to miss the adventure of the untried steamboat's maiden voyage. What are your thoughts about Lydia? Have you ever taken such risks yourself? Would you, do you think, if you had such an opportunity?

5. After all the wild adventures of these two voyages, Lydia seems to have settled into a more conventional life, raising her children and becoming deeply involved in community. How do you understand that seemingly drastic change? How do you see her making such an adjustment?

6. The New Madrid Fault is not located at a juncture of tectonic plates, such as the fault that caused the 1906 San

Francisco earthquake, which is familiar to us all. Instead, the New Madrid Fault is a seismic zone within *the interior* of a tectonic plate. Geologists believe the fault to be the result of plate separation that began in the Devonian age but was never completed. The continent remains connected, but in such a way that it periodically goes through a violent seismic readjustment. The New Madrid earthquakes of 1811–12 are barely known in spite of the vast crevasses that formed, the river shores that collapsed, the massive lake that was formed, and the river tsunami that caused the Mississippi to run backward for as long as perhaps twenty-four hours. Small tremors in the region, unfelt by human beings, continue to register on the Richter scale. However, several centuries may pass before there is another major episode of quakes in this seismic zone. Why do you think the New Madrid quakes of 1811–12, exponentially more severe than the 1906 San Francisco quake, are so little known? Now that you have some familiarity with the New Madrid Fault, what do you imagine it would be like if such a seismic event happened there today?

7. The successful voyage of the *New Orleans* did, in fact, change history. With the initiation of paddleboat travel on the river, not only did commerce and trade benefit greatly, but westward expansion also gained momentum. Would you discuss your views and understanding of how those changes affected the history of the nation? Have you been on a modern paddleboat voyage on the Mississippi?

8. The Mississippi River formed the western border of the American frontier around the turn of the nineteenth century. The western bank of the Mississippi marked the be-

ginning of Indian-held land. The timing of the paddle-boat voyage on the river coincides with Native American efforts to unify the tribes. The Shawnee warrior chief Tecumseh was at the forefront of this effort, and so was his brother, the Prophet, who took a more mystical approach. What were your feelings as you read about the unrest on the western shore of the Mississippi in conjunction with the technological advances and the daring first voyage of the steamboat the *New Orleans*? What is your view of Tecumseh's efforts and of the Battle of Tippecanoe? Did you find that any of your viewpoints changed?

9. One of the primary themes of the novel is *memory*, memory that flows through life like the river, like drops of water reaching the sea, evaporating into the clouds to fall and return to the streams and rivers, then back to the sea once more. In doing research for this book, I found all manner of varying or even conflicting information. I chose to work with what I found most plausible. Later in life, Lydia recounted her memories of the steamboat voyage to her younger half brother, John H. B. Latrobe, who wrote an account of the journey. In my own experience, I find that I may be certain of the details of a memory, only to have a friend or relative describe the same memory from a different perspective, with conflicting details they are sure of. How do you experience your own memories? Do you ever find them coming into question? What are your thoughts on the movement of water as a metaphor for memory?

10. When we study history, the people involved tend to become stereotypes of themselves. We know their story. We know the facts, but we don't know them. When writ-

ing reliable historical fiction, the history, the facts, the events, the times must all be thoroughly researched. The task then is to flesh out those people as fully as the facts make possible. As a reader of historical fiction, do you find yourself viewing history differently? In what ways? To what benefit?

Bonus Question: The Great Comet of 1811 created quite a stir, yet most of us have never heard of it. It is mentioned by a character in Tolstoy's classic *War and Peace* as an "enormous and brilliant comet [. . .] which was said to portend all kinds of woes and the end of the world." It was thought to portend Napoleon's invasion of Russia. It is mentioned in *Les Misérables* by Victor Hugo. Tecumseh, who appears in this novel and whose name translates as Shooting Star, considered the comet an omen for his success, although that proved to be false. The settlers along the river saw the comet as an omen of disaster and the end-times. In the novel, Lydia considers it's beauty and timing as a blessing and a guide toward the birth of her child, home, and the success of their venture. What are your thoughts on how that cosmic event was viewed by the people of that time?